## Mara laughed out loud.

The warmth and the sunshine and the pure joy of being with Allan, so far from anybody else, were making her giddy. Beside her, Allan spread out their jackets on the broad, sun-warmed surface of the boulder. Then he lay on his back beside her, closing his eyes in the strong afternoon sunlight.

"Mmm," he murmured sometime later. "Nice, eh?"

"Yes, nice," Mara agreed.

Nearby, the horses grazed placidly, their bits clinking. High overhead, like dark embroidery stitched on pale blue silk, a V-formation of geese winged southward.

After a while Allan reached out and grabbed Mara's long plait of hair, drawing it luxuriously across his face. Then he tugged on it gently, pulling her down beside him and into his warm embrace....

# MARGOT DALTON

# UNDER PRAIRIE SKIES

MIRA

ISBN 1-55166-594-8

UNDER PRAIRIE SKIES

Copyright © 1990 by Margot Dalton.

All rights reserved. Except for use in any review, the reproduction or
utilization of this work in whole or in part in any form by any electronic,
mechanical or other means, now known or hereafter invented, including
xerography, photocopying and recording, or in any information storage or
retrieval system, is forbidden without the written permission of the publisher,
MIRA Books, 225 Duncan Mill Road, Don Mills, Ontario, Canada M3B 3K9.

All characters in this book have no existence outside the imagination of the
author and have no relation whatsoever to anyone bearing the same name
or names. They are not even distantly inspired by any individual known or
unknown to the author, and all incidents are pure invention.

MIRA and the Star Colophon are trademarks used under license and registered
in Australia, New Zealand, Philippines, United States Patent and Trademark
Office and in other countries.

Visit us at www.mirabooks.com

**Printed in U.S.A.**

UNDER
PRAIRIE
SKIES

# 1

Sunlight glinted on smeared windowpanes and played in slow dusty rainbows among the lawn sprinklers. Traffic moved sluggishly, and the prairie city lay quiet and torpid in the mellow warmth. The morning was golden and glorious, rich and sleepy with harvest and fullness and the gentle passing of summer.

Mara leaned on the sill and gazed out the window at the row of houses beyond the school grounds. She had the impression that she was at the core of a vast circle, and all the ugliness of the city spread out around her in concentric ripples, with every block of buildings serving to strengthen and heighten and deepen the barriers that kept her from the beauty of the day. Somewhere out there, far beyond the stores and sidewalks and service stations, she imagined a silent green hillside covered with goldenrod, where she could lie on her back, watch the clouds drift by and listen to the birds while the sun warmed her face. But the walls imprisoned her, and she knew there was no escape.

Mara sighed deeply and brushed a stray lock of hair back behind her ear, fiddling absently with the barrette that was supposed to hold it in place. Her honey-colored hair, worn in a wide plait down her slender back, was very thick and, when it was loose, hung in shining waves to her hips. It was her one vanity, that long, shining hair. Apart from that, she spent very little time on her appearance.

And, to be perfectly honest, she thought with a sudden wry little grin, she probably only kept her hair long because her grandmother hated it so much. If Gran didn't nag all the time about how silly it was to have such a ridiculous mop of hair, she'd get it all cut off and look like Julie Andrews.

Mara stood a moment longer in the sunlight, poised lightly with her hand on the window ledge. Mara was slender and graceful, with a compact, athletic figure. She had, in fact, been awarded the trophy for the best female athlete in her graduating class, but that had been ten years ago, and, these days, sometimes seemed more like a lifetime ago. She had a vivid, fine-boned face with huge gray eyes, dark brows and lashes, and a golden dusting of freckles over high cheekbones. She wasn't actually beautiful, but there was something about her that lighted up a room when she entered, that made people give her a second look and a smile and then go about their business feeling happier somehow for having encountered her.

But just now, for some reason, she felt so trapped and depressed....

She became aware of small murmurings and stirrings behind her, and forced herself to shake off the uncharacteristic blue mood that had overcome her as she stood looking out the window at the late September morning. Then she turned and said with a smile,

"All right, boys and girls, do we have our crayons all put away?"

Rows of bright faces gazed up at her with naked adoration, and shining heads—fair, dark, curly, sleek—all nodded eagerly in unison.

"Good," Mara said. "Now you may put your crayon boxes away on your shelf and get out your library books. Quietly, please, and don't shove!"

They all nodded again, and nineteen little bodies hurried about, whispering, shushing one another, trying to do exactly as they had been instructed. Mara watched them, and her heart ached with love for all of them. They were so little and vulnerable, and they tried so hard to be good, to win her praise and approval.

The bustle subsided, and the room grew silent and expectant. Mara strolled to the front of the class and sat on the edge of her desk, a slight, dainty figure in pale yellow slacks and white eyelet blouse. She held one knee and sat casually, swinging her sandaled foot, looking at the rows of kindergarten students who sat at their little tables, gripping their brightly colored picture books. Deliberately she remained silent a moment longer, letting the suspense build while the five-year-olds watched her, big-eyed and breathless, in an agony of anticipation. Everyone knew what was coming. For the children, it was one of the high points in their morning.

"All right. Worms and Caterpillars!" Mara called out suddenly.

As soon as the words were uttered, the room erupted into sudden, purposeful activity, with children climbing into corners and under tables, while others climbed onto bookshelves, window ledges and boot racks. Within half a minute they were all silently arranged about the room in an incredible variety of positions and locations, looking at their library books.

Mara watched them and smiled.

A knock sounded at the open door, and she turned, still smiling. Milton Parker, teacher of high school French and self-appointed staff social convenor, stood in the doorway, spare and officious, holding a large clipboard and teetering importantly on his toes.

"Hello, Mara," he began, "I'm collecting for..." He paused, staring in bewilderment at the recumbent, contorted forms of small children disposed at random all over the room. "What's happening?" he asked.

"Worms and Caterpillars," Mara responded serenely. "It's our book time, you see. We do it every day for fifteen minutes. They have books from the library, and they get to pretend they're a worm or a caterpillar, so they can crawl or slither or curl up anywhere they like while they look at their books."

"Why would they want to?" Milton asked blankly. "My God, isn't that kid going to roll off the window ledge?"

"He never has before," Mara said.

"And look at that kid curled up under your desk. Isn't it too *dark* to read under there?"

"She has a flashlight."

Milton looked with disapproval at the welter of small bodies. "I wouldn't teach kindergarten for anything. Why can't they just sit at the tables and read like normal human beings?"

"Because this is more fun," Mara said cheerfully. "And a child's first experience with books should be fun." There was a brief pause. "Milt," she prodded gently. "What are you collecting for?"

"Collecting?" He gathered himself together and turned away from his mournful contemplation of the silent children. "For Alicia," he said.

"Alicia?" Mara asked, puzzled for a moment. Then her face cleared, and she smiled at him. "Well, it's about time," she said. "She was at least two weeks overdue. Did she go in last night or this morning? What did she have, Milt?"

"This morning, I gather. Early. It was a boy." He consulted his clipboard. "Two dollars each. We'll send a small bouquet and a fruit basket."

Mara went to get the money from her purse and returned, still smiling at the news. "A boy," she repeated. "How much did he weigh, Milt?"

"Over nine pounds," Milton said. "Rather a *fat* baby, apparently." He said this severely, as if fat babies were quite a serious breach of discipline.

Mara watched him move briskly down the hallway to the next classroom, and thought of Alicia, the bubbly, extroverted English teacher, with her fat baby boy. Her smile was fond and more than a little wistful as she wandered back into her own classroom and sat on the desk again. She glanced around at the quiet children, and her smile faded. "Oh, no," she murmured softly.

Hoisting herself lightly off the desk, she walked over to a little boy who sat alone at one of the miniature tables with a book open in front of him. "Michael," she said gently.

His shoulders stiffened, and his small hands tightened on the book he was holding, but apart from this he made no response.

Mara stood beside him, looking down at him in helpless silence. He was neatly dressed in jeans, sneakers and a plaid shirt, all obviously newly purchased for the school term and all very clean. His dark, shining hair was carefully combed and parted, and the hands clutching the book were scrubbed and well tended. At least somebody took care of him, she thought. He wasn't neglected.

"Michael," she repeated.

Again Mara saw the tension, the almost imperceptible tightening of those thin shoulders. She lowered herself into the child-size chair beside him and put her arm around him. He kept his face averted, rigid and unresponsive to her touch. "Michael, don't you want to play Worms and Caterpillars? Don't you want to find a special place to curl up with your book?"

The little boy muttered something, and Mara leaned closer, unable to hear him. "I beg your pardon, Michael? I didn't hear you, dear."

"I said, this is okay."

"But wouldn't you rather play? It's fun to pretend." She paused a moment, thinking. "Michael... you live on a farm, don't you?"

He nodded tightly, looking down at his book.

"Well, you must see lots of worms and caterpillars on your farm. Do you ever see them, Michael?"

Another brief nod.

"Do you see them on tree branches and under leaves and curled up on the ground after it rains?"

He looked up at her, and she caught a flash of animation in his wide blue eyes. "Once I saw—" he began, and then broke off abruptly and looked down at the table again.

"What, dear?" Mara coaxed. "What did you see? Did you see a worm or a caterpillar?"

But Michael, as if regretting his lapse, kept his eyes fixed resolutely on the book in his hands and didn't answer.

Mara looked down at him, feeling baffled and helpless. "You're sure you don't want to find your own special place and be a little worm like the others?"

"This is okay," he repeated with a tone of finality.

Mara lingered a moment, stroking his hair tenderly, then got up and moved back to her desk, painfully conscious of the stiff, unhappy little figure at the table.

*I've got to do something about him,* she thought. *But what can I do? He just won't respond to anything.*

Her vivid face was still troubled as she picked up a box of autumn leaves on her desk and began to sort through them, picking out the best ones for the children to dry and mount in their nature books.

The hall was crowded with students jostling one another, shouting and standing around, happy to be released from classes for the lunch hour. Mara wove her way among them with practiced ease, carrying a pile of books and worksheets, and paused in the office to search through a huge metal filing cabinet for Michael Williamson's file.

*Not much here,* she thought in disappointment, leafing through the sparse contents of the manila folder. *I doubt that this is going to be any help.*

Adding the folder to her pile, she left the office and walked briskly down the hall to the teachers' lounge, opening the door and stepping inside with relief. The peace and silence in the big comfortable room was a welcome respite from the noise and tumult of the hallway.

Most of the teachers in the huge school complex went home for lunch or ate out, and there were only about fifteen people in the lounge, all reading, eating, relaxing or pursuing various quiet interests of their own. As Mara entered and took her lunch bag from her cubicle, a big, striking woman—easily six feet tall, with a wild head of frizzy red hair—looked up and beamed at her.

"'Lo, sweetie," the redhead said cheerfully. "Heard about Alicia?"

"Milt told me," Mara said. "Isn't it great? Alicia wanted a boy this time, too. Let's go visit her on the weekend, shall we? We can make faces at him through the nursery window and see if he's got Bob's nose."

"Sounds great," Jo said, chuckling. "Talk to me Friday and we'll go Saturday afternoon. I'll pick you up, okay?"

"Okay," Mara said. "How's it going?"

"Not so good," Jo said gloomily. "I can't get the

damn headlights to fit in these housings. I think they gave me the wrong ones.''

Mara paused by the worktable to look at the model Porsche that Jo was building, admiring the exquisite skill and dexterity with which she handled such tiny, delicate pieces of plastic. ''You'll figure it out, Jo. You always do. You're a marvel.''

Jo snorted, and returned to her grim study of the offending headlights.

Smiling, Mara crossed the room, passing behind another table, where the bearded principal and a slender blond man were poring over a chessboard.

''It's the fearless leader of the Little People,'' the principal commented. ''Hi, Mara.''

''Hi, Fred. Watch out. Your bishop's in danger.''

The other man reached over to tug at Mara's long plait of hair, but she neatly evaded his outstretched hand. ''So how's every little thing in Lilliput?'' he asked.

Mara ignored him placidly and moved to her accustomed place by the window to eat her lunch.

She had to endure a great deal of this good-natured teasing because she occupied a unique position in the school. Thomas Carlton Composite was actually a high school, one of the largest in Calgary, Alberta. Because of zoning bylaws, population distribution, overcrowding in the elementary schools and so on, Mara's two kindergarten classes had been tucked away in an empty classroom in the huge, sprawling high school complex. Mara had difficulty understanding all the factors involved but, like all teachers, was required to accept her situation.

She could still remember the dismay she had felt six years earlier, as a beginning teacher, when she had learned that she was to work in this vast, intimidating building where many of the students were bigger than she was, and it seemed that miles of echoing corridors had to be traversed to get from one part of the school to another.

But, in fact, the situation had worked well for everyone. Her tiny students, with the amazing versatility of the very young, had adapted quickly to the enormous building, and their presence in the school was a good influence on the teenage occupants. The kindergarten kids were the school pets, receiving the goodies baked in the Home Economics classes and the toys built in the woodworking shop. And their tender, eager innocence as they trotted across the school grounds and through the hallways, clutching their crayons and their coloring books, seemed to have a gentling effect on the most hardened of high school discipline problems.

In her six years at the school, Mara herself had, with tact, patience and competence, won the respect of her colleagues, even though her teaching duties and responsibilities were quite different from those of the other teachers. When she had started at her job, they had all treated her rather like an endearing child. Now, although they still teased her, the banter was tempered with professional respect.

She settled into a chair beside a plump, gray-haired woman who was knitting placidly on a tangled skein of lurid purplish yarn.

"Hi, Irene."

"Hello, Mara, dear. How are you?"

"Fine. How's the knitting?"

"Almost finished. This is the last sleeve." Irene held up the bilious length of magenta, regarding it with enormous satisfaction.

"Which granddaughter is this for? You told me, but I've forgotten."

"Tracy, the youngest. It's her Christmas present. I'm doing Jennifer's next. I already have the yarn. It's a beautiful chartreuse."

Mara wondered briefly where Irene found the dreadful colors that she was forever knitting into sweaters and scarves and inflicting on her helpless family.

*Surely they don't* stock *colors like that,* Mara thought. *I'll bet the shops have to special-order them.*

She smiled to herself, patted Irene's arm and gave her a cheerful smile, and then settled back, munching on a sandwich and paging through Michael's file.

As she had suspected, there was little information that she didn't already have—just his preliminary test scores, indicating extremely high intelligence, and a few sketchy biographical details. He had been born in Calgary and now lived on a farm about twenty miles from the city, riding back and forth on the bus every morning for his half-day session in her classroom. The fact sheet made no mention of a mother or of brothers and sisters. His father, Allan Williamson, aged thirty-three, was listed as the custodial parent.

*That might explain part of it,* Mara thought, pondering the brief summary. *But I don't know…lots of*

*them come from broken homes and single-parent fam-*
*ilies, but none of them are as terribly withdrawn and*
*frightened as Michael seems.*

Irene was looking with concern at Mara's troubled,
preoccupied face. "Is something the matter, dear?"
she asked gently.

"Oh, Irene, I don't know. I have this little boy in
my morning class. His name's Michael, and he's such
a sweet little fellow, but he just seems terrified of
everything, you know, and he won't ever participate
in playtimes."

She was interrupted by a chuckle from the vicinity
of the chessboard.

"Mara's such a lucky girl," the slim blond man
was saying. "All her troubles are little ones."

She looked at him blankly.

"Take me," he explained, waving his arm expan-
sively. "Here I am, trying to decide what to do about
this rotten kid who's been caught for the third time
smoking marijuana in the janitor's closet. Mara, on
the other hand, is agonizing over a little fellow who
*won't participate in playtime.*"

Mara glared at him. "Well, Colin," she retorted
with spirit, "let me tell you something. If there were
more kindergarten teachers concerned about children
who are withdrawn and won't participate, I'll bet that
eventually there'd be fewer high school students
smoking marijuana in the janitor's closet!"

Colin considered this and smiled. "You're probably right. As a matter of fact," he added cheerfully,
"I'll bet *all* the problems we're dealing with here are

because of incompetent handling at the kindergarten level. Right, Mara?''

Mara grinned back at him, but refused to rise to the bait. This was an indication of her concern over the little boy in her morning class. Normally she enjoyed a good argument with Colin. In fact, she and Colin had dated a few times. They'd had a lot of fun together, the two of them, in a platonic kind of way, but he had been unable to withstand the force of Gran's disapproval.

Not that Gran was easy to withstand, Mara thought. Her face clouded briefly as she remembered the dreadful embarrassment of Gran's rudeness to Colin. He was still friendly with Mara, and they enjoyed their contact at work, but he had never asked her out again after that one humiliating encounter with her grandmother.

"Have you spoken to his parents?" Irene asked. She was still thinking about Michael, and her motherly soul was clearly troubled.

"No...well, actually, I'm not even sure if he has two parents. Just his father is listed on the registration form. He's a farmer, from west of the city."

"Didn't you meet him on registration day?"

"No. I wasn't here for registration day. Gran was sick, remember? And I had to stay home, so Jeff looked after registration."

Irene nodded curtly, her disapproval of Gran written clearly in her expression. "Yes," she said briefly. "I remember."

"I guess I could phone him," Mara said doubtfully. "But I hate to bother him if I don't have to. Farmers are awfully busy all the time, aren't they?"

"Not too busy to deal with their children's problems, I should hope," Irene said.

"I know, but it's so early in the term. Maybe he's just really shy and he'll open up later. Lots of them take a long time to get over their shyness."

"Mara..." Irene looked at her steadily over her granny glasses. "You *do* think there's something wrong, don't you? You don't really believe it's just shyness."

"No...you're right, Irene. I have a feeling there's some kind of serious problem. I just have no way of knowing for sure."

"Then go with your instincts. You're a good teacher, with years of experience behind you. If your instincts tell you there's something wrong, then you'd better talk to his father."

"You're right," Mara said with sudden decision. "I will. I'll call him right away, as a matter of fact."

Irene nodded her satisfaction and settled back to her knitting. Mara suited actions to words by jumping to her feet, tidying away her lunch things and heading back down the hallway to the school office, unlocking the door with her master key.

The office was quiet and deserted for the lunch hour. Mara dialed the number and listened in growing dismay to the ring signal—two long, one short, repeated over and over.

*Oh, no,* she thought. *It's a party line!* She pictured other receivers being picked up all along the line and other ears listening in on the conversation.

*Even if I can get hold of him, I'm not going to be able to talk about it on the telephone.*

"Hello?" a strong masculine voice said suddenly.

"Hello...Mr. Williamson?"

"Speaking."

"Mr. Williamson, this is Mara Steen. I'm Michael's kindergarten teacher. I wanted to talk to you for a moment about...about Michael."

"What's the matter? He isn't hurt or anything, is he? I'm waiting for the bus right now, but it hasn't come yet."

"No, no, nothing like that," Mara said hastily, struck by the instant concern in the man's deep voice. "He should be arriving at the regular time. I just wanted to talk with you about his...his adjustment to school."

There was a brief silence, "But not on the phone," Allan Williamson said.

"No, preferably not. I know how busy you must be, but I wondered if you could possibly find the time."

"Would this afternoon be all right? I have to come into town to pick up some baler twine."

"Yes, fine. My afternoon class leaves at three-thirty, and then I supervise a high school study class at four, but I do have that half hour free, or I could—"

"I'll be there at three-thirty."

Clearly, Mara thought, this was a decisive man and not one to waste time, either. "That's fine, then, Mr. Williamson. I appreciate your cooperation."

"Miss Steen?"

"Yes?"

"I'll have to bring Mick with me. There's no one else to look after him, you see. Would you have some way to occupy him while we talk?"

"Certainly. He can play outside in the kindergarten playground, and I can keep an eye on him from the window."

"Good. I'll see you this afternoon. Thanks for calling."

Mara hung the phone up slowly and then stood for a long time gazing out the window, her face thoughtful and concerned.

"Home time" was Mara's favorite part of her teaching day—the brief period at the end of each morning and afternoon class when the school day was over and most students took a moment before leaving to have a little chat with her and show her a new toy or whisper a secret in her ear.

At three-thirty she was kneeling on the floor by her desk, saying goodbye to her afternoon students. Lavishly she distributed hugs, kisses and praise while she tied shoes, buttoned sweaters and listened to a dozen children who were all trying simultaneously to capture her attention. Finally the last one was dealt with and she shooed them all out the door, laughing and waving. Then she looked up and froze.

Michael Williamson stood quietly in the doorway, gripping the hand of a man who had to be his father. Mara stared up at the man and then, realizing belatedly that she was still kneeling on the floor, she scrambled hastily to her feet, brushing at the knees of her slacks to hide her confusion.

Allan Williamson was, somehow, not at all what she had visualized. Well over six feet tall, lithe and athletic in faded jeans, riding boots and a gray plaid shirt, he had lean hips, broad muscular shoulders, a tanned, clean-cut face and a springing shock of thick, sandy hair. His eyes, Mara noticed, were deep blue, almost startling against his sun-browned skin, and when he smiled at her, a sudden, surprising dimple appeared in his left cheek.

"Miss Steen?" he asked.

"Yes, I am. I assume you're Mr. Williamson?" She extended her hand, which was immediately enveloped in a hard callused palm. "I'm sorry to have kept you waiting," she murmured, retrieving her hand, which still tingled from his firm grasp. "I didn't realize you were here."

"That's all right. I was enjoying watching you. You sure seem to love those little guys."

Mara hesitated, then looked down at Michael, who stood quietly beside his father. "Hello, Michael," she said. "I don't usually get to see you in the afternoon, do I? I'm lucky today."

Michael was silent.

"You said something about the playground?" his father asked.

"Yes, it's just outside the window, there," Mara said, indicating a small grassy area beside the school, equipped with swings, slides and monkey bars. "Michael, would you like to run out and play for a few minutes while I talk to your dad?"

The little boy looked hesitantly up at his father, who nodded. "Just for a little while, Mick. I'll be right here."

The tall man knelt and zipped his son's jacket up to his chin, adjusting the collar and brushing the boy's hair back from his forehead. Mara looked on, and the gentle tenderness in those big hands made her throat tighten suddenly. Together they watched Michael walk down the hall to the outside door. Then they entered the classroom, where Mara sat behind her desk and indicated the only other adult-size chair in the room.

"That's all right, thanks," he said. "I'll just stay here where I can see him." He leaned back easily against the window ledge, his long legs crossed, his booted feet casually extended.

Mara hesitated, fiddling with a pile of worksheets on her desk and searching for the right words to begin.

"You've got a problem with Mick?" he prompted. "Has he been misbehaving, doing something he shouldn't be?"

"No, no, not at all. It's just the opposite, actually. He isn't doing anything at all. I just can't get him to respond and take part in things. I thought maybe it was just shyness, but he's been here almost a month now, and it doesn't seem to be improving. I've tried everything."

Allan watched her silently.

"He's very polite and well behaved," Mara went on. "He just…he won't play or get involved in anything we're doing. He's so withdrawn all the time. I wonder if he…he doesn't like me for some reason, if he might do better with another teacher.''

She paused, glancing up at the tall man. He looked out the window for a moment, watching his son, and then turned back to her.

''It's not that, Miss Steen. Mick loves you. He talks about you a lot at home. The way he is, it's just…it's something else.''

Mara watched as he crossed the room and lowered his long body to sit on one of the children's little tables, facing her.

''Miss Steen, this is something I don't like to talk about to anybody. I prefer my personal life to remain private. I'll tell you about it now, for my son's sake, but I would like this to be entirely confidential.''

''Of course, Mr. Williamson.''

He took a deep breath and looked directly at her with those vivid blue eyes. Mara held his gaze steadily.

''You knew that Mick's mother is dead?'' he asked.

''Not really. I just knew that you were listed as the custodial parent.''

''Well, she died a year ago last spring when he'd just turned four.''

Allan got to his feet and began to pace restlessly around the room. Mara watched him, fascinated by the easy grace of his movements and the impression of controlled power in his lean, muscular frame.

''She was pregnant,'' he began. ''It was spring-time, and I had so much work to do. It was hard for her, being alone so much, because she'd been raised in the city, and I don't think she ever really got used to the farm. She used to say…''

He paused and looked at Måra. ''Sorry,'' he said briefly. ''None of that's very relevant, I guess. It's just a hard story to tell.''

Mara nodded encouragingly, and he went on.

''As I said, she was pregnant. About six months along. I was out in the field, seeding, and she was doing a wash. She went out onto the back porch to hang some sheets out on the line and leaned against the railing. It was loose, and it gave way, and she fell—about four feet.''

He shook his head briefly, as if to clear the painful memories, while Mara watched him quietly.

''I knew it was loose,'' he said. ''I warned her about it all the time. I'd been planning to fix it, just as soon as I got a spare minute, but it seemed like there never were any spare minutes. There was always more work to do than there were hours in the day.''

He paused and looked back at Mara. ''My parents were killed in a hotel fire in Italy, the year before I was married. The first real holiday they ever had, that trip to Europe, and that's how it ended. I inherited the farm and all the equipment, but my sister in California got all the cash.'' He smiled grimly. ''You have to work damn hard these days if you're trying to hold a farm together without a good cash reserve.''

Mara nodded, fascinated.

''Anyway, when she fell, she…ruptured, internally, because of the pregnancy, and started to bleed heavily right away. Mick was there, playing in the yard, and she told him to run and get me. He ran so hard, the

poor little guy—it's almost a mile out to the field—
and when he got there he was so..."

He glanced at Mara again, and she was stunned by
the look of agony on his tanned, handsome face.

"God," he muttered, "I hate talking about all this.
I'm sorry...."

"Please," she whispered. "That's all right. Please
go on."

"There's not much more," he said, coming back
to sit on the little table again. "By the time Mick got
to the field, and I figured out what he was trying to
tell me, and we came back to the house in the truck,
it was too late. She'd bled to death right there in the
yard. I tried to keep him from seeing her, but I
couldn't. He jumped out of the truck while I was
phoning for help, and God knows how hard it must
have been on him to see her like that and all that
blood...."

His voice broke, and he was silent for a moment,
looking out the window at the playground where Michael sat quietly on a swing, touching his small feet
to the ground.

"When he came running to get me out in the
field," Allan continued when he had his voice under
control once more, "he was screaming, crying, hysterical. But after it was all over and they'd taken her
away, he quit talking. Neighbor women came over
and helped out, looked after him while I was out
working and so on, but for three months he wouldn't
talk at all. Not even to me."

"That's understandable," Mara said. "Did he ever
have any professional help or counseling?"

"When he was a little better, I started taking him to a child psychologist here in the city. They said he felt that it was his fault because he hadn't come to get me fast enough, that he was to blame for her death." Allan paused, looking at Mara in anguish. "I hate to think of him bearing that kind of guilt. God knows, I've felt enough guilt over the whole thing myself and thought a thousand times that if only I'd done this or not done that...you know?"

Mara nodded gently. "That's only normal, of course. But that kind of guilt is so much more traumatizing to a child."

"That's what they told me. And he was so terrified by the sight of blood...still is, actually. Even if he gets a little scratch on his hand or something, it just horrifies him. The psychologist said he was supposed to draw pictures, act things out. I guess you probably know the procedure."

Mara nodded.

"But he always seemed worse after those sessions, more upset than before. So after a few months I stopped taking him and just hoped that time would heal his wounds."

Mara gave him a questioning glance, and he flushed slightly beneath his tan. "That's not as foolish as it sounds, you know. He *is* getting better, Miss Steen. I can see improvement all the time. He's always been shy, and he's particularly nervous around women he doesn't know. But he really does love you. He talks about you all the time. I think he's just scared to get close in case you get hurt or disappear or something."

Mara nodded slowly, considering. "So if he can really learn to trust me and believe that I'm going to stay here..."

"Right. I think that's what it's going to take. If you have the patience, that is, and if it doesn't upset your class too much to have him here."

"Oh, Mr. Williamson, it's never been a problem to have him here! I was just concerned that...but now I understand so much more."

"I'm learning to understand, too. Over the past few years I've read everything I can find on child psychology. You know, Erickson says—"

Mara glanced up suddenly, startled.

He grinned at her, and the dimple popped into view in his tanned cheek. "What's the matter, Miss Steen? Are you surprised that I'd be reading Erickson? Did you think I'd spend all my time reading *The Farmer's Almanac* or something?"

She smiled back at him, relieved to break the tension of the preceding interview with its tragic revelations. "I don't know what I expected," she confessed. "I guess I thought you'd be wearing bib overalls and a tractor cap and be chewing on a straw or something."

He looked at her, surprised, and then grinned. "Well, then, we're even, Miss Steen. Because when I asked Mick what you were like on the first day of school, he said you were 'really nice, but pretty old.' So all this time I've been picturing a nice elderly lady with blue hair and sensible shoes. But now that I've met you, I've certainly had to readjust my mental image of how you look."

He regarded her with a frank, admiring gaze, and Mara instantly regretted her earlier moment of familiarity. It was unprofessional to be too familiar with the parents of students, she knew. Especially parents with tanned, handsome faces and blue, blue eyes....

"Well," she said crisply, looking down at the papers on her desk, "I think our perceptions of each other aren't really all that important, are they? It's Michael we're concerned about."

Allan Williamson sat thoughtfully for a moment, studying her bent head and the dark fan of eyelashes on her smooth cheek with its golden dusting of freckles. "Do you have children?" he asked suddenly. "Of your own, I mean."

"No," she said. "I've never been married, Mr. Williamson."

"That's a shame, you know. That you don't have children, I mean. You seem to love them so much, and you're so good with them. Yet you spend all your time looking after other people's kids. A woman like you should be raising her own."

"That's highly unlikely," Mara said flatly. She got to her feet, glanced out the window at Michael and then moved toward the door, her slender body tense, her face cool and distant.

"What's highly unlikely?" he asked, following her.

She paused in the doorway, looking off down the hallway so that he could only see her profile. "It's highly unlikely that I'll ever be raising children of my own," she said quietly.

"Look, Miss Steen—" he began.

"Thank you for coming," she interrupted in a tone of polite dismissal. "I'll try harder with Michael and keep watching for progress."

Mara turned away and walked back toward her desk.

"Thank you, Miss Steen. I really appreciate your concern."

She nodded without looking at him as she gathered her papers together.

Allan Williamson paused in the doorway a moment longer, watching her. Then he turned and walked rapidly down the hallway to the door.

# 2

Mara watched through the window as the tall man found his son on the playground, took his hand and walked out of sight around the corner of the building. She stood by her desk for a few moments longer, trying to compose herself, wondering why the ending of the interview had upset her so much and why she had reacted so badly.

*He was just making conversation, after all,* she thought, *and I acted like a schoolgirl with the sulks....*

All at once she gave herself a little shake, looked at her watch in horror, grabbed a pile of books and ran out the door and down the hallway. Three days a week, as part of her teaching contract, Mara was required to supervise a senior high school study class from four o'clock until five in the afternoon. This extra duty, it had been explained to her, was to compensate for the fact that her working day was shorter than the other teachers' and apparently also to express her gratitude to the school board for finding a place for her to work at all.

In theory the study class was an opportunity for students to remain at school and do extra work in a supervised setting. In reality many teachers used it as a dumping ground for their discipline problems.

"Mara, sweetie," they'd say, "I gave detentions to four little stinkers in English Lit and I absolutely *forgot* that I had a dentist's appointment. You won't mind if they just drop into your study class, will you? Thanks, you're such an *angel*...."

The result was that her study class was often a curious aggregate of earnest honor students doing extra projects for scholarships and hardened school criminals serving time for various offences. At first, accustomed to her tender five-year-olds, Mara had been terrified to confront these large, loud, pimply adolescents. But, to her surprise, she soon discovered that they seemed to like her and that she had no trouble controlling them. She tried sometimes to analyze this and had decided that they perceived her as being on their side—an adult who was neither their teacher nor their parent and who could, therefore, possibly be their friend.

Lately Mara sometimes reflected that in just a few more years her first kindergarten class would have grown old enough to be in high school, attending the study class. The thought made her feel deeply sad and alarmed by the swift passage of time. She tried not to dwell on it.

As she hurried into the classroom, which seemed even fuller than usual, and crossed the front of the room toward the desk, a small cheer went up.

"Yo, Teach!" a boy sang out from a desk near the back. His faded denim jacket hung open over an Iron Maiden T-shirt, and his dirty blond hair, with one vivid, orange-bleached streak, tumbled to his shoulders. He wore tinted wire-rimmed glasses, and a gold cross dangled from his left ear.

Mara smiled at him. "Hi, Jason. How's your turtle?"

The boy looked immediately troubled and not nearly so tough. "I dunno, Miss Steen. I got some stuff from the vet, like you said, and put it on his eyes, but they're still all scaly and gummy, kinda, you know?"

Mara nodded. "Just keep putting it on and be sure to handle him gently. It takes a few days."

"Hey, Miss Steen!" A plump girl in the front row waved her hand. "Look at Kevin's hair, Miss Steen. You ever seen anything like that?"

Kevin, thin, dark and intense, gave Mara a glance that was both defiant and pleading. His hair had obviously been recently cut—shaved, actually, on the sides and stood up in a black brush about four inches high on the top.

Mara studied him in thoughtful silence while he shifted uneasily in his desk. "I like it," she said finally. "It makes him look bright and alert."

The class whistled and cheered, and Kevin gave her a shy, grateful smile before burying himself in his book.

"How 'bout me? You think *I* look bright and alert, Miss Steen?"

Mara sat on the desk, resigned to the fact that they were never going to settle down to work until they had their customary few minutes of conversation and banter with her.

She looked over at the boy who was questioning

her. "Stefan," she said, examining his pale face and red-rimmed eyes, "you *might* look bright and alert if you ever got a full eight hours sleep at night—for about a month or so."

"Yeah, sure," he said agreeably. "But when does a guy sleep? I deliver pizzas till two-thirty in the morning, then do my homework, and I get up at seven to catch the bus to make it here on time. So when do I sleep?"

"I don't know," Mara confessed. "I don't know how you manage, all of you. How many of you work?" she asked the class.

Almost all of the hands went up, and a chorus of voices answered her. She looked thoughtfully at the roomful of teenagers.

"Didn't you work when you were in high school?" a girl asked.

"No," Mara said. "Very few of us did, actually. I was on the volleyball team, and the gymnastics team, and I was studying for scholarships and just...busy being a high school student, I guess, and enjoying it. You kids all seem to carry such heavy loads of responsibility."

"Yeah, well, probably *your* parents were rich."

Mara shook her head. "Not at all. In fact, my grandmother raised me, and we weren't rich at all. She worked full-time in a hardware store to support us, and when I went to university she took in sewing, besides, to help pay the expenses." Mara was silent a moment, remembering. "It's a different world now, I think. But I feel sorry for all of you sometimes. It seems to me that you're too tired and overworked to be enjoying your high school years. I wonder if it's worth it, the money you earn.''

The students all looked at her quietly, thinking about her words.

"Well, enough talk," Mara said, smiling. "Get to work, all of you, while there's still a few minutes of class time left.''

Chairs scraped, books opened and the room grew silent. Mara checked worksheets for a while and then got up to move quietly around the room, pausing here and there to answer a question or give a word of praise or encouragement.

Near the back of the room she stopped at a desk where a girl was carefully drawing a map, her pale blond hair falling in a shining curtain to cover her face.

"Hi, Lisa," Mara said softly.

"Hi, Miss Steen," the girl said, glancing up and then lowering her head again quickly.

Mara stood silently, looking down at Lisa's golden head. Something, she was sure, was troubling the girl, but she had no idea what it was.

Lisa was an honor student in her final year of high school who had been coming to Mara's study class regularly for three years. Often, as well, when she had a free period, she came to the kindergarten class to help with the children and enjoy their company. She and Mara had grown to be genuine friends, and Mara loved the girl's brilliant intellect, her quiet, impish humor and her serenity and composure amid the tumult of adolescent life. Also, she sympathized with Lisa's home situation, which in some ways was similar to what Mara's own had been. Lisa was an only child whose young mother had run away to Florida with another man when Lisa was little more than a baby. Lisa was being raised by her stern, distant father, now almost in his sixties, and Mara knew all too well the kind of entrapment and isolation that a child could feel in such a situation.

But she had a feeling that Lisa's present unhappiness had little to do with her home situation. Mara knew that there had been a boyfriend over the summer. She had seen Lisa with someone once or twice in the park, and walking to the swimming pool. She had, in fact, expected to hear all about the summer romance once school started again, since Lisa liked to confide in her. But Lisa had seemed tense and preoccupied most of the month and had made no effort to seek Mara out for a conversation.

Mara hesitated now and then murmured, "Lisa, is anything the matter? I haven't seen much of you lately."

Lisa shook her head, staring down at the map she was working on.

"Well," Mara said, "if you ever want to talk to me about anything, you know where to find me."

Lisa glanced up suddenly, and her delicate, pale features had a look of such agonized pleading that Mara was shaken, almost frightened. But the girl lowered her eyes again instantly, and returned to her careful work on the map, her curtain of hair falling forward to hide her once more.

Mara lingered a moment longer, touched the girl's shoulder and then walked back to her desk at the front of the room. She stood, gazing out the window, thinking how strange it was that Lisa's reaction just now had been almost identical to little Michael's earlier in the day.

There were so many of them, she thought, with so many different problems, and there was so little that a person could do to help them....

Shaking herself a little, as if to free herself from the worry of all these troubled children, Mara turned away from the window, sat down at her desk and began to read.

When the study class ended, Mara returned to her own classroom and worked late, resolutely putting everything else out of her mind, occupying herself with lesson plans, project designs and record keeping. Finally, when she was too hungry to work any longer, she gathered up her sweater, handbag and daybook, locked the classroom door and trudged through the deserted school toward the teachers' parking lot.

Beside her little car she paused for a moment, gazing at the sky. The sun was low in the west, slipping behind the mountains, and the sky glowed a soft shell-pink and heliotrope, lit by fingers of gold where the waning light rayed down through rifts in the clouds. As always on the prairie, the sunset hues weren't confined to the western sky, but swirled all around the vast horizon, bathing the world in luminous color.

Mara lingered, yearning for some nameless something, possibly for wings, so that she could fly up, up, beyond the tinted clouds and soar away into that realm of splendor, free from all the problems and responsibilities that anchored her to earth. She indulged the fantasy for a little while, imagining how it would feel to rise and fly over the mountains and ride the warm wind into that glowing bank of clouds and never, never return....

A car horn sounded in the next street, brakes screeched, a child shouted in the distance, and the spell was broken. Mara unlocked her small red Nissan, tossed her books onto the front seat and backed the car slowly out of the parking lot.

As she drove through the quiet, dusky streets toward home, suddenly, unbidden, Allan Williamson's face materialized inside her mind. She could see him as clearly as if he were in the car beside her—his thick sandy hair, those vivid blue eyes, the charming, unexpected dimple in his cheek, his strong chin and firm, sculptured lips. She saw his big square hands, gently adjusting the little boy's collar and smoothing his hair, and she heard him saying, "A woman like you should be raising her own children."

Then she heard her own voice, curt and dismissive, almost rude, saying, "That's highly unlikely."

The rare depression that had been haunting her all day came flooding back, making her feel bleak and desolate. Suddenly her life seemed empty and devoid of meaning, her future sad and hopeless. All at once the heavy burden of responsibility she carried seemed to be more than she could bear, and she was almost crushed by it. But with characteristic self-discipline she squared her shoulders and thrust aside her gloomy thoughts. She pushed a tape into the deck, turned the volume up and forced herself to sing along with

Roger Whittaker as the houses, parks and shopping malls flowed past her window.

Mara parked in the garage and ran lightly up the steps, unlocking the side door of the roomy old two-story house, set in a big shady yard on a quiet residential street.

"Hi, Gran," she called as she stepped into the silent kitchen. "It's me. I'm sorry I'm—"

She paused, listening.

Something was wrong. The house was dark and still, with nothing cooking on the stove, no radio playing, no footsteps, no activity.

No Gran.

Mara was puzzled and felt a small stirring of concern. She hurried through the darkened kitchen and down the hallway toward the bedrooms.

"Gran?" she called. "Gran! Where are you?"

There was still no answer. Her fear mounting, Mara ran out the side door and around to the backyard. There, with a flood of relief, she saw her grandmother's small, spare figure out in the garden, barely visible in the deepening twilight. Gran was toiling, puffing with exertion as she raked the mounds of bright autumn leaves littering the yard and garden. Mara stood for a moment near the corner of the house, watching the old lady in puzzled concern.

Gran was wearing an old housedress, a ragged brown cardigan and a sturdy pair of running shoes. She worked with dogged energy, filling baskets of leaves and tossing them onto the pile that was now considerably higher than her head.

*My God,* Mara thought. *She must have been work-ing all day, and she hasn't even stopped for supper.*

"Hi, Gran," Mara said, walking toward the tow-ering mountain of leaves. "I'm home."

Her grandmother grunted something inaudible and bent to heave at the loaded basket.

"Pardon, Gran?"

"I said, it's about time."

"Oh, am I that late? I'm sorry. I was working and I had so many papers to mark...."

Gran continued to work silently, heaving the basket of leaves onto the pile.

"Gran," Mara said gently, "stop now. Come in and have supper."

The old lady ignored her, grabbing the rake and stabbing angrily at a drift of leaves scattered at the base of the pile. Her small, spare body was tense with some kind of emotion, and she refused to look at Mara.

With quiet firmness, Mara took the rake from her, held her arm and guided her toward a pair of wrought-iron lawn chairs beneath a big poplar tree near the house.

"Something's wrong, Gran. Something's happened to upset you. Now I want you to just sit here and tell me what the problem is."

She looked over at the old lady's profile, stubborn and unhappy in the dim evening light. Mara sat back for a moment to study the wrinkled, troubled face. At seventy Agnes Steen was still an attractive woman, with a cloud of silver hair framing a soft, delicate face, and the same small, spare, compact body that

Mara possessed. Her eyes, also like Mara's, were large and gray, and still clear and expressive. She turned finally to meet her granddaughter's concerned gaze, and Mara was surprised to see in the older woman's eyes a look of fear and almost childlike supplication.

She felt a sudden deep weariness accompanied, strangely enough, by an almost unbearable flood of love and tender compassion.

Other people, those who disliked Gran and were so angered by her rudeness and her sharp tongue—those people never saw her like this, alone and vulnerable, helpless, upset and entirely dependent on Mara for her care and comfort.

Others were all too aware of Agnes Steen's strength. Only Mara witnessed her times of weakness.

"Gran, has something happened to upset you? Did you talk to someone on the phone today or have company?"

Agnes shook her head stubbornly, avoiding Mara's probing gaze.

"Look, Gran," Mara began, trying not to lose her patience, "I've had a long day. I'm tired and hungry, and I don't feel up to this right now. Something's the matter, and you might just as well tell me so we can talk about it. All right?"

Agnes hesitated, closing her eyes and resting her head wearily against the high cushioned back of the chair.

"Gran!" Mara said, exasperated. "*Tell* me!"

Agnes opened her eyes, and a tear squeezed out,

rolling across her furrowed cheek. "Rachel has to move," she whispered.

"Move?" Mara asked blankly. "Where? Rachel's almost eighty years old. Where's she going to move?"

"Into a *home*. Into that awful place up on Blackfoot Trail that looks like a giant termite mound. That's where Rachel's going." Gran's voice was suddenly vigorous again, much more like her usual self, and vibrant with anger. "That selfish Delores, she says Rachel's too much trouble to look after, with the diabetes and all, and what can Wayne do... Rachel's his mother, but he has no say in anything, so Rachel has to leave her house, poor soul, and this neighborhood and all her family and go live in that...that awful..."

Agnes paused, flushed and breathless, and sank back onto the cushions, closing her eyes wearily.

Mara looked over at her in distress. "Gran..."

Agnes opened her eyes. "And," she went on, "it's not true at all, really, you know. Rachel's no trouble. She just has to take her medicine and watch what she eats, that's all. It's just that they want to be free to travel and enjoy themselves, and Rachel's too much of a burden!"

"Gran," Mara repeated.

"And then," Agnes whispered, "you were so late, and you didn't come and didn't come, and I got so worried, and then I just started feeling so unhappy...."

"Oh, Gran," Mara said helplessly. She leaned over and hugged the small, frail body, pressing her cheek against her grandmother's seamed, tearful face. "Gran," she said, "you know you don't have to worry. I'll never leave you alone. You know that. And I'll never, ever make you go and live in one of those places. We've been through all this before, Gran."

"Promise?" Agnes asked, gazing up at her piteously. "You promise, Mara?"

"Yes, silly, I promise. Now, do you think you could stop all this nonsense and have something to eat?"

"Well…" Agnes said, forgetting her unhappiness and sitting a little more erect in the chair, with her chin beginning to assume its customary imperious angle. "Well, maybe just a little."

"Shall we just warm up last night's casserole?" Mara asked, getting out of the chair and leaning Gran's rake against the shed.

"All right," Agnes said, starting across the lawn toward the house. She paused and looked back at the mountain of leaves, towering against the velvety purple sky. Then she turned to Mara and grinned, her eyes sparkling wickedly. "It's going to make a dandy blaze, isn't it?" she said.

Mara looked dubiously at the pile of leaves. "I don't know, Gran," she said. "Are you planning to burn them all at once?"

"Certainly," her grandmother said calmly. "With any luck at all that silly Delores will call the fire department again, like she did that other time, and make a complete fool of herself."

Mara smiled back at her. "You're an awful woman, Gran."

"I know that," Agnes told her placidly, opening the door to the house.

Later, when their meal was finished and they were doing the dishes together, Agnes returned to the topic of Rachel, her oldest friend, and her forced move to the nursing home.

"Old people are so helpless," she said bitterly. "They get tossed around like sacks of potatoes, and they have no say in things at all."

"That's not true," Mara argued, polishing a dish and putting it away in the cupboard. "People make their own choices, after all. Everybody does."

"Oh, is that so? And what choice does Rachel have?"

"Well, all right," Mara conceded. "Maybe Rachel's choices are limited because of her age and her health and all. But yours certainly aren't. You're as capable of looking after yourself as I am."

"What do you mean by that?" Agnes said sharply. "I thought you said you wouldn't ever leave me alone!"

"Gran," Mara said, looking at her in surprise. "I didn't say I was going to leave you alone. I just said your options aren't limited by your age, that's all."

"You left me alone once before," Agnes muttered. "You went away to live with that boorish lout for two years, Mara, even though I tried to tell you he was no good. And look what happened?"

"What happened, Gran?"

Agnes swirled the dishcloth angrily through the water and refused to answer.

"David wasn't a lout, Gran," Mara said quietly. "He was a teacher in my school, and we cared about each other. We had a good relationship."

"Until he ran off and left you," Agnes said cruelly.

The unfairness of this left Mara momentarily speechless. She struggled to control herself and keep from making a sharp response. And as she did so, she remembered....

Gran had been almost incoherent with shock and anger when Mara, after two years of living at home and working, told her grandmother as gently as possible that she was going to move in with David Jensen, the handsome physical education teacher at Thomas Carlton.

"You can't!" Agnes had shouted. "They'll fire you! They won't stand for teachers carrying on like that!"

"Gran," Mara said patiently, "those days are long gone. A teacher's private life is her own business. And I do have a right to live my own life, Gran."

After that the memories grew even more painful....

David, his dark, handsome face tight with anger, arguing passionately. "Come *on*, Mara! It's the last weekend of good skiing this winter. And everybody's going. Why can't *you*?"

"David, I've told you a thousand times. I'm all she's got. And she sacrificed her whole life for me. I owe her everything. Is it so much to ask that I just spend one day a week with her? Just Sunday, that's all. She's expecting us, David."

"Yeah, sure," he said bitterly. "And does it ever occur to you that there's things I'd rather do with *my* weekend than sit around all afternoon in a stuffy house with an old lady who hates my guts?''

Standing by the sink, clutching the dampened linen dish towel, Mara closed her eyes and tried to block out the memories. But they came crowding in....

David, flushed and triumphant, waving the final papers for their exchange-teaching program in Germany. ''I've got them, Mara-Bear! Here they are! We're going, babe! Tomorrow we buy the tickets!''

Her own face, glowing with excitement and happiness. ''Oh, David...''

And then, finally the call from the hospital, the cold, terrible clutch at the stomach, the awful reality of it. ''It was a bad fall, Miss Steen. Her hip is fractured and will take several months to heal. It'll require extended hospitalization or competent home care. She indicates that you're her next of kin.''

Furious arguments with David. ''Why *can't* she stay in the hospital? It won't kill her, for God's sake, to spend a few months in the hospital.''

''Yes, David, it could. She hates being away from her home. She can't stand it in there.''

''Well, then, why *you*? Hire a nurse. Hell, I'll pay. We can do it. Just don't back out on me, babe. Don't do this.''

''But, David, oh, David, you *know* she couldn't stand to have a stranger around her, handling her and taking care of her. She just couldn't. Please, David...''

And, at the end, his cold, bitter anger as he left alone for Germany. They both knew on the windy, rainy day when he boarded the plane that it was over.

That had been more than two years ago now, and Mara hadn't heard from him again. He wrote occasionally to Jo and her husband, though, and Mara knew from them that he had met an American girl in Germany and that they were planning to be married....

As for Mara, she had never managed to move out on her own again after Gran was fully recovered. Gran got so terribly upset whenever she broached the subject that eventually she just quit making the effort and stayed on in her old second-floor bedroom in this house where she'd lived almost all her life.

The girls she had known in high school and college were all married now, raising children, talking about orthodontists and dance lessons and chicken pox. And the men she met these days, it seemed, were either married or swingers. The few who might have been suitable were soon discouraged by Mara's aloofness, and Gran's acid tongue.

"What are you daydreaming about?"

"Pardon?" Mara asked, turning to look at her grandmother, who was wringing out the dishcloth and wiping the sink with quick, decisive movements.

"I asked what you were daydreaming about. You were a million miles away. Are you *still* mooning over that man?"

"No, Gran, I'm not mooning over that man. I got over him a long time ago."

"Good," Agnes said with satisfaction. "He wasn't worth anything, anyway. None of them are. Men are nothing but trouble and sorrow, girl, and if you're smart, you'll stay away from them altogether and not let yourself get hurt.''

"That's not fair!" Mara said heatedly. "Sure, maybe I was unlucky. Maybe I had a bad experience. But I'm not prepared to write off all the men in the world because of it!''

Agnes looked coldly at her granddaughter. "Like I said, you would if you had any sense. And if you want to make a fool of yourself, just don't bring any of them around here. *I* don't want to have any part in it.''

"Gran…''

"You're a good girl, Mara," Agnes said with sudden, surprising gentleness. "I just don't want to see you hurt again, that's all. I don't want you to go away. I just want us to go on the way we are, living here together. We have a good life, don't we? What more could a person want from life than what we have here?''

Mara looked at the older woman, trying to think of a response that would be truthful but not upsetting to her grandmother.

But Agnes avoided Mara's gaze, turning aside briskly and starting across the kitchen toward the hallway. "I'm tired," she announced. "I'm going to have a bath and go right to bed. Good night, dear.''

"Good night, Gran." Mara said mechanically, folding the dish towel and hanging it neatly away on the rack.

A few hours later, with Gran bathed and sleeping comfortably in her bed and the house clean and tidied,

Mara wandered into the living room to relax. She built a small fire in the fireplace, put her favorite Vivaldi album on the stereo, dimmed the lights and curled up on the couch, comfortable in a fleecy jogging suit and socks. She hugged her knees and stared at the soft, leaping flames, thinking about Gran's strange, contradictory emotions.

Incidents like the one they had just experienced were, she realized, growing more frequent. As Gran got older and more terrified of being alone and helpless, it was almost as if a mysterious reversal of roles had begun taking place. Gran, who had always been Mara's rock, her tower, her protector and comforter, was suddenly shrinking, becoming unpredictable and childlike. It was Mara now who was assuming the role of parent, who provided care and kept the dangers at bay.

Mara closed her eyes and let the rich, lilting strains of the music wash over her, soothing and lifting her spirits. But the effect was short-lived. When the record ended, she sat on the couch in silence, gazing with brooding eyes at the gently flickering flames... remembering.

As far back as her mind could travel, there had always been Gran. Only Gran. Nobody else. Mara's mother, Emily, was just a shadow, not real at all. She was a faded image in an old photograph album, a quiet, sensitive face in a silver frame on the piano.

Emily had been seventeen when she had gotten pregnant with Mara, and Agnes had been over forty, a widow, fiercely proud and independent, working at the neighborhood hardware store to support herself and Emily, her only child.

Emily had kept her secret to herself, terrified to confide in her mother until it was too late for an abortion. "Even if I would have considered such a thing," Agnes said much later to Mara.

With uncharacteristic stubbornness, Emily refused to reveal the identity of her baby's father, even under intense pressure from Agnes, who had never even thought that Emily had a boyfriend.

"He wasn't a boyfriend," Emily said over and over. "He didn't really care about me at all."

"But, Emily," Agnes persisted with the rock-hard morality of her own generation, "you have to tell me his name. I have to talk with his parents. He's got to marry you."

"*Marry* me!" Emily laughed hysterically. "He doesn't even *like* me!"

Agnes never found out his name.

Ignoring the stares and whispers of the neighbors, she kept her daughter at home, in this same house she had come to as a bride. When Emily's time came, Agnes went to the hospital with her and sat by her bed, holding her hands and crying with her when the pain was too great to bear. And when she finally saw Mara for the first time, she knew that it had been worth every moment of suffering. Her anger over Emily's betrayal ebbed away and vanished, and she began suddenly to look forward to the years ahead when they would bring their sweet new baby home from the hospital and raise her.

But Emily never came home from the hospital.

All these years later Gran's voice still thinned and trembled when she spoke of it to Mara. "It was a mild infection, the doctor said. A minor postnatal complication. He said she should be better in a week or two. But she didn't want to get better. She just turned her face to the wall and died."

So Agnes brought her tiny granddaughter home to the old two-story house when she was a week old, and Agnes raised her all alone.

During her adolescence, Mara thought sometimes about the poor tragic child, forever seventeen, who had been her mother. What had she been like? How had she felt, pregnant and alone in a generation where such a condition was still so shameful and humiliating? And what selfish, insensitive boy had she been protecting with her stubborn silence?

Less frequently she thought about him. He would probably be close to fifty now, maybe still living right here in the city, possibly even one of her neighbors. But Mara had no curiosity about him at all and very little actually about her mother. They were both as unreal as shadowy figures in a dream, remembered weeks later. They had no dimension, no substance.

Only Gran was real.

There had always been Gran. As far back as Mara could remember, Gran had been the one, stable, vital, powerful reality in her life.

Gran, twice as old as everybody else's mothers, beaming in the front row at Mara's primary school Christmas concerts.

Gran, wincing with pain while her swollen and arthritic fingers labored over tiny, exquisite clothes for Mara's dolls.

Gran, gray-haired and puffing, running alongside and shouting encouragement as Mara rode her first wobbly, triumphant few yards on a shiny new two-wheeler.

Gran, in a lawn chair at the edge of the playing field with a thermos and her knitting bag by her side, yelling and cheering while Mara made city history by becoming the first girl ever to pitch in a Little League championship.

But, as the years passed, some of the images of Gran grew sharper and less pleasant....

Gran, with heavy sarcasm and an ill-concealed antagonism, embarrassing the shy, tongue-tied high school boys who came to the front door to call on Mara.

Gran, disgusted and appalled when she visited Mara at university in her co-ed dorm and saw for the first time the easy, casual way that the young men and women lived together on campus.

Gran, so furiously and coldly angry over her decision to move in with David and so subtly rude to David whenever she had the chance to say something cutting and sarcastic...just as she had been rude to Colin on the one occasion that Mara had brought him to the house....

Still hugging her legs, with her forehead resting against her knees, Mara rolled her head from side to side like an animal in pain, remembering, as she had earlier in the day, Gran's rudeness to Colin.

Suddenly the telephone shrilled, sounding unnaturally loud in the silent, darkened house. Mara ran to the kitchen and grasped it, hoping desperately that it hadn't wakened Gran. After these hours of sleep, Gran might well be feeling rested and in the mood for a snack and a long chat, and all that Mara wanted, just now, was to climb into bed and pull the covers up over her head.

"Hello?" she said breathlessly.

"Hello. Is that Miss Steen?"

Mara's heart began to pound wildly, and her face flushed. She knew that voice. She had already heard it once before on the phone, and once in person, and she wondered if she would ever be able to forget it. She gripped the receiver, and her free hand tightened into a fist, squeezing so hard that the nails dug into the palm.

"Yes," she heard herself saying. "Yes, this is Mara Steen."

"Miss Steen, this is Allan Williamson calling. I spoke to you earlier today about my son Michael."

As if she could have forgotten! She murmured some sort of acknowledgment, and he continued. "I've been thinking, Miss Steen, and it occurs to me that I was out of line in some of the things I said to you. I had no right to be so familiar, and if I upset you, I'd like to apologize."

The quiet frankness of his voice was so compelling that she felt herself relaxing and feeling immediately more at ease. "Please, Mr. Williamson," she said earnestly, "don't worry about it. It didn't concern me at all. As a matter of fact," she lied, "I haven't even given it a second thought."

He laughed, a warm, cheerful sound in the quiet of the evening. "Well, then, I guess I was flattering myself. If I'm *that* forgettable, I don't have anything to worry about, do I?"

Mara laughed with him. "I didn't mean I hadn't given *you* a second thought. I just meant that I wasn't upset by anything you said." She paused, and then, overcome by a sudden need to be honest with him, she added, "Well, maybe I was a little, but just because you were right. What you said was true."

There was a brief silence. "Miss Steen...I really do appreciate your interest in my boy. And I could certainly use your help and advice. I was wondering if you might consider getting together sometime, say, over dinner, to talk and compare notes, so to speak. Maybe even this weekend. Would that be possible?"

Mara was startled into silence. She knew exactly what was being offered to her. She could see the handsome, manly look of him, almost feel his strong arms around her and his long, hard body against hers, imagine the pleasure of entering a crowded room with such a man beside her and the pure joy of talking and laughing and sharing her thoughts with him.

But, woven all through these fantasies, like a sour, flat note in a piece of lovely music, was the other reality: Gran's panic, her anger, her inevitable, humiliating rudenesses to him, and the constant need to lie and explain and apologize.

With a kind of dull horror, Mara realized that she had reached the point where the delight of a relationship with a man was outweighed by the knowledge of the terrible price that it would exact.

And that means, she thought, that I'm twenty-eight years old, and my life is over....

"Miss Steen?"

She pulled herself together and forced her voice to behave normally, even though her throat was tight with emotion. "I think not, Mr. Williamson. It's very kind of you to suggest it, but I don't think it would be a good idea. But please feel free to contact me at school whenever you're concerned about Michael."

"Thank you, Miss Steen," he said courteously. "I'll do that."

They said their goodbyes with formal politeness, and Mara hung the phone up slowly, staring at it for a long moment before she lifted her hand from the receiver.

# 3

Allan Williamson hung the phone up and sat gazing thoughtfully into the distance. He was disappointed but not discouraged. Allan was an intelligent, perceptive man, and he had noticed and correctly interpreted Mara's moment of hesitation before she refused his invitation.

*She wanted to say yes,* he thought. *She was thinking it over and she was tempted, but something made her change her mind at the last minute. I wonder what it was.*

Still musing over their conversation, he sat for a moment longer in the spotless kitchen of his small farmhouse. Then he got up and moved restlessly around the room, pausing to stare out the window at the wide prairie sky, a rich black velvet spangled with stardust. His lean, muscular body looked large in the tiny room, but his movements were spare and graceful, his clean-cut features quiet and intent.

Finally he settled again in a chair by the round wooden table beneath the window and picked up his jackknife and the block of wood that he was whittling. He began to work methodically, while curls and shavings of wood fell onto a sheet of newspaper covering the tabletop. A dog's head and body was beginning to emerge from the wood, and Allan labored carefully, carving with quick, easy strokes. He was making a gift for Michael's birthday—a dog, with a whole litter of puppies yet to be created in the months ahead. The house was cluttered with Michael's toys, some of them very complex and ruinously expensive, but best of all, Michael still loved these simple toys his father made for him.

Despite his apparent concentration, though, Allan's mind wasn't really on his work. He was still thinking about Mara and analyzing her reactions on the telephone.

If she was in a serious relationship, he reasoned, or committed to somebody at all, she wouldn't even have hesitated. She would have said no right away. You could tell she was a woman who didn't play around. And if she couldn't stand the sight of him, she would have been honest about it, but kind. She wasn't one of those who just pretend to like a man while waiting for something better to come along....

His strong, masculine features were composed and thoughtful as he chipped delicately at the wood around the dog's ears. Suddenly he smiled to himself, and the dimple that Mara had found so appealing became clearly visible in his left cheek.

God, but she was an attractive woman, he thought, remembering how she had looked during their brief personal exchange. His smile grew more tender as he pictured her bent head with the soft pink glow on her cheeks and the heavy plait of wheat-colored hair.

He had only spent a brief time with her, but he recalled her with vivid clarity. She was, in his opinion, completely adorable. She was the kind of woman that a man wanted to gather up in his arms, and hold forever. There was something about her that was just so sweet, so utterly desirable.

She had seemed kind of shy, he reflected, and she certainly wasn't a flirt. Quite the contrary, she was a sweet, gentle woman who had a sense of fun. He could tell that when she smiled at him. If she were relaxed in a relationship and comfortable with her man, Allan was willing to bet she'd be so much fun in bed....

He closed his eyes briefly and pictured her again as she had been that afternoon when she smiled and teased him about the bib overalls. And suddenly, without any conscious choice on his part, he was seeing a different picture—himself, lying and holding her while her slender, naked body burned his skin, and she was laughing, tickling, whispering in his ears, climbing all over him....

Numb and shaken with a sudden storm of longing, and vaguely annoyed with himself for this errant fantasy, he flexed his wide shoulders and returned to his work.

"We won't give up, will we, pal?" he said aloud to the pensive dog's face that was beginning to gaze back at him from the rough-hewn block of wood. "She said no, but we're not going to pay any attention to that, are we? We'll just keep trying. After all, she's—"

His monologue was interrupted by a muffled sound from another room, and he tipped his head, listening intently. Then he hid the wood carving beneath the folded newspaper, got to his feet again and walked softly into Michael's bedroom.

The small boy was tossing in his sleep, muttering and crying, his face flushed and troubled. Allan sat on the bed beside his son and touched his shoulder gently.

"Mick," he said. "Mick, you're having a nightmare. Wake up, son."

The little boy's eyes flew open and focused on his father's face. "Dad?"

"It's okay. You were just dreaming. It's okay. I'm right here and everything's fine. Just go to sleep."

Michael looked at his father blankly for a moment and then nodded, clutched the big hand on his shoulder and holding it tightly, snuggled back into his pillow again, falling asleep almost instantly. Allan sat on the bed until he was sure the boy was deeply asleep. Finally he gently disengaged his hand and tiptoed back into the silent kitchen, retrieving the dog from beneath the newspaper and settling back to work.

Beyond his kitchen window, the harvest moon illuminated the prairie with a spare, pure radiance. Far off to the east an owl hooted—three mournful notes repeated over and over. Allan worked on, lost in his thoughts, as night blanketed the countryside and the soft swishing of his knife blade was the only sound in all that vast stillness.

Delicate mare's tails of cirrus cloud swirled across the incredible, endless arch of prairie sky, while the sun shone warm and golden on the autumn fields. In the city trees and shrubs were riotous with color, and the breeze carried a crisp, smoky tang that was reminiscent of childhood and of long-ago, leisurely days.

Mara lifted her face to the sun, laughing with pleasure. She turned to smile down at Michael Williamson, who stood beside her on the playground, holding her hand.

Well, not *exactly* holding her hand, Mara thought. It was probably more accurate to say that she was holding *his* hand, and he was allowing it....

His small hand lay passive and unresponsive within hers as they stood side by side in the screaming, laughing circle of children. Michael was silent, watching.

It was outdoor playtime, and the activity today was dodgeball, a simple game played with a large rubber ball. One child stood in the center of the circle, while the ones around the perimeter threw or kicked the ball at him, trying to hit his legs. As long as the child in the center could dodge the ball, he remained where he was. When he was hit, the one who had thrown the lucky ball was allowed to take the center position, and the vanquished hero returned to the sidelines.

Jeff was in the center now, his dark curly hair glistening in the sunlight, his agile body leaping and twisting. Laughing, he teased and taunted the children. "C'mon, hit me! Can't you do any better than that? Hit me! Let's see you do it! Can't *any* of you hit me?"

The children screamed with laughter, dancing and jumping in a frenzy of excitement, but nobody could hit Jeff. He was too fast.

Mara laughed again, watching his muscular, leaping body. Jeff was her teacher's aide and, she often thought, one of the best things that had ever happened to her. He lightened her teaching burden, brightened her days, dealt patiently and skillfully with the children, listened to Mara's troubles and worked competently and without complaint all the time.

In fact, she sometimes found it hard to believe that he had only been with her for a month. She had already come to depend on him as if he'd been around for years. Jeff was barely twenty years old, a sophomore at the University of Calgary, with a major in early childhood education, and the two or three days a week he spent with Mara's kindergarten classes were part of a work-for-credit program being pioneered by the Faculty of Education. His schedule, Mara knew, was fairly heavy, because his labs and classes had to be fitted around his work days at the school, but he never complained.

He was paid, of course, for the hours that he worked with her, but Mara doubted that he had any pressing need for the money. His parents, who were both doctors, lived in a palatial residence on the outskirts of the city, and Jeff himself shared a luxurious downtown apartment with three other college boys. Their life-style, Mara guessed from occasional remarks that Jeff dropped in casual conversation, was interesting but highly irregular.

"There was a horse in our living room this morning when we woke up," he had commented one day about a week earlier.

Mara had stared at him, openmouthed. "A horse? In the living room?"

"Yeah. Just a little one, actually. Kind of a Shetland pony."

"But," Mara asked, stupefied, "but what was it doing in the living room?"

"Eating the house plants. Wiped out a whole begonia and most of a rubber tree."

"I mean, you idiot, how did it *get* there?"

"Oh," he said vaguely, "some other guys brought it up there in the freight elevator, I guess. It wasn't a very big horse. But we're not sure where they got the key."

"Why on earth would they do such a thing?"

"Well," he said evasively, "just to…get even, you know?"

Mara was wise enough, at that point, not to inquire what atrocity the friends were getting even for….

She smiled now, remembering, as she watched Jeff teasing and playing with the children in the bright autumn sunlight. Knowing what she did about his living conditions, she often wondered, in a motherly fashion, how he ever managed to sleep and eat properly and find time to study.

But he was always buoyant and cheerful, his tanned face sparkling with a permanent grin and, miraculously, he kept his position near the top of his class every time the grades were posted. He drove a bright red Corvette, and to the high school girls at Thomas Carlton, he was a glamorous and irresistible figure. It amused Mara to observe their flimsy excuses for visiting the kindergarten class on Jeff's working days, and their clumsy, sultry attempts at seduction. Jeff ignored them staunchly or treated them like a tolerant older brother.

"C'mon, Jody!" he shouted now. "You swing like a rusty gate! Put some life into it! Missed by a mile! Laura, you're a big girl. Kick that ball! Look, I'll even stand still. Let's see you hit me if I stand still."

Laura watched Jeff, biting her lip in concentration. He stood facing her, his dark handsome face laughing, his wiry athletic body lightly poised. She flung back and threw the ball with all her strength, and it sped toward his sneakered feet, looking as if it would surely hit him. But, just before it reached him, he leaped straight upward in a high, twisting spiral, and the ball rolled harmlessly beneath his feet. The children shouted with laughter.

The ball continued to tumble across the circle, rolling directly toward Michael. Mara gripped his hand and leaned down toward him. "Come on, Michael," she urged. "Give it a good kick! Let's see you get him!"

She glanced across at Jeff, who winked. Michael's ball, they had agreed earlier, would be allowed to hit Jeff so that the boy could be drawn into the center of the circle. But Michael shook his head and stood passively as the ball rolled past him out of the circle.

Mara's heart sank. It had been a week since her revealing discussion with Allan Williamson. Since then she had tried even harder with Michael. Her heart yearned over the shy, withdrawn little boy with such tragic memories locked inside his head. But none of her efforts had any noticeable impact. He remained just as remote, just as politely silent and uninvolved as he had been on the first day of school.

The game went on. Jeff allowed himself to be hit finally, and little Tracy, flushed with triumph, took her place in the center. Mara held Michael's hand in the sunshine, amid the shouts and squeals of excitement, and watched the graceful sea gulls wheeling overhead....

Everything happened so fast that it was over before she realized it. One moment Michael was beside her, standing quietly with his hand in hers. The next thing she knew he was kneeling on the ground with his hands over his face and his thin little shoulders shaking violently.

Children crowded around him, pushing and shouting.

"It was Jamie! Jamie kicked it, and it hit Michael smack in the nose!"

"I bet his nose is broke!"

"Hey, Michael, is your nose bleeding?"

Mara knelt beside the huddled form of the little boy, while Jeff herded the other children off and got the game started again.

"Michael," she murmured, hugging him. "Michael, it's all right. You're all right, dear. Let me have a look at your face. Take your hands away and let me look."

Reluctantly he removed his hands from his face, looked down at them and stiffened in terror.

Both hands were covered with blood.

He looked up at Mara with a horrified blue-eyed stare before he buried his face in his bloodied hands again and began to tremble uncontrollably. Mara watched him in anxious silence, thinking of the terrible memories that the sight of blood would release in his mind.

"Michael," she said urgently. "Michael, it's all right. It's just a nosebleed. Let me help."

She tipped his head back, peeled his hands gently away from his face and pinched his nostrils together, holding them firmly. "Breathe through your mouth, Michael. The bleeding will stop right away."

His eyes were closed, and there was no way to tell if he heard her. He still shook and twitched spasmodically, and his lips were beginning to take on an alarming bluish tinge. Mara checked to make sure the nosebleed was stopped, wiped her bloodied fingers on a tissue in the pocket of her cardigan and then whipped the heavy sweater off and wrapped it around the little boy's hunched, quivering body.

Jeff jogged over and dropped to one knee beside them, looking down at Michael in concern.

"Did you get the bleeding stopped?" he asked Mara.

She nodded.

Jeff touched Michael's trembling shoulder and gave her a questioning look.

"It's the blood," Mara whispered. "I think the sight of it upset him. He had a bad experience a while ago."

True to her promise, she had told nobody, not even Jeff, the details of Allan Williamson's story.

Jeff frowned in sympathy. "Did he? Poor little guy. He looks like he's going into shock." He was silent for a moment, looking down at Michael. "What time does the bus come?"

"Not for another hour," Mara said, checking her watch. She sat back on her heels, thinking. "Jeff, I'd better take him home. I'm sure he's not really hurt, but I'm concerned about the way he looks. Can you take care of things for the rest of the morning?"

"Of course. But do you know where he lives, Mara? It's somewhere out in the country, isn't it?"

Mara shook her head. "I just have a vague idea. I'll have to get the directions. Could you bring him in for me and get him cleaned up a little, then get the others settled in the classroom? I'll run and call his father to tell him we're coming."

But, as she'd half expected, there was no answer at the Williamson number. Hurriedly she leafed through Michael's file and called the number of their nearest neighbor, a Mrs. Hilda Schultz, whose name was listed as a contact in case of emergency. Immediately she found herself talking to a pleasant, motherly sounding woman, who was clearly concerned.

"You're sure he's not badly hurt, Miss Steen?"

"No, it's just a nosebleed, but it was quite a bad one, and he seems to be partially in shock. He was terrified by the sight of the blood."

There was a brief silence at the other end of the line. "Yes," Mrs. Schultz said finally. "Yes, I can imagine that he would be. Poor little fellow."

"Do you happen to know if his father is home, Mrs. Schultz? I'd like to bring him home instead of sending him on the bus, but I don't know if Mr. Williamson is there."

"Yes, Allan's home. Elmer was just over there an hour ago to pick up some eggs, and he says Allan's building some new corrals. He'll be working right near the house."

"Good. Can you tell me how to get there?"

"Of course. It's simple, really...."

Mara listened, jotting down the directions, and thanked Mrs. Schultz for her help.

"It's nothing. Poor little dear. You just get him home, and Allan will look after him. He'll be all right then. He's the salt of the earth, you know, that boy is. Just wonderful. The world should have more like him, I always say to Elmer. We've been his neighbors for thirty years, lived right here on the next farm ever since he was born. He's a wonderful boy."

Mara was briefly puzzled until she realized that Hilda Schultz was talking about Allan, not Michael. "Yes," Mara said, surprising herself. "Yes, I think I agree. Thank you again, Mrs. Schultz."

Outside the school, Jeff helped her to settle the pale, trembling little boy in the front seat of her car, then returned to the other children.

Mara glanced across the car at him. "Okay, Michael?" she asked.

He stared straight ahead at the dashboard and made no response. Jeff had cleaned his face and hands, but his T-shirt was soaked and discolored, and the thick, metallic smell of blood lingered in the confined space. He was still huddled inside Mara's heavy cardigan, his face white and pinched, his dark blue eyes enormous, filled with nameless terrors.

Mara turned the key in the ignition and began talking casually, trying to calm and reassure him. "We're going to your house, Michael. And we're going to see your dad. Mrs. Schultz says he's building corrals today."

She backed out of the parking lot and headed for the freeway that would bypass the city traffic and get them to the outskirts as quickly as possible.

"I'm really excited, Michael," she went on. "I'm so glad I'll get to see your farm. You know, I just love farms, and I haven't been to one for a long time. I'm really looking forward to this."

*And, Michael, I'm excited about seeing your dad again,* an inner voice whispered silently. *Because, you know, Michael, I think your dad is the most exciting man I've ever met, and just the thought of seeing him again makes me feel all trembly inside.*

"Is this the right turnoff, Michael? Is this the way to your farm?" she asked aloud, although she already knew the answer from Hilda Schultz's careful directions.

Anything to quell these thoughts that she seemed to have so little control over, and to help free her mind of the image of Allan Williamson's strong, sun-browned face.

She looked over at Michael again, but he was staring silently out the window, watching the buildings thin and disappear as they left the city limits.

Mara gave up, lapsed into silence, and eventually found herself, despite the circumstances, beginning to enjoy this strange but welcome interruption to her working day. A drive in the country, even on a weekend, was a rare treat for her. These days she seldom went anywhere alone, and Gran hated the country.

"It's so boring," she would complain whenever Mara would wistfully suggest a drive out into the countryside surrounding Calgary. "All that flat prairie and nothing but sky, sky, sky. Let's go shopping."

But Mara loved the country, especially this sweep of prairie where the land flowed in clean, pure lines right up into the sky, and the horizon was visible all around, tinted near the earth with subtle bands of color. As they drove westward, the crowded industrial sector gave way gradually to rich, rolling farm and ranch lands, golden and serene beneath the warm October sky. In the distance the Rocky Mountains shimmered along the skyline, while cattle and horses grazed placidly behind fences and cultivated fields lay clipped and bare, their crops harvested, machinery stilled for another season.

Mara began to hum, loving the sunshine and the peaceful stillness all around her. After a few more miles, they turned south off the main road allowance and headed down a long, straight, gravel road.

"Two red granaries," Mrs. Schultz had said. "Watch for two red granaries and then turn left."

Birds perched on fence posts watched them pass, and dust billowed out in a wide plume behind the little car. The road was lined with tall native grasses and autumn flowers growing wild along the barbed wire fence. Off to the west two antelope in a field near the road flung their heads up in a graceful, wary gesture to watch the car approach and then drifted off across the prairie, running effortlessly with delicate, springing bounds. Charmed and excited, Mara pointed them out to Michael but got no response.

Finally a cluster of buildings came into view at the end of the lane, and soon they entered a large farmyard, impeccably tidy and ringed by neat, freshly painted buildings, pens and fences. Mara parked in front of the small frame house, painted white with dark green trim. She got out, hurried around to open the door and bent to help Michael with his seat belt.

As she stood erect and turned, she saw Allan Williamson down near the corrals. He stared in their direction for a moment, and then dropped the hammer he was holding and came running across the farmyard toward them.

Mara watched him approach, her heart thudding in her chest until she was afraid that it might be audible.

*Dear God,* she thought, *he's been on my mind all week, but I'd still forgotten what a gorgeous man he is.*

He wore scuffed work boots and jeans, an old faded blue flannel shirt and a denim jacket with a long rip in one sleeve. Beneath the peak of his stained, dusty cap, his blue eyes were piercing as he stared at Michael, still huddled in the front seat of the car, and then back at Mara.

"He had a little accident at school," Mara explained quickly in response to his unspoken question. "Nothing serious. A ball hit him in the face and he got a nosebleed. He's not really hurt, but he was so upset...."

Allan nodded and reached in to lift his son out of the car. Safe in his father's arms, Michael's reserve finally broke, and he clung like a limpet, his arms gripping tightly, sobbing aloud against that strong, tanned neck. Allan held him, rocking him gently, murmuring to him and kissing his cheeks and hair.

Mara stood looking on, deeply moved by the love and tenderness in the man's voice and actions. Tears flooded her own eyes, and she brushed at them furtively, turning away to look around at the farmyard until the little boy's sobs gradually subsided.

When Michael was finally calm, resting against his father's broad chest with his face still hidden, Allan looked over the small dark head at Mara.

"Thanks," he said simply. "It was good of you to bring him home."

"I didn't really want him to wait for the bus," Mara said. "He seemed so upset, and I thought..." Her voice faltered.

His eyes were so blue, and he was looking at her with such intensity....

"I just thought," she murmured, glancing away across the rolling fields, "that it would be best to bring him myself. And now," she added briskly to cover her confusion, "I'd better be going. I left my teaching aide alone with the class, and I really should be getting back."

"Not yet," Allan said calmly. "You're not getting away that fast, not when we've got you right here. Right, Mick?" He set the little boy on his feet and brushed at his hair. "She can't leave yet, can she?"

Michael shook his head. He was still very pale, and his face was stained with tears, but his lips had lost their frightening blue tinge, and his eyes were looking less strained.

"Right," Allan said placidly. "Miss Steen is going to join us for lunch."

"But I can't," Mara protested. "Really. I have to get back."

"No, you don't. By the time you get back, it'll be lunch time, anyway. And since you've got to eat somewhere, you might as well eat here. Come on inside."

As if in a dream, Mara allowed herself to be led inside the little house.

"Why...this is beautiful!" she exclaimed, forgetting herself for the moment and looking around with pleasure. "It's all so cosy."

The farmhouse was, indeed, a delight. Every room was tiny but immaculately clean. The living room, which they entered first, contained soft leather sofas and chairs, scattered with bright knitted afghans and grouped cosily around a wood-burning stove. Navaho rugs glowed on the polished hardwood floor, and the walls were filled with bookshelves and oil paintings of western scenes. Through two doors that opened off the living room, Mara glimpsed the two tiny bedrooms, obviously belonging to Allan and Michael. Beyond a third door lay the small kitchen. These rooms evidently comprised the whole home, as bright and inviting as a doll's house.

In the living room and in the sunny kitchen where Allan led her next, everything was sparkling clean and neat. Mara looked out the kitchen window at a large garden in the backyard, bordered by a white picket fence, with the prairie beyond sweeping off toward the quiet sky.

She turned back to see Allan, who had disappeared briefly to wash his hands and hang up his jacket, filling a saucepan with water. Michael, too, had changed into a clean T-shirt and was setting three places at the table beneath the window.

"Who looks after all this for you?" Mara asked. She indicated the shining floors and counters, the neat cupboards and the gleaming cutlery. "It's all so clean. Does somebody come in to do your housework?"

Allan grinned at her. His eyes crinkled at the corners, and the elusive dimple appeared once more in his cheek. "My cleaning lady, you mean?"

Mara nodded.

"You're looking at her."

Mara stared at him in surprise. He had rolled his flannel sleeves up over his muscular brown forearms and was moving easily around the small room, seeming, in his work clothes, even bigger and taller than she remembered.

"You mean," she asked, "you do all this yourself?"

"Mick helps a lot," he said. "Do you prefer chicken noodle or cream of mushroom?"

"Chicken noodle, please," she said automatically, and then laughed in embarrassment. "This is ridiculous," she protested. "Isn't there something I can do to help instead of just standing around while you two wait on me?"

"Sure," Allan said cheerfully. "You can make up some egg salad sandwiches. There's hard-boiled eggs and mayonnaise in the fridge and some lettuce. Mick, get out the bread and butter, okay? Look sharp, lad!'' he added with mock severity.

Michael smiled and bustled over to the counter. Mara watched him, startled. It was, she realized, the first time she had ever seen Michael smile.

The three of them had a cheerful lunch, sitting around the sun-dappled table and eating their soup and sandwiches. Allan entertained Mara with stories of the small farming community and all its eccentric characters, and she told him about her teaching colleagues, about Milt's organizing and Jo's model cars and Irene's poisonous knitting yarns. They laughed a good deal, while Michael looked on, still silent, but pink-cheeked and smiling occasionally.

Mara examined herself in amazement. She was normally quite shy and reserved in company and took a long time to feel comfortable with new acquaintances. But it seemed so natural to be here in this room, with this particular man and small boy. She felt as if she had known them both forever, almost as if she belonged here.

Allan pushed his chair back and got up to clear the table, declining firmly when Mara offered to help.

''You just stay there and drink your coffee,'' he said. ''There's not enough room for two people to work in this kitchen, anyhow. We'd be bumping into each other all the time.''

He smiled down at her, standing near her chair as he reached across for Michael's plate. He was so close that she could smell the pleasant scent of him— of dust and shaving cream and strong, healthy male.

Her heart began to race again, and her cheeks burned.

*It's his eyes,* she thought. *I've never seen eyes so blue. And that dimple...*

She sensed a small movement nearby and looked down to see Michael's hand resting on her knee. The little boy stood beside her chair, looking up at her solemnly.

"My cat has kittens," he said. "They're in the barn."

Mara was aware of Allan growing suddenly tense at the sink. She looked over to see him watching them, his face intent, his body taut. He flashed her a significant glance, and she nodded slightly. Both adults were painfully aware of the importance of the moment, of Michael's first shy, tentative outreach.

Mara covered his small hand with her own and smiled down at him. "Does she, Michael? How old are they?"

"They're just real little. Do you want to see them?"

Mara began to answer, but Allan interrupted. "Mick, I don't think that's such a good idea. It's all dusty up in the loft, and Miss Steen has her good clothes on. She'd better not climb way up there."

Michael's face fell.

"How about," Allan suggested, "if you go get one of them and bring it up here to show her?"

The little boy brightened immediately. "Okay! Which one, Dad? Which should I bring her?"

Allan paused, considering. "How about that one

you like so much...the black one with all white paws?"

"Blackie? Yeah! She'll love Blackie!" Michael grabbed his jacket from a hook near the door and was gone across the yard, his arms swinging, his small legs pumping.

Allan stood in the doorway watching him and then turned back to Mara. The strong planes in his lean, sculpted face softened, and his blue eyes were filled with tenderness. "That," he said, indicating the direction in which Michael had disappeared, "is a miracle. And you, Miss Steen, are a miracle worker."

"Hardly," she said. "I think you were right. It's mostly just the passage of time and the stability in his life that's helping him."

They were silent for a moment.

"Please," she said, almost as an afterthought, "call me Mara. Only the children call me Miss Steen."

"Mara." He tried it on his tongue. "Mara. What a pretty name. It suits you," he added with a smile. "Graceful and beautiful."

She looked down at her coffee cup, hating herself for this awkward, tongue-tied feeling that she hadn't experienced since adolescence.

Allan studied her bent head with its delicate bone structure, the golden dusting of freckles on her smooth cheeks, and the long, thick braid of honey-colored hair.

"Do you live alone, Mara?" he asked suddenly, "or with a friend or what?"

She looked up at him. "I live with my grandmother."

He raised an eyebrow in surprise. "Really?"

Mara nodded. "She raised me. My mother died when I was born and I never knew my father. Gran always looked after me. And now," she added with a small, mirthless smile, "I guess I look after her."

Allan considered this, drying a glass carefully with a red gingham dishcloth. "And that's a pretty big job, I guess," he said, not looking at her, his voice innocent. "Keeps you busy all the time, like evenings, weekends...?"

He cast her a teasing glance, and she looked up at him, meeting his eyes directly.

"No," she said quietly, "it's not a particularly big job, but it *is* a big responsibility. My grandmother had an accident a couple of years ago when I was away from home and she was living by herself. She fell and broke her hip and was alone and in pain for a long time before help came. Now she has an almost pathological fear of being alone and helpless. She's very dependent on me, and I...I don't really know how to..."

"How to break away and live your own life without feeling terrible guilt about it?"

"Something like that," Mara said, feeling warmed and grateful for his understanding.

"What's she like, your grandmother?" Allan asked, pausing to wring out the dishcloth and wipe the table and countertop with neat, deft movements.

"Oh, I don't know...she's kind of...difficult, I guess you'd say. I mean, she doesn't like to have people around much at all, except for me, and often she's not very nice to people. And she'd die, I think, before she went to live in a nursing home or seniors' complex. She's so terrified of being alone, and yet in company she's just so…so…'' Mara lapsed into silence, defeated by the task of trying to describe Gran.

Allan wiped a soup bowl in thoughtful silence, put it away in the cupboard and appeared on the verge of saying something further.

Mara drained her coffee cup nervously and was relieved when Michael reappeared, carrying a black-and-white ball of fluff with extreme care in his two cupped hands.

Mara peered down at the kitten and smiled in delight. "Michael, isn't he darling! He's so tiny.…"

"His eyes aren't even open yet," Michael said proudly. "Dad says they should open this weekend."

Mara lifted the kitten carefully from his outstretched hands and held it, surprised by the precious, fragile feeling of the tiny bundle of bones and fur. The kitten stretched and rolled in her hands, flexing its soft pink paws and mewing piteously. Mara held it up to her face, sniffing the clean, warm scent of straw and fur, murmuring endearments, while Allan and Michael stood side by side and beamed at her.

"How many kittens are there?" she asked Michael.

"Five. There's two gray stripy ones and this one. This is Blackie. And one that's all black and one that's all different colors."

"Calico," Allan explained to Mara.

"Just wait till their eyes are open," she said to Michael. "They're going to be so cute, and they'll all want to play with you. You're going to love them."

"I should bring them to school," Michael said eagerly, "and show the other kids. Can I, Miss Steen?"

Mara looked doubtfully at Allan, who grinned wickedly. "How about it, Miss Steen?" he teased. "You want five kittens, none of them housebroken, roaming around your classroom?"

Michael was gazing from one adult face to the other, bright-eyed and expectant. Mara hesitated.

"Well, Michael, not *all* of them, dear. But I think you could bring just one of them someday...after their eyes are open, that is," she added hastily.

"What a soft touch," Allan scoffed, addressing the ceiling.

Mara gave him a severe glance. "And your dad," she said firmly, "can make a nice little box for him to ride in on the bus and to stay in while he's in the classroom. He'll need air holes so he can breathe...."

"And a little bed," Michael planned happily, "and a window and a door and some pictures on the walls and a table and...."

"Hold it!" Allan said. "I'll go as far as air holes, and maybe a bit of old blanket. No windows, no tables, no pictures. You two quit bullying me!"

Michael laughed and hugged his father's long, denim-clad legs.

"The other kids will like me, then," he said shyly to Mara. "They'll all like me if I bring Blackie to school."

"Michael," Mara said gently, "the other kids like you already. You know that, don't you?"

Michael took the kitten from her and stood looking

at her gravely, his huge blue eyes questioning. "Do they? I thought they didn't."

"Certainly they do. They all like you. They just wish you'd play and do things with them. They want you to have fun, too."

"And Jamie didn't throw the ball at me on purpose?"

"No, of course not. He felt terrible when you were hurt. He even cried. Didn't you see him crying?"

Michael shook his head, still thoughtful. "Did he cry? Poor Jamie." He considered for a moment. "I'm going to give Jamie one of my Hot Wheels. Can I, Dad?"

Allan chuckled. "Mick, there's so many Hot Wheels in this house that you could give one to every kid in Calgary and have twelve left over."

Mara laughed and got to her feet, reaching for her sweater and handbag. "I'd better be going," she said. "I'll be late for my afternoon class."

"So soon?" Allan asked with a look of genuine disappointment. "I was hoping to show you around the farm."

"Oh, I'd like that, but I really can't spare the time. I have to get back. I've been away far too long as it is."

Allan followed Mara through the house, holding the outside door for her while Michael ran off across the yard to return the kitten.

The two adults stood on the shady veranda, watching his small figure disappear inside the barn, and then turned to each other and smiled. Their eyes met and held until Mara finally turned away and began searching nervously through her bag for her keys.

"You left them in the ignition," Allan told her gently. "This is a mixed farm," he added in a casual, conversational tone. "I do a little bit of everything, just to keep my books in the black. Mostly grain farming, but I have cattle, too, and some pigs... He grinned down at her. "Even chickens. We raise a few chickens, and it's Mick's job to look after the eggs."

Mara nodded, shading her eyes against the slanting rays of autumn sunlight, and looking around at the tidy, well-maintained farmsite. "How much land is there?" she asked.

"About eight sections. Mainly pasture, of course."

"Section?"

"Square mile. About five thousand acres."

She looked up at him, her eyes wide. "Square *miles*? You own eight square miles?"

He nodded. "Not a lot, really, in this area. Just an average farm. But it's a nice location."

"And you do it all alone? All this work?"

"Sure. At this stage I can't afford to hire help."

"Is it really that bad?" Mara asked. "The economic situation, I mean? We keep hearing on the news about the terrible plight of the prairie farmer, but I really know so little about it."

Allan nodded grimly, leaning against the veranda post with folded arms and gazing out across his fields. "It's pretty bad, I guess. But I'm luckier than most. Lots of farmers these days barely make enough to pay the interest on their bank loans. At least I own all my land and machinery. I have some small capital operating loans, but a few good years will have them all paid off, and then I'll be in a strong profit position.''

"You really are lucky, you know," Mara said, lingering on the step and looking wistfully at the grove of trees surrounding the windmill and the quiet prairie flowing away to the horizon. "No matter how hard the work is, you're so lucky to be able to live here. I'd give anything to live in a place like this and just go into the city to my job."

"So why don't you?"

She looked up at him blankly.

"Why don't you live in a place like this, if that's what you like? Life's so short. People should live their lives the way they want to, shouldn't they?"

"Only in fairy tales," Mara said with a sudden grim edge to her voice. "In real life people spend their lives doing what's required of them and fulfilling their responsibilities, whether they like it or not."

She started down the walk toward her car, and he strolled beside her, his sandy hair lifting and stirring in the warm autumn breeze.

Mara paused beside the car as he held the door open for her. "Thank you for lunch," she said politely. "I really enjoyed it." She bent to get into the car, but was arrested by his voice.

"Mara," he said.

She turned and looked up at him.

"Will you come back and visit?" he asked, reaching out and holding her arm gently. "Not everybody can own a farm, but you can sure borrow this one. Feel welcome to drop in anytime." His smile was lazy and casual, but his blue eyes were intense as he looked down at her.

She met his gaze for a moment and then looked away.

"As a matter of fact," he continued, "I think you should promise to come back. I think it's your duty as a teacher. Look at the good it's done Mick having you here."

"All right," she said with an awkward little laugh. "I promise I'll come back."

Anything, she thought, to escape that stirring blue gaze and the big hard hand that seemed to burn her skin even through the soft fabric of her sweater.

But as she waved and drove off, heading through the mellow autumn beauty of the countryside and back into the noisy, teeming city, she knew that she had lied to Allan Williamson.

She wouldn't be coming back. Not ever.

# 4

Mara was caught in a lunch-hour traffic jam just off the city bypass and arrived back at the school, hot and flustered, almost an hour after the opening of the afternoon class. She rushed into the school and down to her room, full of apologies, to find the classroom silent and peaceful and Jeff sitting serenely cross-legged on top of her desk, watching a roomful of children laboriously copying words from flash cards.

"Jeff," she said breathlessly. "I'm so sorry. I got tied up out there at Michael's home, and then on the way back there was a traffic jam just off Sixteenth Avenue. I was so frustrated. I just had to sit there and sit there, and it seemed like forever...."

"Relax," he said. "Everything's under control. No problem at all. Whatever gave you the idea you were indispensable?"

Mara looked at the bent heads of the children, working in silent concentration at their little tables.

"No problems?" she asked. "Really?"

"Oh, you know," Jeff said cheerfully. "Just the usual. Lesley threw up in the corner of the playroom, Sean pulled his front tooth out and bled all over the place, and Jason hid Marcie's Cabbage Patch doll in the boy's washroom, and she had hysterics."

He vaulted lightly off Mara's desk and gathered up a pile of blunt and broken pencil crayons from the work table.

Mara stared at him while he carried the pencils over to the sharpener on the window ledge and began, methodically, to sharpen them.

"No problems?" she repeated incredulously, following him. "You call that 'no problems'?"

"Nothing I can't handle, my girl. Playroom's cleaned up. Tooth is wrapped up in Kleenex, ready to go home to the Tooth Fairy. Kidnapped doll has been restored to rightful owner."

Mara smiled her gratitude. "Jeff," she said fervently, "you really are a marvel. You're worth your weight, such as it is, in gold."

He chuckled. "Yeah? I hope the school board agrees with you. A glowing report like that would do wonders for my grade point average. How's Michael?"

"He's a lot better. He was fine, really, as soon as I got him home to his father. He really loves his father."

"What's he like? The father, I mean? I must have met him on registration day, but there were so many kids and parents crowded in here that day that it's all just kind of a blur."

"Oh," Mara said vaguely, "he's...nice, I guess." She turned aside quickly to check the attendance sheet on her desk.

Jeff followed and gave her a searching look. "Nice, hey?" he asked. "*How* nice, Mara?"

"Oh, Jeff," she said evasively, "don't be silly. He's just…nice, that's all."

Jeff arched a dark eyebrow, grinned knowingly and went back to his pencil sharpening.

"What are they doing, exactly?" Mara asked, looking at the rows of thick pencils gripped in small, sweaty hands.

"They're copying their own names off flash cards. Feel some sympathy for poor little Nathaniel O'Halloran."

Mara chuckled. "How long have they been at it?"

"About ten minutes. Nearly the limit of their concentration, I'm afraid. I find that a five-year-old's attention span isn't a great deal longer than mine."

"That's true," Mara said. "I think we'd better do some action songs next. I'll get out my guitar, and you can take a break if you like, Jeff."

"Good. I could use one, actually. I have a few theorems left to work up before my psychology tutorial tonight."

"Take all the time you want. In fact," Mara said, checking her watch, "go home if you like. You've done enough for one day."

"What?" he asked in mock outrage. "And miss Play Dough time? Not on your life!"

Mara laughed, then watched affectionately as he gathered up his formidable pile of college texts and notebooks.

"Three grade eleven girls came down just after lunch," he said casually, pausing in the doorway. "I said I didn't need any help and sent them away again."

"Good," Mara said. "I don't really like having them in here, anyway, when I'm not in the room."

"Yeah, I know." He hesitated, his dark curls shining in the hallway light, his boyish, handsome face serious for once. "Another girl came down, too," he said. His voice was still carefully casual, and Mara looked at him with sudden attention.

"Really?" she asked. "Who was it?"

"I don't know. Someone I've never seen before. Older than the others, I think, and really beautiful. Tall and slim with pale blond hair."

"That's Lisa," Mara said, pleased to hear of the girl's visit. "Did she say anything?"

"Not really. Just asked to see you and said she'd come back later. What did you say her name was?"

"Lisa," Mara said. "Lisa Stanley. She's graduating this year and going on to major in languages. She gets high grades in everything, but she's a real whiz at languages. She wants to be an interpreter at the United Nations."

Jeff was silent for a moment, absorbing this information. "I wonder why I've never seen her around before," he said. "A guy could hardly miss a girl who looks like that."

"I've wondered about her, too, lately," Mara said. "She used to come down here a lot, just to visit and help with the children. She loves them and she's so good with them. But she hasn't been here once this fall. Until today, that is," she added.

"Maybe she heard about me being down here and decided I was unfit to associate with," Jeff said with a cheerful grin.

"Actually," Mara said, "I think she's been associating with someone else. At least she had a boyfriend during the summer. I saw them together quite a bit."

"Who is he?"

"Kevin Donner."

"The quarterback? That girl's dating the *quarterback*? I figured she'd go more for the president of the debating team or something."

"I don't know if she's still dating him," Mara said. "I haven't seen them together for quite a while, and Lisa seems so unhappy lately...or at least really withdrawn...."

"Maybe she's finding out that quarterbacks aren't all they're rumored to be. Do you think I'd have a chance?"

"With Lisa?" Mara hesitated. "I don't know, Jeff. Lisa takes her schoolwork really seriously. I don't know if she goes out much at all. I can't remember seeing her with anybody but Kevin."

"Imagine that," he mused. "A girl who's every guy's dream come true, and she'd rather stay home and study."

"Or date quarterbacks," Mara added, teasing.

"Yeah. What a shame. Oh, well," he said, "I can't be fraternizing with high school girls, anyway, can I? It's unprofessional to date students, right?"

Mara considered. "Well...maybe not so much for you. Now it would be unprofessional for *me* to date my students," she added solemnly.

Jeff chuckled. "Well, then, you'd better watch out.

Because Trevor over there told me in confidence, just half an hour ago, that he's planning to marry you.''

"Don't you have work to do?" Mara prompted.

He started off, and then turned back. "How unprofessional is it for you to date your students' *fathers*?" he asked with an exaggerated wink and a wolfish grin.

"Go away!" Mara said. "Now!"

She watched, smiling, as he sauntered off down the hallway toward the teachers' lounge. His jeans, faded almost white from countless washings, hung on his lean, muscular hips, and his college sweatshirt was getting a little frayed at the elbows.

*You'd never guess, to look at him,* Mara thought fondly, *that he's an honor student and that his family belongs to the city's social elite.*

Still smiling, she went back into the room, where restless little stirrings and mutterings were becoming audible, and hurried over to the closet to get out her guitar case.

Later that same day, Mara sat opposite her grandmother in their bright, warm kitchen, eating dinner. Gran's chicken stew with dumplings was, as usual, an absolute joy. Mara finished her second helping, sighed with pleasure, then looked in dismay at the piece of hot apple pie with ice cream that appeared instantly in front of her.

"Oh, Gran, really, I don't think I can."

"Eat it," Agnes said calmly. "Every bite. If I'm going to work all afternoon to make a nice meal, the least you can do is to eat it."

"But, Gran, I—"

"Eat it!"

Obediently Mara picked up her fork and began to eat. "Mmm!" she murmured in ecstasy. "Gran, you make just the *best* apple pie...."

"Of course I do," Gran agreed placidly. "Everybody says so. And I know how much you love it. You always have, ever since you were a little girl."

Mara smiled at her grandmother. Gran was looking especially nice tonight, pink-cheeked and cheerful in a blue gingham housedress and a voluminous white ruffled apron. Her hair, which Mara had cut and permed just a week earlier, was a fluffy mass of soft white curls.

"You're looking awfully chipper, Gran. Have you had a good day?"

"Oh, the usual," Agnes said, sitting down and pouring tea into cups. "I raked leaves in the backyard and burned another big pile of them in the morning. Then I went over on the bus to the nursing home and had lunch with Rachel...."

"Did you?" Mara interrupted. "How is she?"

"Well, I guess she's all right. You know Rachel," Agnes added with a fond smile. "She already has her room reorganized to suit her, and Wayne's smuggled in her old sideboard, and a hotplate so that she can make tea, and all her ornaments and things, so it looks just like her room at home, almost."

Mara stared at her grandmother. "Not even Rachel could manage to smuggle in a *sideboard*," she said. "I've seen that sideboard. It's as big as a deep freeze."

"I know. I think the nurses indulge her, just because she's such a darling."

"She is, isn't she?" Mara asked. "I'll bet she already knows all their names and their life stories and all their troubles." She sipped her tea. "I'm glad she's happy, anyway. I know she wasn't anxious to move."

"She's not all that happy," Agnes said with a sudden sharp edge to her voice. "She's making the best of it, but I know she misses her house and the neighborhood and all her friends. Poor Rachel."

Gran was silent for a moment, swirling her tea and gazing thoughtfully into the depths of the cup. Finally she looked up at Mara again.

"I hate it there," she said. "No matter how nice they try to make it, it's still just another institution, and they're all like prisoners in there, really."

"Oh, Gran, that's not true. A lot of those older people are happy to—"

"I'd die," Agnes interrupted her. "If I had to go live in one of those places, I'd rather just die. I couldn't stand it."

This was a familiar topic of conversation and one that Mara had no wish to pursue at the moment. "I'd really love another cup of tea," she said to divert Gran's attention. "What did you do after you came back from Rachel's?" she asked, watching her grandmother pour the last of the tea.

"Well, first I went down to Harry's and bought some meat—"

"Gran, I thought we agreed that Harry's prices are

far too high, and it's so much better to get our meat at the supermarket.''

"But I *know* Harry," Agnes protested. "I like to know who I'm getting my meat from."

"Gran…"

"And, besides, I can handle Harry. You should have seen the fatty round steak he tried to palm off on me today. I just said to him, 'Harry, you of all people should know better than to…'"

Mara tuned out and let Gran ramble on about all the gossip from Harry's corner store, which was a meeting place for Gran and her cronies.

Mara's mind drifted, picturing a cosy little lighted farmhouse, solitary on a broad sweep of silent prairie under a starry black velvet sky, and a pair of blazing blue eyes in a lean tanned face….

"And what did you do today?"

There was an expectant silence.

"Pardon?" Mara asked with a start.

"My goodness," Agnes said affectionately, "what a daydreamer you are. I was just asking what *you* did today."

"Oh, nothing much. I just…"

Mara hesitated, wondering if she should tell Agnes about her day and her trip to the farm. Gran was being so nice, and Mara knew she would be interested in the story about Michael. Mara wanted to tell her about Allan, too—like all women, she was experiencing a powerful urge to talk about the man she found so attractive, just to have the pleasure of saying his name aloud and discussing him with another person.

But with Gran you could never be sure what might

trigger a negative reaction, especially where men were concerned.

"Well?" Agnes asked impatiently. "Did something happen or not?"

Mara decided not to risk it, and got up quickly to clear the table. "Nothing much. Just the usual. You know."

Agnes looked at her with sudden suspicion. Mara pretended to ignore her grandmother's penetrating gaze, turning aside to stack dishes in the sink. Agnes sat at the table, sipping her tea and watching Mara's slim, rigid back.

"Nothing else?" she asked. "You look funny, Mara. *Did* something happen? Why won't you tell me?"

"No, Gran," Mara said, turning on the faucet and spraying detergent into the jet of hot water. "Nothing happened. It was just a normal day."

"You're keeping something from me," Agnes said plaintively. "I can always tell. You know how I hate it when you keep things from me, Mara. I get so worried, and then I don't sleep well, and then I start to feel so—"

"Really, Gran," Mara interrupted wearily, "there's nothing to tell. Nothing happened. Nothing at all."

The autumn days slipped by. Early frost draped the trees and shrubs with filmy lace in the morning, and the shadows lay long and still across the prairie in the slanting afternoon sunlight.

Mara moved mechanically through her days, trying to suppress the loneliness and the helpless, trapped feelings that lay just beneath the surface of her thoughts. Her days were filled with the concerns and problems of her students, but her evenings were long and her dreams were haunted by troubling visions of Allan Williamson's tanned face, the feel of his lips and hands upon her, the line of his cheek and the strength of his body.

She woke from these dreams feeling sadder than ever, and then found herself longing for sleep so that she could dream some more.

She entered her high school study class on an afternoon in late October and noticed with relief that Lisa was back in her usual desk. Since her conversation with Jeff, Mara had been especially conscious of the girl, to the point of becoming genuinely concerned when Lisa had failed to turn up in study class for two consecutive weeks. But now she was back, looking pale but serene in a soft blue angora sweater, her golden hair pulled back and fastened with a blue clip.

Mara responded to the usual jokes and teasing, had her customary brief conversation with the class and got them settled to work. Then, as was her habit, she left her desk and began to move quietly around the classroom.

As she neared the back of the room, Lisa looked up and smiled at her, and Mara was struck, as always, by the girl's extraordinary beauty. Lisa's skin was translucent and exquisitely pale, and her deep blue eyes and silvery blond hair combined to give her an appearance of extreme delicacy. At eighteen she already had the poise and composure of a woman twice her age. She seemed, somehow, set apart from her rowdy, wisecracking classmates.

Mara, however, knew from past experience that Lisa had a vibrant, mischievous sense of humor and could be overcome by a fit of giggles just like any other schoolgirl.

Now, as she smiled back, she studied Lisa's face and sensed that something was wrong. Lisa looked as calm and lovely as ever, but there was a stillness behind her eyes, and a closed, shuttered look about her young face that had never been there before.

"Hi, Lisa," she murmured.

"Hi, Miss Steen. How are all the little kids?"

"They're fine. You should come down and meet them, Lisa. We have some real sweeties this year."

Lisa smiled wistfully. "I'll bet. I've been wanting to come, but I've been...really busy." She blushed scarlet and looked down quickly, fiddling nervously with the ring binder on her notebook.

"Jeff told me that you came down the other day when I was away," Mara said casually. "I was sorry I missed you."

"He's your teacher's aide, isn't he?" Lisa asked.

"Well, sort of. I call him that, but he's actually going to university and working with me for credit towards a degree in early childhood education."

"Really?" Lisa asked with interest. "He seemed... he seemed really nice."

"I often wonder how I ever got along without him," Mara said with a smile. "But," she added, "he's an awful tease sometimes. He's got a real off-the-wall sense of humor."

Lisa smiled back at her briefly with a little of the old sparkle. But it soon faded, and she dropped her eyes nervously, staring down at her books. Mara looked gently at the girl's bent head.

"I was a little concerned, Lisa," Mara said, "when you missed study class these past couple of weeks."

"I know. I wasn't feeling well. I'm better now, though." Lisa looked up and smiled again, but it was a halfhearted effort. Her face looked as if it might crumple into tears at any moment. "Miss Steen?" she whispered.

"Yes, Lisa."

"I'd...I'd like to talk to you about...something. Could I come down to your room on...I don't know...on..."

"Anytime, Lisa. How about Thursday afternoon? I don't have study class Thursday, so we can have a nice long talk."

Lisa gave her a sad little smile. "Long, maybe. I don't know how nice it'll be." She paused, and her fine skin flushed pink again. "Thanks, Miss Steen."

Mara smiled back, patted her slim shoulder and then hurried across the room to settle a dispute that had just flared up near the windows, concerning the ownership of a squashed, ripped bag of potato chips.

Next day, in the morning, Mara sat at her desk and glanced out the window at the playground. Then, conscious of something out of the ordinary, she got to her feet to look more closely. The children were beginning to arrive for their morning class, and a number of them were clustered together near the monkey

bars, clearly excited about something. Mara could just
make out Michael Williamson's red jacket and sleek
dark head in the center of the group.

Feeling again the pang of protective concern that
always accompanied her thoughts about Michael, she
took her soft woolen jacket from the closet, tossed it
over her shoulders and went down the hall and out
onto the playground. As she approached, a few of the
children noticed her and began shouting and pointing.

"Look, Miss Steen! Look what Michael's got!"

"Hey, Miss Steen, his name's Blackie! Come
look!"

"Oh, Miss Steen, he's got the cutest little pink
paws. Just look!"

Mara entered the throng of children, smiling down
at their bright, animated faces. Michael stood nervously in the center of the group, carefully holding a
cardboard box close to his chest. When he saw Mara,
he gave her a shy smile. She smiled back, and he
dropped his eyes quickly.

In the two weeks that had passed since Mara's visit
to the farm, Michael had come a long way, although
he was still far from being a normal, outgoing five-
year-old. He was never as relaxed and spontaneous
with her at school as he had been in the security of
his own home, but he did smile at her occasionally
and sometimes even answered her questions. And he
had tentatively made friends with Jamie, another shy,
thoughtful little boy. They played gravely together at
quiet, complicated games of their own invention.

Wordlessly Michael held the box up toward her,
and she opened the flaps to peer inside. Blackie glared

up at her, blinking angrily in the light and immediately attempted to escape. Mara closed the flaps quickly, becoming aware of detailed, colorful markings all around the outside of the box.

On closer inspection she saw that the box had been decorated to resemble a little house, by someone surprisingly skillful with pen and crayons. There were small leaded glass windows drawn on the cardboard, complete with frilly curtains and window boxes full of flowers. Neat lines had been drawn to resemble siding, and the impressive front door sported a tiny peephole, a brass handle, and a door knocker. Mara peered more closely at this item and laughed. It had been drawn, in careful miniature, to represent a cat's face.

"Michael," she asked, "who did the artwork?"

"Dad did," Michael said proudly. "He said you'd like it."

"Well, I certainly do. I think it's just beautiful."

"But he said he got kind of carried away," Michael admitted.

Mara chuckled. "Yes, it looks like maybe he did, all right. But you can tell your dad that I think Blackie's house is really terrific."

She took the box and carried it into the school, followed by a laughing, dancing crowd of children.

Because they were all so excited about the kitten, Mara scrapped her lesson plans for the morning and centered all their activities around cats. The children drew pictures of cats, sang songs about cats and played a game in which they pretended, by turns, to be cats, and the class had to guess what "cat thing" they were doing. This last was such a rousing success that they continued the game right until lunchtime and were reluctant to stop when the bell rang. It was Mara's turn, and she was down on her hands and knees, stroking at the floor with her hands and then shaking both hands violently in the air. The children crouched around her in a circle, shouting out their guesses.

"You're washing your paws!"

She shook her head.

"You're fighting with another cat!"

"Wrong again."

"You're trying to catch a fish, and it keeps getting away!"

"Good guess but wrong."

"You're batting a ball of wool around and getting all tangled up in it," a deep voice said far above their heads. "And you're going to be in deep trouble."

Mara threw her head up and stared, openmouthed.

Allan Williamson was lounging in the doorway, laughing down at her.

# 5

Mara knelt, startled and speechless, overwhelmed by Allan's sudden and unexpected appearance.

"Every time I come here," he said cheerfully, "you're down on your knees."

She was still too stunned to respond. He looked different today and, again, even more handsome than she had remembered. He was wearing polished shoes, dark brown dress slacks and a brown tweed jacket with a striped tie. Except for his weathered tan and callused hands, he looked like any young executive on his way out to a business luncheon.

"Had an appointment with my banker," he explained, indicating his apparel. "I have to make an effort to impress him with my solvency. Here, Miss Steen, let me help you up."

He extended his hand, still grinning. Mara ignored it, getting to her feet with an attempt at dignity.

As Mara hurried the children into their hats and jackets, Allan crossed the room and leaned against the window ledge, followed by Michael, who was chattering to him with great animation about the morning's activities. Allan listened to his son, but his eyes followed Mara's slim, dainty figure as she moved about the classroom, getting her students ready for departure.

She wore a soft corduroy shirtdress, the color of faded rose petals, that clung to her rounded hips and her high, firm breasts. Her tawny hair, as usual, fell down her back in its heavy plait, and he tried to imagine how it would look if it were hanging free. Just the thought of it was almost enough to take his breath away....

Finally the last child was gone, and she turned to look at Allan.

"I was in town anyway," he explained, "so I thought I might as well come by and pick these two up. I'm not sure how excited the bus driver was about his extra passenger." He indicated Blackie's box, which Michael was holding protectively near his chest.

Mara nodded, trying to think of something to say.

"And," Allan went on casually, "since I'm here, and it's noon, I thought I might as well take you out for lunch."

"Oh, Mr. Williamson, I'm sorry, but I have to—"

"Call me Allan," he interrupted firmly, "and don't argue. This is a celebration. You should see what great shape I'm in with my banker. Paid off one of my loans, got a new line of credit..." He paused, grinning. "As a matter of fact, I'm so rich right now that you can have cheese on your hamburger if you're one of those expensive women."

Mara laughed in spite of herself. "Really, Mr. Williamson...Allan...I'd love to, but..." She hesitated, trying to think of something pressing that she absolutely had to get done on her lunch hour.

"Please, Miss Steen," Michael said shyly, gazing up at her with imploring blue eyes. "Please come. It'll be so much fun."

She looked down at him dubiously.

After all, she argued with herself, what harm can it do? It's only lunch. And it's important now to be friendly with Michael when he's finally beginning to respond....

"All right," she said finally. "All right, I'll go."

Allan's big green four-wheel-drive truck was at the curb in front of the school, immaculately clean but still carrying a faint, pleasant scent of hay and cattle. The three of them drove to a nearby Italian restaurant, parked and went inside.

As they wove their way among the crowded tables, with Allan's hand protectively on her elbow, Mara realized with a little shock of surprise that a lot of the younger women in the restaurant were looking at her with genuine envy. It shouldn't surprise her, she knew. Allan, with his fine, clean-cut face and big erect body, was an enormously appealing man.

*They assume we're married,* Mara thought with a little inward thrill. *They think he's my husband and Michael is our son....*

They found a booth, and Michael scrambled up beside his father, beaming across the table at Mara. Michael was delighted with the unexpected treat of lunch in a restaurant, and overjoyed to have his two favorite people together with him.

Their meal was noisy and cheerful, with a good deal of joking and teasing and, Mara felt, it was over far too soon. She was amazed, as she had been earlier, at how easy it was to talk with Allan. He seemed to understand what she was thinking before she said it, and his insights and offbeat sense of humor were surprising and delightful. She was sorry when the bill came and Allan began searching in his pocket for change.

"We're going to the zoo," Michael told her, his face bright with excitement.

"Are you, Michael?" Mara asked. "When?"

"Right now. This afternoon. Dad promised."

Allan gave Mara an eloquent glance. "Kids," he said briefly. "Never forget a thing, do they?"

Michael looked alarmed. "Aren't we, Dad? You said you'd have time this afternoon."

"Yes, Mick, we're going. I know I promised." He smiled at Mara again. "The poor little guy never gets to go anywhere, really, because I'm always so busy, it seems, and he's always just playing by himself in the house. So I thought we'd have a treat just this once."

Mara smiled back at him, and then looked at Michael. "Will Blackie be all right while you're at the zoo?" she asked.

"I brought some milk from home for him," Allan said, "and I'll park in the shade. It's not too hot today."

Michael bounced on the padded seat of the booth, beaming. "Do you like the zoo?" he asked Mara.

"I love it," Mara said. "I always have."

She held Michael's hand, following Allan to the front of the restaurant and standing nearby while he paid the bill.

"What's your favorite animal there?" Michael asked.

Mara frowned, considering. "I think I like the penguins best," she said.

Allan held the door open for them, grinning, and they went out into the clear autumn sunlight.

Michael paused beside the truck. "I wish you could come with us," he said to Mara.

"Oh, Michael," she said wistfully. "Wouldn't that be nice?"

"It sure would," Allan said. "Can't you play hooky just for one afternoon and come with us?"

She looked up at him suddenly, her eyes wide and startled.

"What is it, Mara?" he asked. And then, with his seemingly uncanny ability to read her mind, he said, "You *are* free this afternoon, aren't you? You don't have to work, right?"

"Actually," she confessed, "I don't. I'd forgotten about it until just now when you said—You see," she explained, "Jeff has to handle the class alone one afternoon a month. His supervisor comes out to watch him, and I'm not even supposed to be in the room. I was planning to spend the afternoon in the staff room, making up lesson plans."

Michael stared up at her, wide-eyed, and Allan smiled in delight.

"Would you get into trouble if you were to leave the school, do you think?" he asked.

Mara considered for a moment and then grinned at him, her eyes sparkling. "Not," she said slowly, "if I were to use part of the afternoon to talk with the staff at the zoo about bringing the children over on a field trip. It's something I've been planning to do, anyhow, now that I have Jeff to help me."

"Well, Miss Steen," Allan said, opening the truck door with a formal bow, "I believe this is the perfect time to make those arrangements."

"Mr. Williamson," she said solemnly, "I believe you're absolutely right."

Allan and Mara strolled side by side along the winding, tree-lined path leading to the aquariums. His tie was gone, his shirt open at the throat and he had his jacket slung carelessly over one shoulder. Beside him, Mara carried a large bag of popcorn, liberally soaked with butter stains at the bottom. Michael raced ahead of them, his face smeared with chocolate, mustard and other substances less easily identified, carrying a large balloon shaped like a panda bear.

Allan reached over casually and helped himself to a handful of popcorn from Mara's bag.

"Hey!" she said indignantly. "Stop that! Just because yours is all gone you can't start eating mine, you know."

"Mine was a smaller bag," he argued.

"It was not," she said firmly. "You had just as much as I did. And if you don't have any more self-restraint than that…"

He turned and looked down at her. She was laughing, and her gray eyes shone with happiness. Her cheeks were as pink as the soft corduroy dress she wore, and little wispy strands of hair had escaped their barrettes, catching the sun and curling around her face in a golden halo.

"Mara," he said softly. "Oh, Mara, if you only knew how much self-restraint I'm exercising right this minute."

Their eyes met, and she gazed up at him, her lips slightly parted, her face open and gentle. For a long moment they stood looking at each other, and then Mara turned away quickly.

"Michael," she called, rummaging in her bag for a tissue. "Michael, come back here and let me clean your face."

She paused to wet the tissue in a water fountain beside the path, and the little boy ran back toward them, standing in front of Mara and lifting his face obediently while she wiped him clean. Mara smoothed his hair tenderly and bent to kiss his cheek.

"This is the best day I ever had," he told her solemnly. "Ever in my whole life," he added, then ran off down the path again, waving his balloon.

Mara watched his small dancing body. Her throat tightened suddenly and her eyes blurred with tears.

"Oh, Allan," she murmured, "just look at him...."

Allan put an arm around her and held her against him. "I know what you mean," he said huskily.

She stood quietly for a moment within the circle of his arm, trembling at the feel of his long, hard body against her own. She was almost overcome by the surging flood of emotion that washed over her—of warm, rich happiness and a deep urgent longing that left her feeling strangely weak.

She'd never felt this way before. Not even with David. There had never been a man who affected her the way Allan did.

She looked up at him again.

He was gazing down at her, his eyes serious and intent. He lowered his face toward her, and her lips parted, waiting to receive his kiss...

"Come on!" Michael shouted, running back toward them. "Come down here! There's penguins down here and they're playing on a slide!"

Mara and Allan drew apart awkwardly, turning to follow the little boy down the path.

"Damn penguins," Allan muttered.

Mara laughed, and hurried ahead of him to catch up with Michael.

Finally the afternoon ended and they drove reluctantly back to the school. Michael drowsed sleepily in Mara's lap, worn out from his day of fun, and she and Allan talked casually of unimportant things.

At the school Allan parked by the curb, got out and held the door open for her, courteously assisting her down to the sidewalk.

"Goodbye, Michael," she called. "See you tomorrow. Goodbye, Blackie."

Allan walked with her to the doors of the school and paused inside the vestibule, turning to face her.

"Thank you for everything, Allan," she said. "I had a lovely time."

"May I call you this weekend?"

Mara stared at him in alarm. "No," she said hastily. "No, please don't call me."

He looked down at her in silence.

"It's...my grandmother," she explained lamely. "She gets so upset if I..."

"So what's the deal, Mara? You have no life of your own at all, is that it? You can't ever see a man because your grandmother wouldn't like it?"

Mara reddened. "No, it's not like that. Of course I can have a life of my own. I'm almost thirty years old. It's just that I don't want..." She paused, searching for words, and then looked up at him, meeting his eyes with a level gaze. "You don't know what it's like, Allan. I love my grandmother, but she can be just awful sometimes. And she panics if she thinks there's any possibility that I might be...getting involved with someone or even seeing someone. She's so terrified that I'll go away and leave her alone, and she..." Mara hesitated.

"She uses emotional blackmail," Allan said. "She makes a big fuss and makes your life so unpleasant that she winds up controlling you and getting you to do what she wants. Right?"

"Not entirely," Mara said quietly. "I mean, I know that she's manipulative, but I also know that she's *my* responsibility. There's nobody else to help me with it. And she's going to keep on being my responsibility for a long, long time, Allan. That's just the way it is. I'm not the kind of person who can walk away from a responsibility."

"Fine," he said calmly. "Believe me, Mara, I

know all about responsibility. I just don't see why it has to prevent you from leading a normal life.''

"Look," she said, irritated by his calm, reasonable tone and the truth of what he was saying, "just because I don't want you to call me at home, doesn't mean I can't live a normal life! I can do just as I please!"

"Great. Come and visit us at the farm, then. You promised over two weeks ago that you'd come. You promised, Mara, and you never have."

Her anger ebbed away as quickly as it had flared, and she looked up at him, her wide gray eyes pleading. "Allan, please don't press me. You just don't know what I have to live with."

"No, but I can imagine. And I'm telling you that if you don't come, then I *will* call you. And if that doesn't accomplish anything, then I'll come myself and have a little talk with your grandmother."

Mara trembled in horror, picturing the dreadful embarrassment for everybody concerned that would result from any confrontation between Allan and Gran. She stared at him, her eyes dark with panic.

"Allan," she whispered.

"I mean it," he told her relentlessly. "Either you come to my place or I'll go to yours."

Mara gazed unseeingly at his broad chest, wrestling with her turbulent thoughts.

"I mean it, Mara," he repeated.

"All right," she said in defeat. "I'll come."

"This weekend," he insisted.

"Yes," she agreed helplessly. "This weekend."

"Good. Can you ride?"

She looked up at him, startled. "A horse, you mean?"

"Yeah," he said, grinning at her. "A horse."

"Well...sort of. One of my girlfriends in high school kept horses outside the city, and I used to love going riding with her."

"Good. Come out real early Sunday morning, then. Can you make it about...say, eight o'clock?"

Mara gave him a small, grim smile. "I guess I don't really have much choice, do I? You're calling the shots here, after all."

Allan serenely ignored this. "We're gathering cattle in the community pasture on Sunday," he said. "We'll be riding most of the day. You're going to love it...right?"

"Right," she agreed mechanically. She was still dazed by the shameless, skillful way that he was manipulating her and the fact that she seemed unable to do anything about it.

He smiled down at her cheerfully. "That's what I wanted to hear. I'll see you Sunday morning. Goodbye, Mara."

She nodded wordlessly.

Allan reached out and cupped her cheek gently in his strong brown hand, looking directly into her eyes. Then he bent and kissed her mouth—a long, tender, searching kiss.

"See you Sunday," he murmured huskily against her cheek. "I can hardly wait."

He looked down at her for a moment longer, smiled again and was gone, striding briskly up the sidewalk to his truck.

Mara stood in the vestibule, her hand to her cheek, her heart pounding, and watched him walk away.

All through the next day Mara went about her duties automatically, her mind whirling. Part of her resented the high-handed way Allan had moved in and taken over her life. But another part of her—a girlish, tremulous, long-buried part—was singing, "Sunday...Sunday...Sun- day...." And sometimes she found herself smiling for no reason at all.

Fortunately, though Jeff had been away all morning to write an English exam, he was there in the afternoon to help with the children. He cast her a few suspicious glances and asked some probing, pointed questions, which she ignored, until he finally gave up and concentrated on the children's activities.

"Something's going on. I can tell," he muttered on his way out to the playground for recess. "But never mind. I'll get it out of you later."

Mara just smiled.

She watched out the window as Jeff organized a game of tag, and then she left, walking briskly through the school corridors to Jo's drama classroom. A dull roar emanated from within, and Mara had to knock several times before a student answered the door.

Finally Jo herself appeared, statuesque and striking in a jungle-print caftan with a matching headband on her wild red curls.

Mara smiled up at her. "You look so exotic," she said. "I just love it."

Jo beamed and patted the top of Mara's head.

The noise from within the classroom accelerated, and a dull thumping and scraping became audible, as well. Jo turned and bellowed into the room, "I said to *lift* those desks! Don't drag them."

She turned back to Mara and explained in normal conversational tones, "We're clearing a space to act in. It's Improvisation Day. Skits written by the students. Wanna come in and watch?"

"Well..."

A boy ran past the open door, wearing, Mara was certain, nothing but a lace-trimmed teddy and a pink lamp shade.

"I'd love to, Jo," she said with genuine regret, "but I have to get back to my room. We're going to be starting finger painting in a few minutes. I just came down to ask a favor of you."

Something in her face impressed Jo, who shouted, "Quiet!" into the rollicking classroom, then stepped out into the hallway, pulling the door shut behind her.

"Yeah?" she asked with interest. "What kind of favor?"

"I have to be away from home on Sunday, and I can't tell Gran where I'm going. Can I say that I'm with you?"

Jo studied her friend's face in thoughtful silence. "Mara," she said finally, "you're getting far too old for this kind of crap, you know. Why can't you tell your grandmother where you're going?"

"Jo, you know what she's like. Everybody says, 'Don't put up with it. Don't let her run your life....' But what can I do? What choice do I have?"

"Just do as you damn well please. Let her adjust. If she doesn't like it, she can lump it."

Mara shook her head in frustration. "That's always easy to say. But it's not easy to do. I'm not a child and I'm not a coward, Jo. But I believe that at this stage in her life if Gran's left alone or forced to live with strangers or even if she feels there's a danger of that happening, then she'll really, genuinely, either go insane or commit suicide. Now how am I supposed to live with that reality? How, Jo? If I go ahead and do what I want, then how do I deal with the consequences without feeling guilty for the rest of my life?"

Jo's aquiline features softened in compassion. "Jesus, kid," she murmured, "you really are in a trap, aren't you? You should have left with David when you still had a chance to make a clean getaway."

Mara looked up at her but didn't answer.

"Maybe not," Jo added reflectively. "On second thought, David turned out to be quite a louse, too, didn't he? No sense exchanging one kind of trap for another."

Both women were silent for a moment. "What time Sunday?" Jo asked.

"All day. From early in the morning until after supper."

Jo hadn't taught improvisation all those years without learning something. "Okay," she said briskly. "Tell her you're coming to my pool-cleaning party. Tell her half the staff is coming, and my phone's unlisted, so you can't possibly be contacted there."

Mara stared at her. "A *pool-cleaning* party?" she asked incredulously.

Jo smiled placidly. "Certainly. All the best people are having them. On a nice fall day, you invite a bunch of friends over, give them all brooms and brushes, set a bar up near the pool and let them go at it. Gets a dirty job out of the way and everybody has a great time."

Mara chuckled. "Are you really having one?"

"Of course not. I've never heard of such a thing. I just thought it'd make a good cover story for you." Jo hesitated thoughtfully. "Maybe I should. It does sound like fun, doesn't it?"

Mara laughed and hugged the tall woman. "Thanks, Jo."

Jo looked down at her friend's glowing face. "All day Sunday, huh? I assume it's that yummy item you were with yesterday?"

"How on earth did you know?"

"I was in the office, checking attendance sheets after school. I saw you coming back in that big green truck." Jo put one hand to her breast and sighed theatrically. "God, what a man. For a gorgeous creature like that, I'd lie, cheat, steal...possibly kill." She smiled at Mara with sudden tenderness and opened her door again. "Have fun, kid," she said. "God knows, you deserve it."

Mara started to answer, but a solid wall of noise erupted from Jo's classroom, obliterating all other sounds. Jo swirled back into the room, shouting, while Mara beat a hasty retreat up the hallway.

\* \* \*

The afternoon finally ended, and Mara bundled her small students up and sent them off, still smiling. Then she settled to work at her desk, while Jeff vanished outside briefly and reappeared carrying a colorful paper cylinder.

"What's that?" Mara asked.

"Wallpaper. I found it in the back of an old storage closet at our apartment. It's pink and gold brocade. The previous tenants' decorating style was what is referred to as 'Terminal Tacky.'"

"I see. What are you planning to do with it?"

"I'm going to wallpaper the dollhouse," Jeff said with dignity.

"Oh, Jeff," she said in dismay. "What a picky job. Do you really want to?"

"Sure," he said placidly, moving the big dollhouse onto the worktable and assembling glue and scissors. "I like picky jobs, and I sure need a break from studying childhood neuroses."

"How was the English exam?" Mara asked, watching as his skillful fingers measured and cut the tiny pieces of wallpaper.

"Not bad. I missed two of the poetic meters." He looked over at Mara. "Did you know that there are virtually no poems in the English language written in anapestic tetrameter?"

"No kidding," Mara said idly. "What an absolutely fascinating piece of information. You know," she added, looking at the bright scraps of pink and gold, "that's kind of pretty paper, actually."

Jeff chuckled. "My, we *are* in a good mood today,

aren't we? A person would have to be a little out of it to *like* this stuff."

"I didn't say I liked it," Mara protested. "I merely commented—" She broke off, startled by the sudden look of surprise that appeared on Jeff's handsome, laughing face.

Following his gaze, Mara turned to see Lisa standing shyly in the doorway, wearing white slacks and a loose pink pullover.

"Oh!" Mara exclaimed. "Lisa, I completely forgot that you were coming by today. It's so nice to see you."

Lisa came hesitantly into the room. "I can come back another time," she said, "if you're busy, or something."

"No, we're not busy. We were just talking, really. Jeff..." Mara began.

"Sure," he said. "I was just about to leave, actually. Hi, Lisa," he added, tidying up wallpaper scraps and scissors and restoring the dollhouse to its shelf. "I'm Jeff."

"Hi, Jeff. Don't let me rush you away."

"No problem. I have a class at five."

Lisa wandered over to peer into the miniature house, and Mara saw, with private amusement, the tension in Jeff's shoulders as the beautiful girl came and stood near him.

"This is really pretty," Lisa said, reaching out to touch a tiny dining room wall. She smiled. "So this is what they teach you at university," she teased. "I've often wondered."

"And don't think it's easy," Jeff told her solemnly.

"A lot of guys never make it. Even as we speak, two of my friends are flunking Basic Dollhouse 101."

Lisa laughed, and the two young people stood for a moment by the window, smiling at each other.

"Well," Jeff said finally, "I'd better get going. See you Tuesday," he said to Mara, pausing in the doorway. "Bye, Lisa. Drop back in someday when we're doing Play Dough. I may be great at wallpapering dollhouses, but I'm a *genius* with Play Dough."

Together they watched him leave.

"He's just terrific, you know," Mara said. "And he's great with the kids. They really love him."

Lisa smiled, still watching the doorway. "I've been hearing about him ever since school started," she said. "All the girls are talking about how cute he is and about his car and how rich his family is and all that.... I thought he'd be too conceited to stand."

"He isn't, though," Mara said. "He's just as nice and natural as can be."

They were both silent for a moment.

"I think he likes you," Mara added.

Lisa looked over at her with the same expression of naked anguish that Mara had surprised on the girl's face once before.

"Lisa," she said gently, "what is it? What's the matter?"

Lisa sank into a chair and picked up a big rag doll from a shelf nearby.

Mara watched silently, waiting for the girl to speak, while Lisa kneaded and pleated the doll's soft fabric arms.

Finally Lisa turned to her with that same expression

of desperate pleading in her wide blue eyes. "I really need to talk to somebody," she said, "and I can't think of anyone else but you."

"Thanks, Lisa. I'll be happy to do anything I can."

"Nobody can do anything," Lisa said. She fell silent again, brooding, and then pulled herself together with a visible effort, took a deep breath and looked up at Mara. "I'm pregnant," she said.

# 6

Mara stared back at her, stunned and speechless. Although she had spent some time speculating on the source of Lisa's unhappiness, for some reason she had never once considered the possibility of pregnancy.

"Oh, Lisa…" she began. All the clichés that were normally expressed at such a time went tumbling through her mind: Are you sure? How long have you known? When are you due? Who's the baby's father? And one by one Mara rejected them until she was left without an appropriate response—completely at a loss for words.

Lisa gave her a wan smile. "Pretty heavy, right? But you just don't know how good it feels to tell someone. It's such a relief to say it out loud after worrying all by myself for so long."

"I'm afraid I'm not much help," Mara confessed. "I just can't think of anything helpful to say." She thought for a moment. "I guess, first, I'd like to know if you're absolutely certain, or if it could possibly be a false alarm."

"I'm absolutely certain. I did one of those home tests a long time ago…almost a month, I guess, and it was positive. And last week, when I missed my second period, I went to the doctor. I'm two months pregnant.''

Her voice trembled a little, belying the calm matter-of-factness of her words. Mara looked at her with concern.

"So," she asked, "what now?"

"That's for sure," Lisa said with a little laugh that suddenly turned into a sob. "What now?"

Tears filled her eyes and trickled down her pale cheeks. Mara took a tissue from a box on her desk, got out of her chair and came to kneel beside Lisa, handing her the tissue and putting her arms around the girl's slender body. Lisa cried silently for a little while, then mopped at her eyes and straightened her shoulders.

Mara got to her feet and sat on her desk nearby, reaching over to pat the girl tenderly on the shoulder.

"Sorry," Lisa said. "There's no need for all this crying. I'm just being a baby because you're so sympathetic. But I've thought this all through, and there's no reason to be crying over it."

"What are you planning to do?"

Lisa glanced out the window with a defiant set to her young face. Then she turned to look directly at Mara. "I'm going to have my baby, keep it and raise it."

"Oh, Lisa…that's a hard path to set out on, you know."

"Sure it's hard. Lots of things are hard. But what else can I do?"

"There *are* other options."

"What? Adoption? Having someone else raise my

baby and never knowing where she is or if she's lonely or cold or hungry or scared...." Lisa shook her head, setting her blond ponytail swinging. "Maybe it's right for other people. I think it's probably even the most loving, generous thing to do. But I could never stand it."

They were both silent while the third option hung in the air between them.

"And I can't do that, either," Lisa said finally. "Abortion, I mean. I've given it a lot of thought, and I just can't."

"Okay," Mara said. "That's a highly personal decision, and you're certainly intelligent enough to make it on your own. So, since you've already made your choice, I guess we just have to deal with ways and means. Do you plan to graduate?"

"Sure. My grades are straight A's, and I'm due at the end of May. I can have the baby and be back in time to write final exams. Pregnant students are no big deal around this school."

Mara nodded, knowing that this was true. She refrained from mentioning, however, that pregnant students of Lisa's stature were still a rarity, even at Thomas Carlton. "How about your plans to go to university?" she asked.

Lisa shook her head. "I guess that's on hold for a few years, at least. It costs money to go to college, and my dad sure isn't going to help. Not now."

"Does he know about the baby?"

Lisa shook her head again. Her face crumpled, and she maintained her composure with an effort. "I'm scared to tell him. He's going to be just awful about it. I think he'll probably throw me out of the house, wash his hands of me and that'll be that.''

"Oh, Lisa, he won't. He loves you."

"In his way, I guess." Lisa went back to her aimless fiddling with the rag doll in her hands. "But he's so harsh, you know? He just can't ever compromise or even try to see things from my point of view."

Mara nodded.

"I think he'll just say, 'That's it. She's a tramp like her mother and she's not raising her brat in *my* house.' He'll feel he has every right to make me live with my own mistakes." Lisa paused, then added honestly, "I guess he *does* have that right, doesn't he? But I'm so scared to face up to what it's really going to be like, trying to look after a baby all on my own with nothing but a high school diploma."

"And the baby's father?"

Lisa's delicate face clouded. "Yes. Kevin. You know him?"

"I've seen him."

"You know, I had a mad crush on him for four years. I never thought there was anyone as wonderful as him. I used to plan my day so that I could be hanging around by his locker when he got back from gym or football practice, just to watch him put his gym stuff away and get his books out. That used to be the high point of my day. Isn't that weird? And this summer, when he finally noticed me, I couldn't believe how marvelous it was. I was just walking on air all the time. You know?"

Mara nodded and smiled with a faraway look in her eyes. "I know, Lisa."

"But when I got to know him, there's just nothing to him. Really. He's just hair and white teeth and a great body. But we can't *talk*," Lisa said in despair. "He doesn't really have a clue who I am or what I think about things or how I feel or what matters to me...."

She broke off and looked over at Mara with a sad little smile. "He's being decent about it. He thinks we should get married."

"And what do you think?"

"I used to think that spending a whole evening with him would be heaven on earth. Now, I think that being married to him, for me, at least, would be pure, absolute hell."

Mara nodded again. "I know all about that, too, Lisa," she said gently. "Are you still seeing him?"

"What's the point? It's all over and we both know it. There was never anything there in the first place, just some person that I fantasized, who never really existed at all. But," she added, "no other guy looks good to me, either, after Kevin. Isn't that strange?"

"Women are strange creatures," Mara said. "So," she went on, "since you're planning to keep your baby, and none of the men in your life are likely to be involved in your decision, how do you plan to go about it? Is there anyone who can help?"

"Nobody. No aunts, no grannies, nobody. And my mom...she keeps moving and forgetting to leave a forwarding address. I doubt that she could be much help. She's barely holding her own life together."

"So you're on your own."

"Right. But I've figured it all out. If I get a job for

minimum wage, waitressing or something, I can earn about seven hundred dollars a month. Figuring two hundred for rent and four hundred for someone to look after the baby while I work, that leaves me a hundred a month for food and diapers and stuff. I can manage.''

Mara stared at her, appalled. "Lisa, you can't manage on that. It's impossible.''

"No, it's not,'' Lisa said stubbornly. "Lots of people get by on less than that.''

"But that's figuring that you can even get a full-time job. And that's not easy when you just have high school. There's lots of competition for jobs, you know.''

"Don't scare me, Miss Steen. I'm going to do it, so I might as well try to be optimistic about it.''

"Optimism is great, Lisa, but it has to be tempered with realism. I'm optimistic about the situation because I think your father will be more sympathetic than you expect. I think he'll help.''

Lisa looked doubtful. "You don't know him, Miss Steen.''

"Well, maybe I should meet him. How about if I go along with you when you tell him about this, and we'll see if I can help to convince him that it's not the end of the world?''

The girl's face brightened with sudden hope. "Oh, would you? I'd never have asked it, but if you would…oh, that'd just be so great!''

"Certainly I will. Whenever you're ready. You just let me know.''

Impulsively Lisa tossed the doll aside, sprang to

her feet and hugged Mara, her face wet with fresh tears. "Miss Steen, you're just the nicest..." She choked, dashed a hand at her eyes and smiled ruefully. "More crying. I'd better get going before I make a bigger fool of myself. Thanks for everything, Miss Steen."

Mara watched the girl's graceful, slender form as she walked toward the doorway. "Lisa," she called suddenly.

Lisa paused and turned.

"Lisa," Mara said softly, "my mother was seventeen when she got pregnant with me. And she wasn't married."

Lisa's blue eyes widened. "Really?"

"Really. She was living at home with her mother. Just the two of them."

Lisa took a hesitant step back into the room. "And...?"

"And I was born and my grandmother raised me."

"But what happened to her? Your mother, I mean?"

"She died soon after I was born. My grandmother says she just didn't want to live."

Lisa's eyes flashed, and her chin lifted. "*I* want to live," she said. "I want to live and raise my own baby."

"Then that's what you'll do," Mara said matter-of-factly, smiling at her. "I have a lot of confidence in you, Lisa. I know how capable you are."

Lisa met Mara's eyes gravely for a moment, gave her a small tremulous smile of gratitude and vanished down the empty hallway.

\* \* \*

Mara woke early on Sunday and ran to her upstairs window, peering out anxiously. The air was crisp and tangy with a dusting of gold and a hint of snow, but the sky was a clear, sparkling blue, with all the clouds washed away by the rich autumn sunlight.

Happily she sang to herself as she washed her face and undid her hair. Unbound, her hair flowed past her hips in a glorious, shining cascade. She brushed it vigorously and then replaited it, reaching behind her head with the ease of long practice to manipulate the three heavy strands. When the braid was started, she pulled it over her shoulder to finish plaiting it and fastened it with a whimsical clip made of two tiny red apples, complete with leaves.

After some deep thought, she dabbed on cologne and a dash of lipstick and dressed in jeans, sneakers, a white shirt and a warm red pullover.

*It sounds like a pretty casual occasion,* she thought. *He said we'd be outdoors all day.... I just hope there won't be a lot of people around.... I wonder what a community pasture is, anyhow?*

Still absorbed in her thoughts, she grabbed a warm down-filled jacket and ran down the curving oak staircase, hoping that, for once, Gran had chosen to sleep late. But her spirits sank when she reached the bottom of the stairs. An enticing aroma of bacon and fresh coffee drifted out from the kitchen, where Gran stood at the stove. Mara took a deep breath, walked into the room, hugged the old lady and kissed her soft, wrinkled cheek. "Something smells good," she said. "How's my favorite little grandmother?"

Agnes's mouth twitched. "Well," she observed, "Aren't we chipper today? What's the occasion?"

"It's Sunday, it's a lovely day, and the world is beautiful, Gran."

Agnes snorted. "Beautiful, indeed. How many eggs?"

"Just one, please," Mara said, pouring herself a cup of coffee. "Are you going to visit Rachel today?"

"Why?"

"Gran, you said you were going to go over and spend the day with Rachel, because I'm going to be gone all day. Remember?"

"No, I don't remember," Agnes said flatly. "Where are you going to be all day?"

Mara took another deep breath.

If she could just be patient, just a few more minutes, she thought, she could get out of here without a fight and be free to enjoy her day. If only she didn't have to lie. *Gran, why do you force me to lie to you? I hate this. It's not right that I should have to tell lies when I'm not doing anything wrong.*

Agnes was standing, spatula in hand, regarding Mara suspiciously.

"Gran," Mara said patiently. "I *told* you. I'm going out to Jo's. She's having a pool-cleaning party and I'll be there all day." The words sounded so ridiculous when she spoke them out loud that Mara wished she and Jo could have come up with something more plausible.

"And what, may I ask, is a pool-cleaning party?"

Agnes thumped a platter of toast onto the table and turned back to the stove.

"Jo says everybody's having them," Mara said, reaching for a slice of toast. "Jo and Stan have that acreage outside town, you know, and they have a big swimming pool, and in the fall, when it's time to close it down for the season, they have all their friends over for the day to help them clean it out before winter. Isn't this just the best strawberry jam you ever tasted?"

But Agnes couldn't be diverted. "A *pool-cleaning* party," she repeated, her voice dripping sarcasm. "Of all the nonsense. Those crazy people would make a party out of anything."

"Life's a party, Gran," Mara said cheerfully.

"Not for most," Gran said darkly. "Not for most."

"Oh, Gran, cheer up. You'll have fun spending the day with Rachel. Maybe," Mara said with sudden inspiration, "the two of you could take the bus over to the mall and do some shopping. Rachel loves shopping."

Agnes brightened momentarily and then looked gloomy once more. "It would be a lot better if you could come," she said. "Then you could drive us to the mall, and we wouldn't have to ride the bus. It's so crowded on Sundays, and they don't run nearly as often, either."

"But you *know* I can't come. I promised Jo. As a matter of fact," Mara added with mock alarm, looking at her watch, "I'm late already. I'd better get going."

"A pool-cleaning party," Agnes muttered again

with deep bitterness. "You'd think grown people could find more sensible ways to spend their time."

Not until Mara had backed out of the garage, closed the door and pulled out onto the street, heading west, did she finally heave a deep sigh of relief and begin to breathe normally at last.

The sun was just rising behind her, and the clouds that hung low over the mountains reflected a soft, rosy glow. Mara drove westward into the country, her heart singing, overwhelmed by a delicious sense of freedom and adventure. She turned at the red granaries and drove south down the long gravel lane into the Williamson farmyard, which was a scene of lively activity.

Allan's big four-wheel-drive truck was parked in the center of the yard with a double horse trailer attached to it. Allan himself was crossing the yard, leading two horses in heavy trailer blankets, while Michael stood on the hood of the truck, peering intently down the lane. When he saw Mara's little car, he began to jump up and down in excitement until Allan called something to him and he obediently stood still, quivering with anticipation.

Mara parked in front of the house, shrugged into her jacket against the early morning chill and walked over to the truck. "Hi, Michael," she said.

"Hi, Miss Steen. We were scared you weren't coming." His face was rosy, his eyes blazing with excitement.

"Of course I came. This is going to be fun, isn't it?"

Michael nodded eagerly. "We're going to the com-

munity pasture, and there's lots and lots of people
there, and there'll be a big picnic, and I get to take
all my trucks, and my bike!''

He stopped for breath as Allan came up beside
them, smiling, wearing blue jeans, riding boots, a
denim jacket lined with sheepskin, and a blue tractor
cap.

"Hi, Mara," he said, pausing near her with the
horses behind him.

"Hello, Allan." She looked up at him and felt her
knees go weak. Every time she saw him she was more
overwhelmed by the sheer masculine appeal of the
man. Now, remembering the breathless pleasure of his
kiss and the warm sensation of his strong arms around
her, she had to fight the urge to walk into his arms,
press her face against that broad chest, kiss his finely
molded mouth....

She dropped her eyes and reached out to pat one
of the horses. "What are their names?" she asked.

"The bay's Cricket, and this little sorrel mare is
called Firefly. You'll be riding her. She's as gentle as
a kitten."

The sorrel mare, as if in response to her own name,
nuzzled at Allan's sleeve, and Mara laughed. "I hope
so. That she's gentle, I mean."

"Here, you hold her, and I'll load the bay." He
handed Mara the halter shank, led the big bay gelding
around to the back of the trailer and tossed the lead
line up over the horse's neck, slapping its rump so
that it stepped into the trailer. Then he went inside
himself, presumably to secure the halter, Mara de-

cided, and emerged almost at once, coming back around to where she stood.

"Any trouble getting away this morning?" he asked.

"No," Mara said. "I lied."

"Yeah?" He cocked an inquiring eyebrow at her.

She told him about Jo and the pool-cleaning party, doing a creditable imitation of Gran's reaction, and he shouted with laughter. Still chuckling, he led the sorrel mare around the truck, loaded her into the trailer and gathered Michael neatly off the hood of the truck.

"Have you got everything?" he asked the little boy. "We won't be coming back, you know. Not till after dark."

Michael nodded.

Allan turned to Mara. "How about you? All set?"

"Well..." she hesitated awkwardly.

He smiled down at her. "Go ahead. The house is unlocked. I have to get the saddles, anyway."

She nodded and ran into the house, grateful for his consideration.

When she came out again onto the wide veranda, Allan was striding up the walk toward her. "I'll lock the door," he said. Then pausing, he reached out to hold her shoulder, looking down at her intently. "You look so beautiful this morning," he murmured, drawing her into his arms and holding her gently for a moment. "I'm glad you're here, Mara."

She smiled tremulously, waiting while he turned to lock the door. Then he draped his arm casually around her slender shoulders and walked beside her down the path to the truck, where Michael waited, bouncing on the seat and beaming out the window at them.

Mara sat in the truck between them, gazing out at the bright morning as they pulled off the road allowance, bumped across a corrugated Texas gate and started up a winding dirt road across the prairie.

Allan drove carefully, swerving to avoid ruts and holes that might jar the horses riding in the trailer behind them. Mara looked up admiringly at his fine tanned profile and, feeling her eyes upon him, he turned to smile down at her.

She smiled back. "What is a community pasture, by the way?" she asked.

"It's a big chunk of land leased from the government. A group of ranchers get together, lease the land as a cooperative, share the work and the expenses and then they're each allowed to run a certain number of cattle in the pasture. That way, you see, we all have access to more land than any of us could have individually."

"How big is the pasture?"

"Ours is ninety-seven sections."

She stared up at him. "But…I thought you said once that a section is a square mile."

"That's right. Our community pasture is just under a hundred square miles."

"Oh, my goodness." She gazed out the window in silence, pondering the vastness of the prairie that these men made their living from.

"It's not really all that big," Allan continued. "It takes a lot of land to run cattle here, especially in dry years. A section is six hundred and forty acres, and you need forty acres to support one cow. That's just sixteen cows to a section or about fifteen hundred in the whole pasture. Now there's twelve ranchers in the group, and most of us run cows and calves together, which uses even more grazing land. What it works out to is about a hundred cows each. Not that many really."

"And what is it that's happening today?" Mara asked.

"This is gathering day. We don't leave cattle in the pasture over the winter, you see. Every year, usually on a Sunday toward the end of October, we all meet out here, ride out and gather the cattle into corrals, sort them out by brands and have them trucked home. Everybody brings their wives and kids and all, and a ton of food, and there's a trough full of beer. It's a combination workday and a big community picnic."

Mara looked alarmed. "Will there be a lot of people?"

Allan patted her shoulder briefly, and then put his hand back on the steering wheel. "Don't worry. They're just neighbors. And besides, they're all going to love you."

Mara was still concerned, thinking about the day ahead. "Should I have brought some food?"

"No way. You're a guest. You're with me, and I've got my contribution in the back."

"What did you bring?"

He grinned at her. "Three cases of beer. The guys who aren't married get off easy."

"Look, Miss Steen!" Michael shouted. "Look at the coyote!"

Mara leaned forward to peer in the direction he was pointing. "Oh!" she said. "I see it, Michael! It's just running out of that gully!"

Allan slowed the truck, and Mara and the little boy both gazed, breathless with wonder, watching the coyote lope up the bank of the coulee. It ran with careless, insolent grace, its tail streaming behind. On the brow of the hill it paused to look back at them with a taunting, mocking air, then vanished over the horizon.

Allan drove on, and Mara settled back on the seat, blissfully watching the ocean of bleached grass that waved and rippled all around them, turning from silver to gold as the sun rose higher in the wide prairie sky. Clumps of sage were dotted here and there, and shy mule deer grazed in sheltered coulees, looking up at them with huge dark eyes as they passed.

"I just love this," Mara said. "Michael, you live in the best place in the whole world."

Michael beamed and extracted two grubby peppermints from his jacket pocket, offering one to Mara. She declined politely, feeling a certain uneasiness about what else might be in that pocket.

Beside her, Allan chuckled softly, but kept his eyes on the road.

After that they drove for what seemed to Mara like an incredibly long time without seeing anything at all—no animals, no buildings, no power lines, no other vehicles. Then, just when she was sure that they'd reached the end of the world, they topped a rise and drove down into a big, sheltered valley that was humming with activity.

A jumbled maze of corrals, pens and fences sprawled across the valley, surrounded by trucks and horse trailers. People moved all around the corrals, saddling horses, repairing gates, moving vehicles about and shouting greetings to one another. Children swarmed everywhere, climbing on fences, playing rowdy games, and galloping about on ponies and bicycles. Mara noticed a small shack set apart from the pens where the women seemed to be congregated, setting up long tables, arranging and covering huge platters of food and shouting commands and threats at passing children.

As they drew closer to all the activity and pulled up near the other vehicles to park, Mara realized that Allan hadn't been exaggerating. A corrugated metal trough near the food table, easily ten feet long, was filled with ice and bottled beer.

Michael bounced on the seat beside her, wild with excitement. "Everybody's here already! Hurry up, Dad! Hey, look, Jimmy brought his bike, too!" Frantically he grabbed for the door handle.

"Hang on, old boy," Allan said sternly. "You just wait till we stop. You've got all day to play."

Allan parked, stepped out of the truck and helped Mara down, calling cheerful greetings to people as they passed. Then he hoisted Michael's bike from the back of the truck, and the little boy vanished instantly, tearing off across the prairie to join the other children. Mara stood shyly near the truck, watching as Allan unloaded the two horses, removed their heavy protective blankets and began to saddle them.

A short, fat woman with red cheeks, frizzy gray hair and a sweet, round face came trotting around the corner of the truck and gripped Mara's arm. "You must be Miss Steen. I'm Hilda Schultz. I talked to you once on the phone. Do you remember?"

"Oh," Mara said, delighted to hear a name that she knew in the midst of all this strangeness. "Yes, of course I remember. It's nice to meet you. Please call me Mara."

"What a pretty name. Allan, she's just a darling."

"Sure she is," Allan agreed, leading the horses around the truck. "Didn't I tell you?"

Mara smiled and then protested, laughing as Hilda marched her away and introduced her to everyone within reach as, "Mara Steen, Allan's friend."

A sea of faces swam in front of her—kindly, practical, weathered faces with friendly smiles and shrewd, far-seeing eyes. Mara felt herself surrounded and examined, swallowed up in goodwill, bombarded with frank questions, passed approvingly from hand to hand.

Finally, to her intense relief, Allan materialized at her side and took her arm. "C'mon, all of you," he said cheerfully. "Take it easy. Mara's not used to prairie hospitality, and you're scaring her." Still, she smiled shyly at all of them and received wide answering grins in return as Allan led her away. He paused beside another trailer, where a lean, tanned rancher, about sixty years old, was fitting protective wrappings on the legs of a tall sorrel gelding.

"Wilson," Allan said, "I'd like you to meet someone."

The older man stood erect and smiled down at Mara. His manner was polite and gracious, and his eyes, in that weathered face, were a brilliant, startling blue, like sapphires embedded in parched earth.

"Mara Steen," Allan said, "this is Wilson Tolman. He's the president of our cooperative."

Mara held out her hand, and the old rancher took it with courtly grace, giving her a keen, friendly glance. "Pleased to meet you, Miss Steen," he said. "Little Michael's a good friend of mine, so I've heard a lot about you. All good."

Mara smiled, warmed and pleased by his words.

"Well," Allan asked, "have you got a job for us, Wilson?"

"Yeah," Wilson said, lifting a clipboard from the fender of the horse trailer. "I figured Mara probably hasn't done a lot of riding before, so I thought I'd get you two to gather the yearlings in the South Five. That's not too many miles to cover."

"Thanks, Wilson," Allan said. "That'll be fine. What's the yearling count?"

Wilson consulted the clipboard. "One twenty-six."

"Okay," Allan said. He smiled down at Mara. "Well, girl, we'd better get going before Hilda decides that you should stay here with the women and butter two hundred buns for the kids' hot dogs."

"Listen," Wilson called as they led the horses away, "just because you got an easy ride, I don't want you two stopping and fooling around out there.

I have to maintain some standards around here, you know.''

Mara looked startled, but Allan threw his head back and laughed. ''Wilson,'' he assured the older man, ''I won't do anything you wouldn't do.''

Wilson grinned broadly and waved them off.

''I don't have riding boots,'' Mara murmured. ''Just these running shoes. Is that all right?''

''Sure. This isn't a long ride, and you're not going to have any problems with this little mare.''

''I hope not,'' Mara said fervently.

''Come on, I'll help you up. I just guessed at these stirrups, but they look about right.'' He lifted Mara's slender body and swung her easily up into the saddle.

She took a deep breath, fitted her feet into the stirrups, picked up the reins and looked around. The sorrel mare stood quietly, her ears twitching. Mara reached forward and patted the rough springing mane, then smiled down at Allan, who was checking the cinch on her saddle.

''Feels okay?'' he asked.

''Feels great.''

''Good girl.'' He gathered his reins and swung up onto his horse. The big bay danced and sidestepped skittishly, alarming Mara, but Allan sat with careless grace, controlling the horse effortlessly. When his mount had settled, he led the way off across the prairie at a gentle walk, and the mare followed, falling easily into step beside the other horse.

All she had to do, Mara realized with surprise, was to sit in the saddle and hold the reins. As her confidence increased, she began to relax and look around with pleasure. The sea of grass stretched endlessly here, and the mountains stood white and stark against the vivid sapphire of the sky. High overhead, like dark embroidery stitched on pale blue silk, a V-shaped formation of geese winged southward, their raucous cries echoing faintly as they passed.

A slight breeze was blowing from the southwest, bringing a touch of color to Mara's cheeks, and her gray eyes shone like stars. Allan looked at her as she rode along beside him, and wondered how long he could keep himself from gathering her into his arms and covering her face with kisses.

From the first moment he'd seen her, sitting behind the desk in her classroom, he had felt an attraction so powerful that it was difficult to control. And the more time he spent with her, getting to know the depths and subtleties of her warm, generous, thoughtful nature, the stronger his feelings grew. But he knew that he had to be cautious. There were, in her mind at least, serious obstacles to any close relationship, and if he pressed too hard, she would draw away permanently.

And that, he thought, would be pretty hard to bear. *God knows, I don't want to lose this woman, now that I've just found her....*

"Everything okay?" he asked, smiling at her.

"Allan, this is just wonderful. I can't remember ever enjoying a day so much."

"Good. I thought you'd like it." He glanced over at her approvingly. "You know, you've got a real good seat on a horse."

Mara smiled, pleased by his compliment.

"Of course," he added with a teasing grin, "you have the advantage of having a really nice seat to start with."

She ignored this with dignity and pointed out a jackrabbit, already wearing its winter coat of white.

After a peaceful hour of riding, they came upon the yearlings, sleeping and grazing placidly around a big prairie slough.

"Easy now," Allan murmured. "We'll just come up on them nice and slow. We don't want to scare them and get them running."

Mara nodded.

They reined in side by side on a small rise of land and looked down at the herd of young cattle.

"There's supposed to be a hundred and twenty-six," Allan said. "Let's both count and see if that's what we get."

They counted silently and agreed that all of the cattle were there.

"Okay," Allan said. "I'll ride around the end there and get them started. You just stay here and keep them headed down along that fence line."

Mara nodded tensely. "I'll try."

He grinned. "Nothing to it. They just follow the fence line naturally. All you have to do is sit here."

He turned his horse and loped off around the end of the slough. Seeing him, the cattle bunched together and headed toward the fence. Allan, mounted on his big bay, waded across the shallow water to gather up a few of the stragglers and moved them neatly off to join the others. When all the yearlings were trotting in loose formation along the barbed wire fence, Allan motioned to Mara, and she rode over to join him, falling into step beside him once more.

"That was easy," she said.

"Sure. And this fence runs all the way down to the corrals. We just have to follow them in."

The sun climbed high in the sky and shone warm and rich upon them. They took off their jackets, and Allan showed Mara how to tie hers onto the latigo leathers at the back of her saddle.

Mara lifted her face to the sun, closing her eyes with pleasure, and breathed in the rich scent of grass and sage, of dust and horse and leather. She found that there was something infinitely soothing, almost hypnotic, about the easy rocking motion of the horse, the gentle bobbing of the cattle's shaggy hindquarters in front of them and the soft clicking of hundreds of hooves.

She began to talk, telling Allan all about Rachel in the nursing home and Lisa's pregnancy and Jeff with his obvious attraction to the beautiful girl.

Allan smiled. "You're just one of those women that everybody tells their troubles to," he said. "Even me. I told you my whole life story the first time I ever met you. And that's something I *never* do."

"I know people like to talk to me," Mara said. "I guess it's just because I'm available. I mean, I hardly every go anywhere. I'm almost always either at home or in my classroom, so I'm kind of a captive audience."

Allan shook his head. "It's not that. It's just you. It's because you really care about people, and it shows. People can feel it."

Mara was silent, enjoying the lulling, rocking motion of the gentle mare and the warm sun on her face.

Allan looked over at her again. "But that's all very well," he said, "bearing everybody else's burdens all the time. When do you ever have time just for *you*?"

"Right now," she said with a smile. "This whole wonderful day. This is just for me."

"And me," he said. "And there'll be lots more of them. Right?"

Her face clouded. "Allan..." she began.

But he shook his head and reached over to touch her hand. "Not today, Mara," he said gently. "Don't tell me anything negative today. I don't want to hear about problems. Okay?"

"Good," she said with relief. "Today I'll just take a break from my problems."

Soon—too soon, Mara thought—the pens and corrals came into view again. They were, however, still far off in the distance and as tiny as a child's farm set tossed carelessly down on a vast carpet of grass.

Allan reined in, stood up in his stirrups and squinted at the corrals. "The yearlings will go on in by themselves now," he told Mara. "And the kids will ride out on their ponies and gather them. Do you want to go in right away and have something to eat, or would you like to rest a little bit first and enjoy the sunshine?"

"I don't want to go back till we absolutely have to," Mara said. "This is just so lovely."

"It sure is. Come on, and I'll show you something."

He turned his horse and rode toward a small hill,

off to the west, with Mara beside him. They topped the rise and looked down into a little sheltered valley. In the center of the hollow was a huge flat boulder about four feet high and ten feet in diameter. The ground was bare and dusty, like an empty moat, all around the base of the massive stone, forming a wide, shallow ditch.

"It's called an erratic boulder," Allan explained. "The glaciers dropped them here and there all over the prairie."

"What made that ditch all around the base?"

"Buffalo. They used to rub on the stone and wallow in the dust beside it to keep the insects off. Now cattle do the same thing."

Mara gazed down at the boulder, fascinated, then followed Allan as he rode down toward it. He reined in nearby, dismounted and lifted Mara from her horse. Then he took a metal stake from his saddle bag, pushed it into the ground and tied the reins of both horses through a ring at the top. Finally he untied their jackets from behind their saddles and tucked them under his arm.

Mara walked around, easing the stiffness from her legs.

"How do you feel?" Allan asked.

"Not bad. Pretty good, actually, considering that I haven't been on a horse for ten years."

"Yeah. You're an amazing woman. Come here." He took her hand and led her toward the big boulder. "Up you go!" he said, lifting her in his arms and tossing her up onto the flat surface of the big rock and then vaulting up after her.

Mara sat cross-legged on the boulder, laughing, loving the warmth and the sunshine and the pure joy of being alone with him, so far away from anybody else. Allan spread their jackets out on the broad, sun-warmed surface, tossed his cap aside and lay on his back beside her, closing his eyes in the strong afternoon sunlight.

"Mmmm," he murmured presently, flexing his long legs. "Nice, eh?"

"Yes. Nice."

The horses grazed placidly nearby, their bits clinking against their teeth. Meadowlarks ran and fluttered in the prairie grass, filling the air with liquid trills of music. A cloud drifted slowly across the sun, throwing long, cool fingers of shadow across the prairie, and the breeze stilled.

Beside her, Allan reached out and held her long plait of hair, drawing it luxuriously across his face. Then he began to tug on it gently, pulling her down toward him.

"Mara," he whispered.

She leaned on her elbow beside him, and their eyes met for a long moment.

"Oh, Mara," he said again, his voice husky. Finally he could no longer resist the yearning that had been tormenting him for so long. He reached up and gathered her into his arms.

Mara nestled beside him, thrilling at the hard-muscled firmness of his long body, trembling within the circle of his strong arms. He lifted himself up, gazing down at her intently, and then lowered his head gently to kiss her forehead, her cheeks and eyes and neck. Finally his lips met hers in a long, searching kiss, and Mara was shaken by the fiery passion of her body's response to his kiss. She clung to him, lost in the thrill of his mouth on hers and the feel of his big, lean body arching against hers.

"Mara," he muttered brokenly. "Oh, Mara..."

His kisses grew deep and lingering, and his hands began to move over her body, fondling, carressing, stroking, cupping her hips and her small breasts.

"Allan," she whispered. "Please..."

She pulled herself free and sat up, flushed and trembling, turning away from him to pat at her hair and adjust her clothing.

He lay quietly, watching her.

"Mara," he said.

"Yes?"

"What's wrong, Mara?"

She turned and met his eyes. "This is just... moving too fast for me, Allan. I'm not ready for this, that's all."

"Why not? Do you have doubts about me? Is there more you'd like to know about me? Ask me, Mara. I'll tell you anything you want to know."

"No, it's not that. It's just..."

"Am I taking something for granted, then? Do you feel that much differently than I do? Tell me now, Mara, if you do. I'd rather know right away."

"No," she said honestly. She turned to look at him directly. "But it's not how I feel that matters, Allan. It's the position I'm in that I have to consider. And I'm just not ready for...for what you want."

Allan sat beside her, gazing with narrowed eyes at
the pearl-gray mass of clouds along the horizon.

"Mara," he said finally, "you can't keep on—"

"Please, Allan," she interrupted him wearily.
"Please don't argue with me. Not today. I get so tired
of conflict, and today I'd just like to enjoy my holiday."

She turned and met his eyes steadily.

"Please," she said again.

"All right." He vaulted lightly off the rock and
reached up to lift her down beside him. "If that's the
way you want it, then that's how it'll have to be. But
you can't hold me off forever, Mara. And I'm not
about to give up. I'm giving you fair warning of
that."

His handsome face was quiet and set, his movements calm and controlled, as he helped her back up
into the saddle and mounted his own horse again. Riding silently, side by side, they headed for the pens
and buildings that lay beyond the vast, rippling ocean
of silvered grass.

# 7

Hours later Mara drove home through the hushed stillness of the autumn evening, while the headlights of her little car picked out a long, solitary ribbon of light on the empty road.

She was still glowing pleasantly from the fresh air, the horseback ride and the easy relaxed fun of the picnic supper at the corrals, with everyone sitting around on rough benches and lawn chairs, eating, drinking and chatting. The ranching community had accepted her with warmth and friendliness, looking on her simply as Allan's girlfriend and giving her the same affectionate respect that they all clearly felt for him.

There had been, however, a good deal of teasing and a few broad, earthy hints that Allan deflected with unfailing tact and good humor. He stayed near Mara, keeping her plate and her coffee cup filled and protecting her from the less than subtle sallies of some of the younger ranchers. When most of the food was gone and the sun was setting, Michael climbed into her lap, drowsy from his long day of outdoor play. Mara cuddled him, stroking his smooth dark hair until he fell asleep in her arms.

Now, as she drove home alone, she could still remember the pleasant sensations of the day—the ride, the sweep of prairie, the delicious, friendly outdoor meal and the sweet weight of the little boy's sleepy body, quiet and heavy in her arms.

But overpowering all was the achingly sweet memory of how it had felt to lie in Allan's strong arms, kissing his mouth, feeling his warm breath on her face and neck and his big hands on her body. She shivered a little, tingling with remembered pleasure, and hugged the thought of him close to her.

"You can't hold me off forever," he'd said. "I'm not about to give up."

She hadn't said anything to Allan but, for a little while, out there on the prairie, alone with him on the big sun-warmed rock, she had really believed that solutions could be found and compromises worked out. It had all seemed so plausible, then, and being in his arms had felt so safe and warm and natural. But now, as she neared the city and the lights and problems and responsibilities came rushing out to meet her, the optimism began to fade.

And, by the time she drove into her own garage and slipped into the house, she was growing increasingly nervous about Gran and about what might possibly await her.

How had it ever gotten so late? It was after ten o'clock. Mara just hoped Gran had gone to bed. She just couldn't stand a scene tonight, after such a lovely day....

She latched the door behind her and tiptoed into the darkened kitchen. "Hi, Gran," she called softly. "Are you still up?"

"I'm in the living room."

Mara felt a stirring of apprehension as she went slowly into the living room where Agnes sat in semi-darkness, watching television.

"My goodness, it's dark in here," Mara said brightly, switching on the floor lamp. "How was your day, Gran?"

"How was *yours*?" Agnes asked bitterly, turning to glare at her.

Mara tensed. "It was fine. I had a lovely time, actually. The weather was so nice all day, but there's a big cloud bank building in the west. I think it might snow tonight. The wind's getting up, and it's cold...." Realizing that she was chattering out of nervousness, Mara stopped talking abruptly and sat down opposite her grandmother.

"You're lying," Agnes said flatly.

"Gran—"

"Lying," Agnes repeated, her voice rising. "I don't think you were at Jo's at all. I think you sneaked away to spend the day with some man!"

Mara struggled to keep from losing her temper. "And what if I did, Gran? I *am* an adult, after all."

"You're a lying little sneak!" Agnes shouted, her face contorted with rage. "Running off to crawl into bed with some filthy man! As if there's any future in that. Men cause nothing but grief, and you're just a cheap little fool!"

"Well, then, Gran," Mara said with cold, deadly anger, "I'll just go right now and pack my things and move out tonight. You don't really want to live with a person like me, do you?"

She looked steadily at Agnes, and the old woman's face crumpled. "Mara," she whispered, reaching out a trembling hand, "don't say that. I'm sorry. I didn't mean it. Don't go away, dear."

"Gran, we can't keep having these scenes. I'm twenty-eight years old. I have to live my own life. I *have* to, Gran."

Agnes muttered something and picked aimlessly at the afghan that covered her knees.

"Pardon, Gran? I didn't hear you."

"I said, I'm just in your way. I'm just a burden to you."

"Gran, I love you. But I need some freedom, too."

Agnes looked up, her eyes blurred with tears. "Freedom to do what? To put me in a home, like Rachel? To go away and leave me alone here to die like an animal?"

"That's just ridiculous, Gran. You wouldn't die. You're as healthy and capable as I am, and everybody on the street knows you. You could manage here on your own with no problem at all."

Agnes shook her head stubbornly.

"Come on, Gran. You could so. You lived here alone when I went to university, and when I was living with David...you managed perfectly well."

"But it's different now," Agnes whispered. "I'm so scared all the time, Mara. You don't know what it was like after I fell and broke my hip and I lay there all day, crazy with pain, screaming and screaming for help, and nobody heard me.... I could have died there, and nobody would have found me for days."

"Oh, Gran..."

"And when I'm here alone, I hear voices, Mara, and things moving around in the basement. I see faces at the window and I'm scared to go into my bedroom, for fear someone's hiding behind the door."

"Someone could live with you here," Mara suggested. "We could hire a companion for you, some nice girl to—"

"No!" Agnes shouted, stiffening in fury. "Some... some *stranger*, living in my house, handling my things, going through all my private papers... No, Mara. Don't even think of it. That would kill me for sure." Agnes pounded her frail, veined fist on her knee, shaking with vehemence. Her mouth trembled.

"All right, all right," Mara said hastily. "Forget that idea. How about if you had a dog, and he could be company for you and bark if anybody came. You could take him out for walks, and Wayne or someone could look in on you every day...."

Her voice trailed off. Agnes was studying her face, with a strange, intent expression. "So," she said softly, "you're really going to do it, aren't you? You've thought it all out, haven't you? You're really going to go away and leave me."

"Gran, I just—"

"That's fine. Go ahead. Have your precious freedom. I won't be a problem to you for long."

"Gran, don't be silly."

"There's lots of ways," Agnes went on, her voice almost dreamy. "Pills and razors and carbon monoxide...all sorts of ways to let you have your freedom."

"Look, Gran," Mara said furiously. "It's rotten of

you to talk that way! It's emotional blackmail, and I won't stand for it! Do you hear me?''

She leaped to her feet and advanced threateningly on her grandmother, her face flushed with anger.

Agnes crumpled against the pillows and began sobbing. ''Mara, I just get so scared when you talk about leaving. Please, Mara,'' she said tearfully, ''don't be mad at me.''

Mara looked down at her grandmother with the old, familiar feelings of pity and frustration. These tears, she knew, were what kept her trapped. It wasn't the old woman's anger and temper tantrums that controlled Mara's life. It was Gran's weakness, her tears and helplessness, the times that she was loving and gentle and defenseless.

*I could walk away from her while she was shouting at me,* Mara thought bleakly. *I could leave and never look back. But I can't walk away while she's like this, and, damn it, she knows it....*

With weary resignation, Mara gathered the frail, hysterical old lady into her arms, rocking her gently and murmuring to her in soothing tones.

''It's all right, Gran. Settle down. It's all right. I'm here.''

''And you won't leave, like you said?'' Agnes asked in a small trembling voice. ''You won't go away and leave me all alone?''

''No, Gran, I won't. I won't go away. Just settle down, please. Stop crying, Gran.''

Gradually Agnes grew calm, and Mara supported her down the hall and helped her into bed. Then she went upstairs and climbed wearily under her own covers, staring at the ceiling in the dark.

The wind was beginning to howl around the eaves of the old house, and the first snowflakes spattered on the windowpane. Mara shivered, even in the warmth of her bed.

She lay still, closed her eyes and tried to recapture the feelings that had flooded her as she'd lain in Allan's arms in the sunshine.

But, back here in her own room in the bleak wintry night, Allan and his world seemed hopelessly far away.

By next morning, snow covered the streets and yards and the city trees were encased in ice. And still the snow fell, for days, muffling city and countryside in a deep, soft mantle of white.

Mara went about her work anxiously, hoping for a break in the weather before Halloween. She hated the years when there was deep snow on Halloween, spoiling the fun for the smaller children, who had to wear coats over their costumes and struggle through heavy drifts to go trick-or-treating.

As if in response to her wishes, a dry, hot chinook wind came howling down out of the mountains the day before Halloween, licking the snow off the prairie like frosting from a cake. Water ran in the streets, and bright little rivers danced and sparkled through the prairie coulees. The sun was high and warm in the sky, a rich, golden, Indian summer sun. By nightfall the streets were completely bare, and only a few patches of snow remained on shady hillsides.

The children came to school in their Halloween costumes, pale and tense with excitement. Mara loved their enthusiasm, forgetting her problems briefly and enjoying the day with them. Jeff, too, was superb, dressed as a pirate, complete with sash and eye patch, pretending to be terrified by the vampires, making wishes for the fairy godmother and nibbling at the gingerbread boy.

Michael, who was a cowboy, paused in the middle of a game of Pin the Stem on the Pumpkin and came to whisper to Mara.

"Dad wants you to phone him. Tonight, he said."

Mara, in her multicolored clown suit and yellow fright wig, looked down at the little boy in troubled silence. She hadn't talked to Allan since the day of the picnic. She wasn't sure, even yet, what to say to him. She felt as if she were being ripped in two, torn between her growing attraction to him and her responsibility to Agnes.

And Gran's behavior in the past few days had made it even more difficult. If she would only be her customary rude and abrasive self, Mara could deal with it better, even fight back. But Agnes was creeping around the house, anxious and timid, trying hard to be good and to atone for her behavior on Sunday. This gentleness was so unlike her, and Mara found it heartbreaking to watch Gran cooking all of Mara's favorite dishes, clipping interesting items from the newspaper to talk about in the evening and working so hard to keep the house clean and shining....

"Miss Steen?" Michael asked.

"Pardon, dear? Oh...." Mara hesitated. "All right.

Tell him I'll call tonight if I can. How is he?'' she asked wistfully.

''He's okay. He cut his hand on the power saw and he's got a big bandage on it.''

''What?'' Mara gripped the little boy's shoulders in sudden panic. ''When? Is it a bad cut?''

''No, he said it was just a scratch. But,'' Michael added thoughtfully, ''it's a pretty big bandage. Hilda put it on. She used to be a nurse.''

Reluctantly Mara released him, and he ran back to the game. She fought off the urge to rush down to the office right that minute and try to reach Allan at home. All at once she realized how much she missed him, how desperately she longed to see him and touch him, to hear his voice and kiss his mouth and feel his arms around her....

''Wake up, Clarabelle,'' Jeff whispered at her in passing. ''You're missing the party.''

Mara pulled herself together, forced a smile and joined a damp, merry group who were off in a corner bobbing for apples in a plastic bucket.

Near the end of the day, when the afternoon class party was still in full swing, Lisa appeared, evoking enthusiastic cheers from the small party-goers. Since her talk with Mara, Lisa seemed much happier and more relaxed. She came regularly to the kindergarten room once again, and all the children adored her. Now she submitted herself patiently to a group who wanted to dress her up as a princess and soon was looking absolutely lovely in a tinfoil crown, with a lace curtain mantle over her shirt and blue jeans.

Totally without self-consciousness, she sat on the

floor in the corner of the room with little Jody on her lap, playing Snakes and Ladders with a group of the shyer children. With the froth of lace over her shoulders, and the bright crown on her silvery hair, she looked, Mara thought, like a young madonna.

Jeff's eyes, Mara noticed, wandered a good many times in the direction of the radiant girl. When she looked up once and smiled at him casually, he swallowed hard and turned away quickly.

Soon the afternoon was over, and all the little ghosts and goblins went their separate ways.

"Be careful crossing the streets tonight," Mara called to them. "Look *both* ways!"

"And don't pig out and get sick!" Jeff added.

When all the children were gone, Mara and the two young people looked around at the wreckage of the room, exchanged dismayed glances and set to work.

"Lisa, you don't have to do this," Mara protested, seeing the slender girl mopping up the apple-bobbing corner. "Really. Jeff and I can handle it."

Lisa, still on her hands and knees, looked up and smiled. "That's not fair. I had all the fun of the party, so I should help clean up afterward."

"Yeah," Jeff said. "But princesses don't scrub floors."

"Oh, yeah?" Lisa said. "And pirates don't pick up peanut shells, so there!"

They laughed together, and Mara, who was on a ladder taking down streamers, smiled down at them, enjoying their cheerful friendly banter.

When the room was finally neat and orderly again, and Lisa had taken off her lace mantle and gone home, Jeff and Mara sank into chairs, exhausted, and looked at one another.

"Well," he said, "that went well."

"It did, didn't it? But Jeff...all that work, and now it's over. Just like that. It seems such a waste of effort, doesn't it?"

"Don't think that way. Think about how they'll remember this all their lives."

"Do you think they will? Do you remember *your* kindergarten Halloween party?"

"Vividly," Jeff said. "I was a squirrel. And I had a bunch of empty walnut shells tied on a string around my neck. And Tracy Simpson ate too much peanut brittle and threw up on my foot."

Mara laughed. "And to this day," she suggested, "you've never been able to stand peanut brittle."

"No, but after that, I never could stand Tracy Simpson."

He took a thermos from his book bag and unscrewed the lid. "Care for a cup of hot tea, Clarabelle?"

"Jeff," Mara said fervently, passing him her mug, "I love you."

"That's what all the girls say," he commented loftily, filling her cup and then his own. "I get so tired of hearing it."

They sipped their tea together in companionable silence for a few minutes.

"That Lisa's some girl, isn't she?" he said finally. "I always think I must be imagining it, you know...that no girl could be that beautiful and still be as nice as she is. Then, every time I see her, I'm more impressed.''

Mara was silent, sipping her tea and looking down at her desk.

"I've asked her out a few times, you know," he went on, "but she keeps turning me down. She seems to be immune to my fatal charm." He poured himself another cup of tea and leaned back, putting his feet up on a table. "Actually, I can't figure out why. We always have fun when she comes down here, and I think she's broken up with the quarterback...."

Mara looked over at him in silence and made a sudden decision. "Jeff," she said, "I have to tell you something.''

"Yeah?" he said idly. "Sounds serious."

"Jeff, Lisa's pregnant.''

He turned pale, staring at her intently, and his feet dropped to the floor with a thump.

"I'm sorry," Mara said miserably. "But you had to know sometime, and soon it's going to be showing. Then everybody will know.''

"It's that guy...Kevin?"

Mara nodded, shaken by the look of pain on his face.

"Is he going to marry her? Does she love him?"

Mara shook her head. "He offered, but she's not interested. She says it's over. She realizes now that she never really cared for him, she was just... infatuated, I guess.''

Jeff thought this over, and his dark, handsome face contracted into an unhappy frown. "Mara, the poor kid. What's she going to do?"

Mara told him what she remembered of their conversation, including Lisa's fears about her father's reaction.

"God," Jeff said in horror. "That's awful! She's going to throw away her whole future—university, languages, the whole thing—and be a goddamn *waitress*?"

"She says she has no other choice."

"Damn!" he exploded.

Mara looked at him. "Jeff, it's not *that* terrible being a waitress, you know. Thousands of women support themselves that way and even put themselves through college, waiting on tables."

"Yeah, but they're not eighteen with a baby to look after."

"Some of them are," Mara said quietly.

"I guess so. But it's hard to picture a girl like Lisa..." He broke off and sat gazing thoughtfully out the window for a moment. "Well," he said, finally, turning back to Mara with a bitter smile, "at least now I know why she wouldn't go out with me."

"And how do *you* feel, Jeff?" Mara asked quietly. "You keep saying how impressed you are with her and how nice she is. Does knowing this change the way you feel about her?"

He met her eyes frankly, his boyish face thoughtful and troubled. "Well, sure it does," he said. "I'd be lying if I said it didn't matter to me. I'm not sure *how* I feel right now. I guess I'll have to think about it."

"She needs her friends, Jeff," Mara told him gently. "Now more than ever."

"I know that. I have no intention of withdrawing

friendship, Mara. I've just been...thinking about something a little more than friendship, you know?''

"I know. But now you're not so sure.''

"Yeah. I'm not so sure.'' He looked at Mara, trying to smile. "Life's pretty rotten, isn't it?'' he asked. "Don't you think life is kind of a mess?''

"No. Life is wonderful. It's people who mess things up,'' Mara said firmly. "And even at that, problems have a way of working themselves out. At least they seem to.''

"Do they?''

"Yes, they do. Every cloud has a silver lining, it's always darkest before the dawn—and all that. Now come on, Sinbad. Let's get to our respective homes before the trick-or-treaters start arriving.''

He nodded and offered her his arm. She accepted with a little curtsey, and they marched off through the school corridors arm in arm, slender clown and tall pirate, heading for the teachers' parking lot.

Allan brought Michael home from his Halloween rounds of the ranching neighborhood, got him bathed and tucked into bed, then settled at the kitchen table with a pile of bills, receipts and record books.

He worked with concentrated attention, jotting down and adding neat columns of figures, making entries in the thick file of documents to be used in filling out his income tax forms.

After an hour, he got up, made himself a cup of coffee and wandered over to look thoughtfully at the telephone. He hesitated for a moment, then picked up the receiver, listened for the dial tone and hung up again quickly, almost embarrassed.

You're as bad as a teenager, he told himself. She doesn't call, so right away you're checking to make sure the phone's working....

He returned to the table, carrying his coffee mug, and started to sift through a huge sheaf of gasoline receipts. But the figures swam meaninglessly before his eyes, and he finally gave up, tilting back in his chair to gaze up at the ceiling as he sipped his coffee.

He had refrained from calling her, knowing that it distressed her to have him telephone her at home. But Allan was a powerful, competent man, accustomed to setting goals and then going after them. This kind of helpless waiting wasn't easy for him.

And, he realized, it was doubly hard because of the depth of his feelings for Mara. He was disturbed, almost frightened, by his powerful, urgent longing for this particular woman. His relationship with his wife had been reasonably amiable, but never very passionate. The marriage had been something he had drifted into because it had just seemed to be the right time in his life to get married. He had loved his wife, he supposed. He must have, to have gone through all the formalities of marriage and establishing a family. But these days he seemed unable to recall her face at all, and the love he had felt for her seemed like a pallid, boyish emotion compared to the shattering longing that washed over him whenever he thought of Mara, of her gentle smile, her quiet, thoughtful conversation, her cheerful teasing, her sweet gray eyes and her slender, curving body...and that glorious, honey-colored hair—

The telephone rang, and he crossed the room in three strides to grasp the receiver.

"Hello?"

"Hello, Allan."

"Mara! It's good to hear your voice. I thought you'd forgotten all about me."

"No, of course not. I just had so many little trick-or-treaters that I was busy all night answering the door. And then I waited for Gran to go to bed."

"I see. How are you?"

"I'm fine," Mara said. She hesitated. "Michael said you hurt your hand."

"Just a scratch." Allan reached out a long arm, drew a chair close to him and straddled it, holding the receiver closer to his ear. "A man shouldn't be operating power tools," he said, "when he's got a woman on his mind."

"Oh, really? Have you got a woman on your mind?"

He grinned, relieved to hear the familiar, teasing note in her voice.

"All the time," he said softly. "Every minute that I'm awake." He paused. "And," he added thoughtfully, "while I'm asleep, too, come to think of it. I've had some very satisfying dreams recently."

"Allan!" she said, shocked, and he grinned fondly, picturing the soft pink color rising in her cheeks.

"It's hell, isn't it," he said cheerfully, "when the most satisfying part of a man's sex life is his dreams?"

"Look," she said severely, "could we talk about something else, please?"

"Okay. Do you want to come out on Sunday?"

"What...what did you have in mind?"

"Nothing special. Just a day at home with Mick and me. We could make popcorn, watch the ball game on TV, play a few hands of Animal Rummy...Mick plays a mean game of Animal Rummy, you know," he added. "Beats me every time."

"Oh, Allan," she said wistfully, "that sounds so nice. But..."

She hesitated. He heard the note of caution in her voice, and his heart ached with sympathy for her, but he knew that he had to persist, even if it was painful for her.

"But what, Mara?"

"Oh, Allan, Gran was so upset after last Sunday, she's just getting over it now. And if I leave her for a whole day, so soon after the last time, she's just going to be so—"

"Mara," he said gently, "I know you don't like to argue about this. But you can't go on letting her dictate your actions. You have to develop more maturity than that."

There was a brief silence, and he held his breath, knowing that he was taking a calculated risk by dealing with her this way.

"So," she said, her voice sounding faraway and cool, "you think I'm immature, do you?"

"Mara," he said earnestly, "to some extent we're *all* immature where our families are concerned. It's easy to be independent when other people are involved, but when it comes to the people who've raised us, people we feel responsible for and love and owe a lot to...then it's harder. I know that. There are so many complicated emotions involved in family relationships. Part of growing up is learning how to deal with them.''

"Allan, I'm not immature. At least I don't think I am. I honestly believe I'm behaving responsibly. I'm just afraid of...of what she might do if she got really upset. She's getting more dependent on me all the time.''

"Well," he pointed out reasonably, "you're not helping when you give in to her all the time. If you want her to develop some independence, then you have to force her to manage on her own a bit.''

"I'm not sure she can.''

"Give her a chance, Mara. She might surprise you.''

There was a long silence while Allan held his breath. He could almost hear her wrestling with her own thoughts, wanting to believe him, but afraid to abandon what she perceived as her responsibility.

"Mara," he said softly.

"Yes?''

"Mara, I want to see you. I'm dying to see you again. I don't know if I can wait any longer.''

"Oh, Allan," she whispered, "I want to see you, too....''

"Then come," he urged. "Come on Sunday.''

There was another long silence, so long that he almost gave up hope.

"All right," she said finally. "All right, I'll come.''

# 8

On Sunday, Mara waited until Agnes was dressed and ready for church and sipping her second cup of coffee, before making her announcement.

"I probably won't be home for dinner tonight, Gran," she said, trying to keep her voice casual and concentrating on the piece of toast she was crumbling between her fingers. "I'm going out of town to visit a friend who lives on a farm. Two friends, actually," she added, smiling to herself as she thought of Michael and his prowess at Animal Rummy.

She looked up and saw Agnes's mouth tighten ominously.

"I see," Agnes said coldly.

"Gran, I wish you could…"

"And are you going to lie to me again and tell me that it's Jo you're planning to visit?"

"No, Gran," Mara said quietly. "I'm not going to lie to you any more, for any reason. It's demeaning to both of us that I should feel compelled to tell lies to you. The truth is I'm going to visit a friend, who just happens to be a man. He's—"

"Don't tell me!" Agnes snapped. "Spare me the ugly details, please."

"Gran, how can you be so harsh? Don't you ever

want me to see any men at all? Don't you want me
to have a home of my own and children and all the
things that other women have? Don't you, Gran?''

"You're such a fool," Agnes said. "You're just
like all those other silly, moonstruck girls, thinking
that a man and babies will make you happy. Well, let
me tell you a thing or two, my girl. Men are liars,
too, and they cause nothing but grief. And as for *babies*, what joy do they bring? What joy did Emily
bring to me? What did you do for her, except to kill
her? Answer me that!'' Gran's face was crimson, and
the veins bulged and throbbed alarmingly at her temples.

"Gran," Mara whispered, appalled, "you don't
mean that. I know you don't mean it.''

Agnes looked up defiantly, her wrinkled old face
twisted with anger and pain. "You've got a good life
here," she said. "You've got a comfortable home and
a good job and friends at school. If you want to throw
it all away for some...some *man*—" she spat the
word out with contempt "—then all I can say is, I'm
glad *I* won't be alive to watch it happening!''

Still in a rage, Agnes grabbed her coat and handbag
and rushed toward the back door, while Mara sat miserably at the table, watching her. Suddenly, as Agnes
was wrenching at the doorknob, she stiffened, gave a
sharp cry of pain and sagged against the doorframe,
clutching her throat.

Mara ran to her. "Gran...Gran, you shouldn't upset
yourself so much.''

Agnes struggled to catch her breath, wheezing and
panting. Her face was gray and ashen, and her teeth

chattered. But for Mara's arms, holding her, she would have fallen to the floor. Feebly she pawed the air and clutched at Mara, muttering broken, incoherent snatches of words and sentences. All at once she quit struggling and collapsed, sobbing, a deadweight in Mara's arms.

"Come on, Gran," Mara murmured. "You'll be all right. Come on, let me put you to bed. You're going to be fine. You've just gone and gotten yourself all upset. Come on, now."

Agnes shifted and muttered in protest, tears streaming down her cheeks, her words still meaningless, barely audible.

She seemed, Mara decided, to be concerned about the kitchen and the fact that the table was still littered with food and breakfast dishes.

"It's all right," Mara said soothingly. "I'll clean up later and do these dishes. You just come and get into your nice bed and I'll bring you some hot tea and biscuits. Come with me, Gran."

Gently, still talking steadily in soft, reassuring tones, she led the trembling old lady down the hall and into her room. Mara helped her undress, touched by the sight of Agnes's frail, pathetic little body, her bony shoulders and thin legs. She slipped a warm flannelette nightgown over Gran's head, turned back the covers, switched on the electric blanket and tucked Agnes into bed. Then she ran into the bathroom to get a glass of water and a warm, dampened cloth to wipe Gran's face and hands.

For a long time she sat by the bed, stroking Gran's

clammy forehead, talking aimlessly about anything she could think of—the weather, the children's Halloween costumes, the antics of the high school students in her study class. When she ran out of things to say, Mara sang softly in a sweet, clear voice the old songs that Agnes had sung to her when she was a baby.

After what seemed like hours, Agnes finally seemed to relax. Her rapid, uneven breathing settled into a slower rhythm and her color improved. Her thin lips were still twitching occasionally, and she moaned from time to time, rolling her head restlessly on the pillow. Mara continued to sing, stroking the old lady's face and hair and, at long last, Gran's thin, papery eyelids fluttered and closed, her mouth dropped open and she slept.

Exhausted and limp with relief, Mara sat by the bed in silence, almost afraid to move for fear that she might disturb her grandmother again. Not until she was certain that Agnes was sleeping deeply did she dare to slip out of her chair and tiptoe around the room, hanging Gran's clothes in the closet.

Then she went back to the kitchen, cleared the table, washed and dried the dishes and scrubbed the countertops. As she worked, she tried to remind herself of how vulnerable Gran was, how much she depended on Mara, how loving and generous and self-sacrificing she had been all through the years of Mara's childhood. But all she could feel was an angry, frustrated sorrow, knowing that she wouldn't see Allan today after all and that soon she would have to call him and—

But Allan would never accept her excuses. She heard his voice once more, so strong and gentle, but accusing, all the same, telling her that she was being immature.

*Maybe he's right,* she thought. *Gran's controlled me for years by staging scenes just like this...but maybe, like Allan says, it's time I got over that fear....*

All at once, as she stood by the sink and wrung the dishcloth into the basin, something snapped inside her, and she felt the growth of a new feeling—a cold, hard stubborn little core of determination.

She *would* go, she decided. She wouldn't keep making sacrifices all the time for the rest of her life. She just wouldn't.

With cool detachment she sat down by the table to consider the situation. Gran was sleeping now. But she'd wake up soon. And she'd be all right when she woke up, just sort of pathetic, as she always was after one of her scenes, ashamed of all the fuss she'd made, sorry for saying such awful things, trying hard to be good.... She wouldn't have enough energy to make another fuss right away. So Mara would just have to be firm and let her know that things couldn't always be the way Gran wanted them....

Mara made a cup of coffee and sat at the table to sip it thoughtfully, looking at the clock. Then she rinsed out her cup, put it away in the cupboard and ran upstairs to bathe and change her clothes.

An hour or so later, when she judged that her grandmother would have wakened from her nap and be feeling better, Mara opened the door to Gran's room and peeped inside. The old lady lay propped against the pillows, eyes open, face wan and pinched.

"Hi, Gran," Mara whispered. "Feeling better now?"

"Well...a little," Agnes said feebly. "I'm sorry, Mara. I just got so—"

"It's all right, Gran," Mara said, coming into the room to smooth the coverlet and plump the pillows behind the old lady's head. "I've turned the thermostat up a little," she went on casually. "And I've left your robe and slippers out, and there's some of the stew we had last night in the fridge that you can just..."

Agnes looked up at her, incredulous, her lips trembling. "Mara," she whispered piteously, "do you mean that you're...you're still planning to go away today and leave me all alone?"

"I leave you all alone every day, remember?" Mara said with forced cheerfulness. "I go to school at eight in the morning and don't come home till supper. Why is it any different today?"

"But...but I'm sick today. You never leave me alone when I'm sick."

Mara looked down at her grandmother's wretched, pleading face and felt a rush of anxious sympathy. But she remembered Allan's words and forced herself to keep her voice light and cheerful.

"Oh, I don't think you're all that sick," she said. "I think you just got yourself all worked up over nothing, and now that you've had a little rest, you're going to be just fine. I won't be late," she added, pausing in the doorway. "I'll leave there right after supper and be home before dark if I can."

Quietly she closed the door behind her and hurried down the hall, grabbing her jacket and handbag as she went.

But, as she pulled her car out of the garage and headed off down the street, she was still haunted by her last glimpse of Gran's pale, anguished, piteous face, so small and helpless against the broad expanse of pillows.

Mara drove into the farmyard, parked and ran up onto the veranda to ring the bell, her heart pounding.

*I'm actually here,* she thought in wonder. *And in just a second the door will open and he'll be standing there, and he'll say...*

"Hi, Miss Steen. I'm building a spaceship with my Lego." Michael stood on the threshold, holding the door open and smiling up at her.

"Are you, Michael? Where's your dad?"

"He's in the barn. A cow's having a calf. He said you should come down to see him when you got here."

"Oh, I see. Well, can I have a look at your spaceship first?"

Michael glowed and led her into the living room, where he was watching cartoons on television, with a bewildering array of colorful plastic building blocks spread across the floor.

"My goodness, you have a lot of Lego."

"I know," Michael said proudly. "My Auntie Diane who lives in California sends me Lego all the

time for Christmas and my birthdays and everything." He settled on the floor again and looked up
at her. "Do you want to stay here and play with me?
I can let you have all those pieces over there. I don't
need them for my spaceship."

"Well, Michael...that would really be fun, but I
think I'd better run down to the barn first and see
your dad. He doesn't even know I'm here."

Michael nodded cheerfully. "He likes you a lot.
He always talks about you. How nice you are and
everything."

"Does he?" Mara asked, absurdly pleased.

"Yeah." Michael frowned, searching for a special
piece, then brightened when he spotted it beneath one
of the leather armchairs.

"Are you all right here all by yourself?" Mara
asked.

He nodded, intent on fitting a tiny gun turret onto
the front of his spaceship.

Mara smiled, ruffled his hair lovingly and went out
of the house.

It was a gray November day with a crisp, bitter
wind blowing and low clouds scudding along the horizon. Mara shivered, pulling her collar up around her
ears and thrusting her hands into her jacket pockets
as she hurried across the yard to the barn.

She unlatched the heavy door and went inside, relieved to be sheltered from the raw wind. For a moment she stood hesitantly, looking around. The barn
was tidy and clean with a concrete floor, rows of mangers along two walls and a bank of high box stalls to
her left. Another full wall was hung with an assort-

ment of saddles, bridles and other equipment. The building was warm and quiet and seemed deserted.

Mara sniffed the pleasant scent of fresh hay, horse, and leather, and stepped into the aisle by the box stalls.

"Allan?" she called. "Are you in here?"

"Over here," he said.

His voice, she realized, was coming from the open door of one of the box stalls. Mara walked over, looked inside and gasped.

A light bulb, suspended from the ceiling on a long cord, hung inside the high sides of the stall, illuminating it with a strong, harsh light. A Hereford cow lay thrashing about on its side in a thick bed of fresh straw on the floor of the small enclosure, and Allan crouched beside the animal, naked to the waist, with his back to Mara.

Mara stared at him, momentarily speechless. He wore only jeans, boots and a cap. The knotted cords of muscle in his long back rippled and flexed beneath the skin, still faintly brown from his summer tan.

"Oh!" she said.

He looked back over his shoulder, saw her and smiled, his cheek dimpling. "Hi, sweetheart. C'mere and pull on this rope for me, would you?"

Hesitantly she stepped into the stall, edging past his outstretched legs, and then put her hand to her mouth in horror.

"Allan..." she whispered.

The animal was quite small, just a young heifer. She was heaving and struggling, flailing helplessly with her head against the bank of straw, her eyeballs bulging grotesquely with the effort of giving birth. Allan's right arm was inserted into the birth canal, almost up to his shoulder, and his face, as he turned back to his task, was grim with concentration.

"Which...which rope?" Mara asked.

He jerked his chin to indicate a coiled length of rope lying beside his body near his bandaged left hand, and Mara grasped it gingerly.

"But," she said, horrified, "but, Allan, this rope goes up...inside..."

Allan frowned, manipulating his arm and then fell back against the little cow's flank and rested briefly.

"The calf's coming out backward," he explained, panting a little, "and it's a great big calf. I have to try to turn it or the mother's never going to get through this. Now, what I've done, I've hooked this rope around the front legs, inside, and I want you to pull on it gently at the same time as I pull on the head."

"How can you...feel things in there?"

He grinned. "Easy. At least I can tell the head from the tail, and I'm *hoping* it's the front legs I've got. Ready?"

She nodded, gripping the rope tensely.

"Okay...not till I tell you.... Now! Pull!"

Biting her lip, she crouched beside him, pulling on the length of rope while he made rotating movements of his shoulder and his unseen right arm.

"Ow!" he yelled suddenly, and collapsed on the floor, closing his eyes and wincing with pain.

"Allan!" Frantically Mara grasped his free arm. "What is it? What's happening?"

He said nothing, shaking his head in agony while beads of sweat sprang out on his forehead. Finally he relaxed his muscles, opened his eyes and smiled at her sheepishly.

"God," he said, "that was awful."

"What? What happened?"

"She had a contraction. Felt like it was going to crush every bone in my arm."

"Oh, Allan."

Mara looked at the terrified little animal, heaving and gasping on the soft bed of straw. Her huge, liquid eyes rolled back in her head, gazing up at the two humans with mute, desperate appeal.

"You poor thing," Mara whispered, touching the cow's warm flank. She turned to Allan with new determination. "Can we try again?"

He smiled at her as he lay resting and rubbing his shoulder. "You're wonderful, you know," he said. "Just wonderful."

"Never mind that now. Let's help her get this over with."

"Okay. Same thing as before. Not yet. Not yet. Now! Good, keep pulling…easy, sweetheart, you're doing great…a little more…a little more.… There!"

Shouting in triumph, he fell back onto his knees and pulled out his arm. It came away covered with blood and mucus, and he plunged his hand and arm into a pail of warm water beside the stall, splashing the water up onto his shoulder and chest, scrubbing briskly with a cake of rough soap. When he was clean once more, he dried himself on a scrap of soft burlap sacking, while Mara watched, awed by the strength and symmetry of his tall body. His shoulders were broad and flat, and his biceps bulged on his big arms. His chest was matted with dark curly hair, running in a dense line down his flat, hard belly and disappearing beneath the blue jeans that hugged his lean, muscular hips.

He felt her eyes upon him and grinned. "What do you think? Will I pass."

"You're okay," she said, looking away and feigning disinterest.

"Good. Your turn. Come on, strip, and let's have a look at you."

"Allan," she said indignantly, "how can you tease like that when this poor little animal is almost dying here?"

"You're right," he said contritely. "Business before pleasure. Let's get this over with."

He took his heavy flannel work shirt from a peg near the door and shrugged it on, buttoning it awkwardly with his bandaged hand while Mara turned to look at the heifer. The little animal was shuddering in the grip of another contraction, twitching her legs feebly and throwing her head from side to side.

"I don't know," Mara said dubiously. "We don't seem to have done her much good."

"Just wait and see what's going to happen in a minute."

Mara stood tensely, staring down at the poor, pain-racked little animal and then froze. "Allan! Look!"

At the heifer's rear, a little black nose was protruding, nestled beside two tiny soft yellow hooves, with the length of rope still attached to them. As Mara watched, they wavered and then vanished back inside again.

"Now *that*," Allan said with satisfaction, "is the way it's supposed to look." He frowned, studying the heifer. "I think she's getting worn out, though. We'd better help her some more." He turned to Mara. "Do you mind, Mara? This isn't much of a way for a guy to entertain his girl on a Sunday afternoon, is it?"

Mara was still gazing, fascinated, at the opening where the tiny nose and hooves had briefly appeared.

"This is marvelous," she breathed. "I've never seen this before, Allan. I wouldn't miss it for anything."

"If you keep this up," he warned her solemnly, "I'm probably going to fall in love with you, you know."

He squatted beside the cow and grasped the rope, handing the free end to Mara. "Next time she has a contraction, we'll both pull. Okay?"

"Won't it hurt her?"

"Not a bit. What's hurting her is all this straining."

"Okay. Just say the word."

"Wait... Now!"

Together they dug in their heels and hauled on the rope, exactly the same, Mara thought, as in a grade-school tug-of-war.

"Rest for a minute," Allan said, and Mara collapsed, panting, against him, and looked at the cow. The calf's whole head was visible now, with the front legs folded neatly beneath.

Mara gazed at its silky little ears and big, dark eyes.

"Allan," she whispered, "can it see us, do you think?"

"Sure it can."

Mara was afraid the head would disappear again, but it remained in position. The calf's expression seemed to implore them to release it from this constricted place.

"Can we pull again?" Mara asked.

"In a second. Get ready...all set?"

Mara nodded.

"Okay...pull!"

All at once the resistance was gone, and Mara tumbled backward and fell onto the piled straw, with Allan tumbling in a heap on top of her. They thrashed briefly in the fragrant straw, a jumble of arms and legs, sneezing and laughing.

With some difficulty, they disentangled themselves, burrowed out of the straw and turned their attention to the newborn calf, lying damp and slick on its bed of hay. The mother was struggling unsuccessfully to rise, heaving her hindquarters into the air and then falling back heavily. Allan removed the length of rope from the calf's front legs, took another piece of sacking and rubbed the little body briskly, all over, until the hide was dry and springy, red-gold in the bright overhead light.

With a final grunt and heave, the cow flung herself to her feet and stood, legs braced, head hanging, swaying unsteadily. Allan grasped Mara's arm and drew her back, and the heifer took a few uncertain steps, paused and lowered her head to nuzzle and lick her baby.

Gently Allan lifted the calf to its feet and propped it on its long, wobbly legs, directing it toward its mother's milk. He released it, and it fell almost a once, and then lay struggling to gather its ungainly legs together. Patiently Allan lifted it and steadied it again, and this time it stood alone, searching the air blindly. When it encountered warmth and skin, it butted and nuzzled and then fastened onto the milk supply and began to suck lustily.

Mara and Allan stood side by side, smiling, while the calf switched its tail and nursed, and the cow gently licked its soft red back.

"Well," Allan said with relief, "a big, healthy bull calf. I'm sure glad that's over."

Mara was still gazing, enchanted, at the pair of animals standing quietly in the warm stall. The small cow continued to nudge and lick her baby, moving her head against his tiny body with an air of brooding tenderness. The calf nursed until it was exhausted, then folded its legs and collapsed on the mound of sweet-smelling straw, and the mother lay nearby, nestling close to warm her baby's body with her own.

"Oh, Allan," Mara said, softly. "Isn't that wonderful? There's something about it that's so…I don't know…" She floundered, searching for words.

As usual he understood what she was trying to say, and turned to smile at her. "I know what you mean. That's what I like about living on a farm. You get to see all the cycles of life and nature, close up, and it makes life seem so real somehow."

Mara nodded, warmed by his understanding. "That's right," she said. "You're so close to it all.

The changing of the seasons, and the cycle of birth and death and rebirth...."

He gave her a brief grin. "And sex and mating," he added innocently.

Mara glared at him. "For a man who's supposed to be in touch with all of nature, you certainly seem to have a one-track mind," she observed.

"Just since I met you. I used to spend all my time thinking about sensible things, like feed bills and crop rotation."

Mara laughed and looked again at the placid pair of animals in the corner of the stall.

Allan turned to her and began to pick bits of straw out of her hair.

"Oh!" Mara said, reaching over her shoulder and pulling out her long braid of hair. "Look at me. I'm a mess."

"You're gorgeous," Allan said. He smiled down at her, his eyes crinkling. "You look like someone who's just had a roll in the hay."

Mara laughed. "Well, so do you."

They brushed off each other's clothes, took a last look at the sleepy pair in their bed of straw and then went back out into the barn.

Allan dropped onto a soft pile of clean burlap sacks and patted a space beside him. "Sit down," he said. "Let's rest for a minute. Did you see Mick?"

Mara nodded, seating herself next to him. "He's fine," she said. "He's making a spaceship out of his Lego. He offered to share some with me, but I said I'd better come down and see you first."

Allan chuckled. "So the calf's all right and Mick's

all right...and how's *your* baby?'' he asked, leaning back and putting an arm around Mara, drawing her close to him.

"My baby?" Mara asked, puzzled. "Oh, you mean Gran?"

He nodded.

"Not as good as Michael," Mara said gloomily. "I think Michael's a lot more independent than my grandmother, actually."

He laughed and began to run his lips softly over her cheek and temple. "Maybe," he murmured against her hair, "we should get her some Lego, too. Do you think that might help?"

Mara laughed in spite of herself and nestled close to him.

"Give me a kiss," he whispered. "We haven't even said hello properly yet."

She lifted her face to him, catching her breath as his lips closed on hers and his strong arms tightened around her. Everything about him was exciting—the warm, rich, manly smell of him, the springing texture of his hair, the sinewy, muscular firmness of his body, the fiery passion of his hard, demanding mouth....

He pushed toward her with gentle, relentless pressure until she was lying in his arms on the soft, springing mound of burlap. He stroked her face and hair, murmuring to her, kissing her with increasing urgency. And she responded, hungering for more, loving the feel of his arms around her, his tongue probing her mouth, his warm breath on her face and neck. He pushed her jacket aside and began to caress her body, running his hands over her skin, reaching beneath her shirt to cup her breasts in his palms.

Mara shuddered with longing, feeling him fit his body to hers. He began to move above her, grinding his hips against her with increasing pressure.

"Mara," he whispered in her ear, still moving his body rhythmically against hers. "Mara, I want you so much...you just don't know how much, darling. I want you all the time...."

"Allan..." Her own voice seemed to come from somewhere far away, muffled against his tanned neck, drowned in yearning. "Allan..."

She felt his hand moving between their bodies, reaching down to release the zipper on her jeans. Everything within her wanted him, needed him. She longed for him to invade and possess her. But she knew she couldn't....

"Allan!" she said again, more urgently.

She struggled beneath him, pushing against his broad chest and rolling away from under his body to sit upright, flushed and breathless.

After a moment, Allan sat up beside her, drawing away from her a little, and looked down ruefully at the painful bulge in his jeans. "You can't keep doing this to me, you know, sweetheart," he said. "I think I'll die."

Mara glanced over at him miserably, then quickly looked away again. "I'm sorry, Allan. It's all my fault, and it's rotten of me. I'm not a tease, you know," she said earnestly, looking up at him. "Not at all. And I want this as much as you do, I think. It's just that I'm..." She paused, searching for words.

"You're not ready," he said quietly. "Still the same problem, Mara? Divided loyalties?"

"Oh, Allan, you can't even imagine what it's like."

"Then tell me," he said gently. "Tell me what it's like, Mara. Let's get this all out in the open. Can we talk out here? Is it too cold for you or anything?"

Mara gave him a wan smile. "Not if you'll hug me."

"Gladly."

They sat close together on the pile of sacks, and Mara snuggled gratefully into the warm curve of his arm. While he listened in thoughtful silence, she told him about Agnes—about her reaction the night of the picnic, her behavior during the week and the dreadful scene that morning. At times her voice broke, and she found it difficult to continue. When she was done, she waited for some reaction from him, but he stared in silence at the opposite wall.

Mara peered cautiously up at him and was frightened by the grim, set look of his handsome profile.

"Allan…?" she ventured.

He looked down at her, then stared off into the distance again. "Christ," he muttered finally.

"Allan, I'm so sorry…."

"Sorry? You? Why should you be sorry? You haven't done anything wrong. I'm the one who should be apologizing. You're going through all this misery because of me."

"That's my own choice," Mara said. "Nobody forced it on me."

"Maybe, but I should still be helping you,

shouldn't I? You shouldn't be dealing with it all alone.''

"How can anyone help?"

"Mara…sweetheart…somebody has to help. This can't go on.''

Mara was silent, suspecting what his next words were going to be, and dreading to hear them.

"I have to meet her, Mara. I want to talk to her."

"Oh, Allan, I know what you're thinking, and I love you for it, but it's just so *hopeless*. You can't imagine what she's like. Nothing is going to change her mind.''

Mara clenched her hands tensely. He reached over, took one hand and unfolded it and began, gently, to play with her fingers until she relaxed. "Listen, Mara. Look at it this way. Nothing's going to be accomplished by letting things continue as they are. You're just going to alienate her more or make her really sick, and then we've got an even bigger problem. Right?''

Mara nodded reluctantly.

"Well, then, having her meet me can't make things worse can it?''

Mutely she shook her head.

"And if it can't make things worse, and there's even a tiny possibility that it could improve the situation, then isn't it worth a try?''

Mara was silent, thinking.

"Say yes," he prompted.

"Yes," she said finally. "I guess maybe it's worth a try. But, Allan, I just dread the thought of it. You don't know how awful she can be. She'll probably be rude to you, and I'll be so embarrassed, and you'll be so offended, you'll never want to see me again.''

"I'm tough, Mara. I can take care of myself. And I hardly ever get into fistfights with little old ladies. Don't worry about me.''

"But…why should you subject yourself to this? Why should you have to endure it at all?''

"That's easy," he said promptly. "I want to clear up all these obstacles so I can get you into my bed and ravage you.''

Mara, who was growing used to this kind of teasing, merely turned a delicate pink and laughed. "There must be easier ways to satisfy your sexual urges," she said lightly.

"Sure there are." He looked down at her, suddenly serious. "But I happen to be a very single-minded man. And I've never wanted a woman the way I want you, Mara. Never.''

His gaze was direct, and the frank passion in his expression was unmistakable. Mara met his eyes for a moment, then looked down in confusion. "When?" she asked in a low voice.

"Whenever you say, sweetheart. How about right here? *I'm* sure ready." He began to nuzzle her ear again.

"I meant," Mara protested, "when do you want to meet Gran?''

"When do you think would be a good time?''

She thought for a moment. "Well…I'd prefer that Michael not be around in case Gran gets really awful. I'd hate for him to be upset by that.''

"Oh. I thought it might help to have him there. Soften her up a little, you know?"

"Not really. If she decides she's going to be upset, nothing will stand in her way. Not even a sweet little boy like Michael."

"Well, then, let me think. How about Saturday? Michael's going over to Jimmy's for a birthday party, and it's going to be a sleep-over. So he'll be gone from noon until sometime late Sunday. That's a good time."

"*This* Saturday?" Mara asked in dismay. "I was thinking…Christmas, maybe, or next summer…."

"Coward. Come on, let's get this over with. Invite me to dine on Saturday, and I'll bring a nice bottle of wine and some flowers and charm the socks off her."

"Oh, Allan…" All at once Mara felt a bright, warm surge of hope. Maybe it could happen, after all. Maybe he could win Gran over, earn her approval, manage to convince her that it was possible for all of them to be happy if Gran could just bend a little and not hold on so relentlessly.

After all, Mara thought, who could resist him? He was just so wonderful.

Impulsively she flung her arms around him and kissed him passionately on the mouth. Before he could respond, she was gone, jumping to her feet and starting off toward the house, while he stared after her with a startled, delighted grin.

Mara unlocked the side door and tiptoed into her darkened house, walking softly down the hall and into

Gran's bedroom.

The room was in semidarkness, lit only by the hall light outside the door. Mara hesitated on the threshold until her eyes were accustomed to the gloom, then saw that Agnes was lying on her bank of pillows, staring fixedly at the opposite wall.

Her robe and slippers were exactly where Mara had put them earlier in the day, and it was impossible to tell if the old lady had been out of bed since Mara left.

Mara switched on the overhead light and came into the room.

"Hi, Gran," she said.

Agnes blinked in the sudden brightness but said nothing.

Mara sat by the bed, reached over to pat her grandmother's spotted, veined hand and looked at her carefully. "You're looking a lot better now, Gran. Did you have a nice rest?"

Agnes's mouth twitched, but she still refused to answer.

"Have you been up at all?" Mara asked. "Have you had something to eat?"

"A lot you care," Agnes muttered bitterly. "You don't even care if I live or die."

"Yes, Gran," Mara said patiently. "I do care. I care a lot. I love you, Gran, and I won't love you less just because there's...someone else in my life, too."

Agnes stiffened and stared rebelliously at the wall again.

"Would you like me to fix you something to eat?"

Mara asked. "Maybe some toast and a poached egg?"

The older woman shook her head stubbornly, refusing to look at Mara.

"Well," Mara said cheerfully, "if you don't feel like eating, and you don't feel like talking, I guess I'll let you get some more rest. I just wanted to see how you felt."

She got up and walked toward the door, then paused, took a deep breath and turned. "By the way, Gran," she added casually, as if in passing, "my friend wants to meet you. His name's Allan Williamson." Aching with sympathy and concern, she glanced at Agnes, but it was impossible to gauge her grandmother's response. "He's coming to dinner next Saturday," she added.

The old woman's eyes still stared at the wall in front of her. At Mara's words they flickered briefly with some indefinable emotion, then resumed their expressionless gaze.

Mara looked at her for a moment longer, hesitating, wondering if she should say something more. But, finally, she turned and went out, closing the door softly behind her.

# 9

As usual, the small gymnasium was musty, over-heated and echoing with the shouts and cries of vanished generations of children. Above the stage a single tattered star rotated disconsolately on a soiled string. Mara stood near the piano, a sheaf of sheet music in her hands, and looked unhappily at the group of small children on the stage beneath the star. She turned to Jeff, who stood nearby, watching.

"The idea, you see," she explained, "is that the reindeer are playing in the woods and then they fall asleep and night comes. The lights dim on stage, you know, and there's just a few blue spotlights, and then the snowflakes fall gently and cover them in the night. It sounded so pretty the way they described it in the book, but *this*—" She waved her hand in despair. "I just hate Christmas pageants."

"You do not," Jeff said. "You love them as much as the kids do." He paused, considering, his handsome face thoughtful. "The problem, I think," he said finally, "is that the reindeer are supposed to dance, and dancing is obviously beyond these little guys. I mean, this isn't the National Ballet we've got here."

"It sure isn't," Mara agreed. "But what can they do if they don't dance? Just run around?"

"Hey, reindeer!" Jeff shouted suddenly. "Get down here!"

The reindeer trotted down off the stage and huddled around his knees, staring up at him. All of them had sad eyes, three had runny noses and one was in imminent danger of losing his antlers.

Jeff regarded them thoughtfully. "How about if they skip? You guys know how to skip, don't you?"

They all nodded, and the loose set of antlers clattered to the floor.

Mara brightened. "Skipping!" she said. "What a good idea. Just set them over there, Tommy," she added. "We'll fix them later. Now, skip. Like this... see?"

She skipped across the gym floor as light and airy as thistledown in her white woolen dress. The small reindeer watched her, their faces brightening.

Jeff watched her, too, sitting on the edge of the stage with his legs swinging. He grinned, thinking how cute she was, skipping like that, and how nice it was to see her looking a little more relaxed.

Normally Jeff knew, she was a calm, unruffled person, dealing patiently and easily with all the crises and problems of life in the kindergarten room. But lately she seemed unusually tense and worried about something. But though he frequently wondered what it was, he knew he had little chance of finding out. Despite her humor and friendliness, she was an intensely private person—easy to confide in, but much more difficult to draw out.

When you were with her, you always wound up talking about yourself, and she just listened. He wondered how she did that....

Jeff leaped down lightly, strolled over to pick up Tommy's antlers, and resumed his perch on the stage, his long, sensitive fingers probing at the faulty plastic binding.

Mara skipped back, flushed and breathless, and divided the reindeer into two groups. She sat at the piano, moved the sheet of music back into position and began to play, giving stage directions at the same time.

"Now, you people go up this side, and you others, up that side. Now skip around in a circle, fairly slow.... A little faster. Listen to the music.... Good! That's good! Now split into your two groups." The music slowed. "Now slower; slower. Now sink down...down...fall asleep... Good! Very good!"

A few of the sleeping reindeer peeped up, beaming, and then carefully closed their eyes again.

"All right," Mara called. "Snowflakes! Your turn!"

The music rippled, slow and dreamy. The snowflakes emerged from the wings, clad in flowing white sheets and glittering headdresses, and drifted among the sleeping reindeer, somewhat in time to the music.

Mara smiled her approval. "Good. That's so much better! Now, snowflakes, fall. Gently...gently... *Gently*, I said!"

Snowflakes plopped on top of reindeer. Eyes bulged, and great gusts of air were suddenly exhaled by crushed reindeer. Faces grew red.

Little Tommy, almost invisible beneath Candace, the largest snowflake, flapped his arms feebly and seemed on the verge of suffocation.

"Candy!" Mara remonstrated. "Snow...flutters! It doesn't thump! Now get off him! You others stay still!"

Mara regarded Tommy's flattened, quivering body as the plump little girl rolled off him, and wondered if there might be some tactful way of changing Candy into a reindeer.

Other reindeer began to mutter and shift in protest. A certain amount of discreet wriggling and tickling commenced. Small bodies, white and brown, began to squirm together on the floor, and antlers clattered.

Jeff leaped down from the stage again, landing softly on his sneakered feet, and strolled over to sit beside Mara on the piano bench. He kept his face sober with some effort, but his eyes danced wickedly.

Mara glared at him, her cheeks flushed. "Don't you *dare* laugh, Jeff, or I'll..." She paused, searching for a sufficiently vile threat, and then gave up. "I just don't know," she said wearily, dropping her fingers onto the piano keys. "It sounded so nice in the book, but this...this is just awful..."

They both turned to see Lisa approaching across the scarred, shining gym floor. She still showed no outward signs of pregnancy, although there was a softer, richer look to her face, and a new glow to her skin that made her lovelier than ever.

"What's happening?" she asked. "I was watching in the doorway, but I can't figure out what's going on."

She looked from Mara's hot, flustered face to Jeff's impish grin, then looked away again quickly, biting her lip and trying not to laugh.

"We're starting to practice for our Christmas pageant," Mara said. "I wanted to get one picked out early, so we wouldn't be so rushed next month, and I thought this one would be perfect because we already had the headdresses and the antlers."

She looked gloomily at the welter of reindeer and snowflakes on the stage floor and explained how the reindeer were supposed to fall asleep in the night, and then be gently covered by the falling snow.

"On your feet, all of you!" she called out to the mass of squirming, giggling children. "Stop that!"

Lisa was still gazing at the stage, eyes narrowed thoughtfully, picturing the scene as Mara had described it.

"What if..." she began, and paused, thinking. "What if the snowflakes came in carrying little white baskets, you know, filled with something...cotton or paper snowflakes or something, and they could just drift around, sort of sprinkling it on the reindeer, and then drift out again? Then they wouldn't be touching each other, and they wouldn't have a chance to fight or fool around."

Mara considered this idea and then glowed. "Marvelous! That'll be just perfect! Lisa, you're so smart." Gratefully she smiled at the slim blond girl and patted her arm. "Jeff and I will start getting the baskets ready right away. This solves everything!"

She turned to gather up her sheet music from the piano, while Jeff vaulted up onto the stage, herding the reindeer together and beginning to remove their antlers.

Lisa watched him, and Mara was startled by the look of yearning intensity on the girl's delicate face. As soon as she felt Mara's eyes on her, she turned away, her expression carefully noncommittal, and Mara almost wondered if she had imagined that look of love and longing.

But she knew that she hadn't.

*Oh, Lisa,* she thought with wrenching sympathy. Now, of all times, to meet someone you really like!

"Tommy wants to be a snowflake," Jeff reported, coming back to them, his arms laden with glittering costumes and headdresses. "Is there anyone he can trade with?"

"I know just the one," Mara said, hurrying off toward the group of children.

Silently Lisa took some of the costumes from Jeff and sat on the piano bench to fold them.

"Thanks, Lisa," he said.

"No problem. I always like helping Miss Steen with the Christmas pageant. The kids are so cute and they all get so excited about it."

They smiled at each other, then dropped their eyes quickly.

"Lisa," Jeff murmured, "Mara told me about... you know."

She nodded without looking up.

"I hope you don't mind. That she told me, I mean."

Lisa threw him a brief smile, then looked away

again. "Not much point in trying to keep it a secret," she said. "By January everybody will know."

"Well," Jeff said, folding and smoothing a snowflake headdress with great care, "I just wanted to say that if you ever need…anything, you know, I'd be glad to help." He grinned awkwardly. "Not that there's much I can do, I guess."

"No," she said quietly. "I guess there's not a lot that anyone can do, is there?" She got to her feet and looked at her watch. "But thanks, anyway, Jeff. And now I'd better get going. I have an appointment with my doctor downtown at four-thirty."

"Who's your doctor?"

"Dr. Gann. In the Professional Building."

Jeff was silent for a moment, gazing down at the pile of costumes, and then he looked up and met Lisa's eyes. "I have some stuff to do downtown," he said casually. "How about if I give you a ride, and then I could pick you up after you're done and we could grab a hamburger or something?"

"No thanks," Lisa said. "I have a bus pass, and it drops me right in front of the building."

"Hey," Jeff said, trying to smile. "Why so crisp? Have you got something against Corvettes maybe?"

"No," Lisa said quietly. "But I have something against charity. You're just offering because you feel sorry for me, Jeff, and in that case, I'd much prefer to take the bus."

She turned and walked rapidly from the room, just as Mara came back holding Candy's antlers.

Jeff looked at her with an awkward grin. "Oh, no,"

he said. "I guess you heard that, did you? Shot down, in front of witnesses," he added miserably.

"I don't think you were shot down," Mara said. "I think she was just telling the truth, as she sees it."

"You mean, that's what she really believes?"

"I think so," Mara said. "Is she right?"

She looked at the boy quietly, and he stared back at her, his face bleak with pain.

"Mara, I just don't know. When I met her, I fell for her like a ton of bricks. I mean, I never thought I'd ever meet a girl who was so beautiful and smart and sweet and funny—everything I ever wanted. And then, jeez, to find out that she's *pregnant*, with some other guy's kid—"

His voice broke, and Mara stood quietly, looking at him with sympathy. She knew that in all of Jeff's carefree, privileged life this was probably the most agonizing problem he'd ever encountered, and she knew, as well, that it was something he had to work through on his own.

"And now," he went on, "I still can't get her out of my mind. I think about her all the time and want to call her, just to hear her voice, but then I think about the...the baby...and I don't know what to do."

"Well," Mara said quietly, "you'd better decide pretty soon. For your sake and for hers."

"Maybe I don't have to," he said bitterly. "Maybe she's made the decision for both of us. From what she said just now, it's pretty clear how she feels about me, isn't it?"

Mara looked up at his troubled, unhappy face and

was tempted to tell him about the look she had surprised on Lisa's face just a few minutes earlier.

Better not get involved, she decided. This wasn't easy for them, but it was something they had to work out on their own. If she interfered she'd just make things worse.

Silently Mara and Jeff gathered up the rest of the costumes and followed the laughing group of children down the hall to the classroom.

"So," Jo said, "what's up?"

She was sitting in front of Mara in the empty classroom, squarely in the middle of one of the little kindergarten tables. She had her legs drawn up, hugging them with her chin resting on her knees, and she fixed Mara with a steady, level gaze.

Mara smiled back at her friend. Jo was wearing gold boots, tight black stirrup pants and a leopard print shift that hung to her knees. She looked wild, exotic and incredibly beautiful.

"With what?" Mara asked, frowning at a crayon drawing that appeared to represent a squashed dog.

"With the hunk. C'mon, Mara. Give. You can't keep a gorgeous man like that hidden in the trunk of your car, you know."

"Wouldn't that be nice?" Mara said dreamily. "Just to keep him in the trunk and let him out whenever I felt like..." She paused, blushing, and Jo pounced.

"Felt like what? A little action, Mara? There *is* something going on, isn't there?"

"Yes, Jo, there's something going on. Not," she

added hastily, "that there's anything going *on*. You know what I mean?"

Jo grinned. "I know. Just a matter of time." She leaned over to pick up a crude clay model of a cat from a nearby shelf. "This is kind of nice, you know," she commented. "What my art teacher at college would have called an 'enchanting primitive.' What a crock that class was."

Mara chuckled, and Jo glanced over at her.

"How's Granny taking it?"

"She isn't. She scares me to death because she just isn't reacting at all. She's normal, cheerful, nice as can be, but as far as Allan's concerned, she just refuses to acknowledge his existence. It's as if he's a...figment of my imagination or something."

"Well, that's not so bad, is it? Why can't things just keep on that way?"

"Because I never know when she's going to flip out. And," Mara added with a little shiver of terror, "because he's coming to dinner tomorrow night!"

She looked up at Jo with eloquent, mute appeal.

Jo whistled. "Wow. That's taking the bull by the horns, for sure. What's the idea? Is he going to ask for your hand in marriage, or what?"

"No, of course not. This was his idea. He just wants to meet her and hopes that once she knows him, she won't be so opposed to us...seeing each other, you know?"

Jo nodded. "Not a bad plan, I suppose. But what's the goal, Mara? I mean, are you content to just date this guy and have someone to hold hands with at the movies for the next twenty or thirty years? Or do you envisage a future together, or what?''

"No, I don't!" Mara said, and then added honestly, "Well, maybe. But there are so many things to consider. It's just far too early to think about anything like that. We've only…''

But Jo was no longer listening. She was staring at the doorway with concentrated attention, her green eyes sparkling wickedly.

"Well!" she said with emphasis. "Well, well, *well*," she added thoughtfully.

Mara followed the direction of her friend's gaze, and her heart gave a great leap and began thudding painfully in her chest.

Allan stood, smiling in the doorway, cap in hand, dressed in boots and work clothes. The hall light behind him made his hair shine like dull bronze and etched his handsome, clean-cut features with gold.

Jo was still regarding him with frank approval.

"*This*," she said solemnly to Mara, "is a quality item. This is a Grade A, number one specimen."

"Hi, Mara. I like your friend," Allan said, strolling into the room and seating himself on another of the little tables.

"Jo Morris, Allan Williamson," Mara said automatically, still a little dazed by his sudden appearance.

"Nice to meet you, Jo," Allan said. "Mara talks about you all the time."

Jo, who had no patience with small talk and believed in getting right to the heart of the matter, grinned at him. "I hear you're about to beard the lioness in her den," she said. "Terrified? Having second thoughts?"

"Of course not," Allan said cheerfully. "I can't imagine why all of you are making such a fuss over a sweet little old lady. I'll bet," he added, leaning back comfortably and extending his long, denim-clad legs, "that she's home right now, knitting me a pair of socks, just as a little gift to show her gratitude to me."

"Gratitude?" Mara asked blankly. "What for?"

"Well," he said innocently, "for taking such a healthy interest in her granddaughter."

Jo chortled. "Yeah, I bet that's what she's doing." She hopped off the table and headed for the door. "Or else," she added sweetly, her hand on the doorknob, "she's home putting arsenic in the sherry. One or the other. Bye, kids. Be good."

She closed the door carefully behind her, and then popped it open and looked in at them. "God," she said wistfully, "I wish I could be a fly on the wall tomorrow at your little dinner party."

"Sadist," Mara said grimly.

Jo laughed and vanished in a swirling, leopard-patterned blur.

Allan smiled at the closed door. "She's certainly an original, isn't she?"

"I love her," Mara said. "She helps me keep my life in perspective."

She looked over at him. "Where's Michael? Why are you in town?"

"I had to bring a calf to the vet, so I left Michael at Hilda's." He grinned. "They were baking gingerbread men when I left, and they were going to use Smarties for the eyes and the buttons,'' he said. ''But, at the rate Mick was going through the Smarties, I doubt that there'll be any left over for the cookies.''

Mara laughed, then looked alarmed. ''What calf did you have to bring to the vet? Not *our* calf?''

He smiled at her fondly. ''No, sweetheart, not *our* calf. Our calf is eating like a pig and wearing his poor little mother to a frazzle, with her running around in circles just to keep up with him.''

''Oh, good,'' Mara said with relief. ''I'll always have a soft spot for that particular calf, you know.'' She paused. ''What calf was it that you brought to the vet?''

''One of the yearlings. He got tangled up in some wire, and he has some pretty bad cuts. I brought him to get stitched up, and he should be ready in—'' he paused to consult his watch ''—in about an hour.''

Allan looked up at Mara. ''So,'' he said cheerfully, ''I've got an hour to kill. Wanna fool around?''

She smiled at him affectionately. ''You just never give up, do you?''

''Never. Come over here and say hello.''

Still smiling, she walked across the room and into his arms. She raised her face to his, shivering as his lips closed on hers and the fiery warmth of desire coursed through her body. He crushed her to him, his big arms tightening around her as if he could never hold her close enough.

''Oh, Mara,'' he whispered. ''You can't imagine how good this feels. I've been out in the cold all day, unloading hay bales, and now I get to hold you, and you're so sweet and warm...."

She pulled away from him, laughing, and sat on the little table. "At least," she said, "it's good to know that being with me is preferable to unloading hay bales."

"Well," he said thoughtfully, "not all the time. Just when it's real cold out."

She laughed again, and he looked over at her. "That's better," he said. "To see you laughing, I mean. You were looking pretty strained when I got here."

Her face clouded again, and he looked at her with concern.

"Mara...you're really worried about tomorrow, aren't you?"

She nodded. "Nobody wants to be in a socially embarrassing situation, Allan. And Gran is entirely capable of creating one."

"You're certain that she's going to?"

Mara shook her head. "No, of course not. With Gran, I can never be certain of anything. She's also capable of being warm and funny and absolutely charming. I just don't know what to expect, and I'm scared."

"Don't you have some hint of how she's planning to deal with me?"

"Not a bit. She just says it's my party and that she's not involved. But she did agree to make an apple pie," Mara added doubtfully. "And her apple pie is just about the most wonderful thing you've ever tasted."

"Well, there you go. She's won over already, and I haven't even met her yet."

He gathered Mara into his arms again, and his mouth began to wander over her cheeks, her forehead and lips and neck, while he cuddled her and stroked her body. Soon he was kissing her fervently with rising passion until at last he broke away and laughed awkwardly.

"God," he said, "this is awful. Let's go for a walk or something, shall we, before I make a fool of myself again?"

Mara smiled, patted his cheek tenderly and went to the closet to get out her jacket.


"Oh, Gran, the pie smells heavenly," Mara said. She opened the oven door and peered inside. "And the chicken is browning so nicely. Doesn't it look yummy?" She glanced at her watch and recoiled in horror. "Oh, my goodness. He's going to be here in half an hour. I think I'll run up and change, and then I'll set the table and make the gravy."

Agnes grunted.

Mara looked at her grandmother, who sat at the table sipping a cup of tea and watching Mara's slim, swift-moving figure as she flew about the kitchen, preparing the dinner.

"Gran."

"Yes?"

"Gran, you'll be nice tonight, won't you?"

"What do you mean, 'nice'?" Agnes asked, her face carefully blank.

"I mean, you'll talk and be polite and try not to say anything too...you know..."

Agnes set her cup down deliberately. "Maybe, if you're so concerned about my behavior, I should just stay in my room. Then you wouldn't have to worry about me. Is that what you want, Mara?"

"Of course it isn't. The whole idea is for him to meet you, Gran. I just want you to be...nice, you know?"

"I don't see why it matters about me. He's *your* friend."

"Gran," Mara said, controlling her temper with an effort, "both of you are important to me. I really want you two to like each other and get along, that's all. And all I'm asking is that you give it a chance."

Agnes sipped her tea in silence.

"Will you, Gran? Promise me you'll be nice."

Agnes stared at the oven window. "That pie should come out soon."

"Gran!"

"Yes, Mara," Agnes said mechanically. "I'll be nice. I'll be polite. I won't spit in his soup or spill gravy on him or laugh at his haircut."

Mara smiled doubtfully, hugged her grandmother and ran out of the kitchen, shedding her apron as she went.

Agnes watched her out of sight and then poured herself another cup of tea, her face a quiet, inscrutable mask.

A short time later the doorbell rang.

Mara, wearing a high-necked, long-sleeved jump-suit of pale yellow silk, finished lighting the candles, gave a last panicky look at the table, wiped her hands on a napkin and ran to answer the door.

"Allan," she said breathlessly.

He stood in the doorway, silhouetted against the frosty night, holding a bouquet of flowers and a bottle of wine, and smiling down at her. He looked, Mara thought, so large and impressive here in her own house in his leather jacket, dress slacks, and tan pullover, with his hair carefully combed and his dimple sparkling.

"Hi, Mara. You look just beautiful."

Mara laughed softly and drew him into the entry hall. "So do you," she whispered. She cast a furtive glance over her shoulder, stood on tiptoe to give him a brief kiss and then led him inside, divesting him of his jacket and taking the wine and flowers on the way.

They paused in the entry to the living room, where Agnes sat, knitting placidly and watching television.

"Gran," Mara said, "this is Allan Williamson. Allan, my grandmother, Agnes Steen."

Agnes picked up the remote control to switch off the television and smiled politely. "Hello, Mr. Williamson. Is it getting quite cold out?"

"Not too bad just yet, Mrs. Steen. But the wind's getting up and it's starting to snow. We could be in for a stormy night."

He moved easily into the room, lowered his tall frame into the chair that Mara indicated and smiled at Agnes. Mara fought an impulse to bend and kiss his tanned cheek, right where the dimple was.

"I guess," she said nervously, "I'd better get back to the kitchen. I have to mash the potatoes."

"Anything I can do to help?" Allan asked.

"No. No, you just stay here and visit with Gran. Dinner will be ready in just a few minutes."

Mara rushed into the kitchen and hurried about, mixing and stirring and mashing, listening tensely to the low murmur of conversation from the other room. Then, incredibly, she heard her grandmother's sharp, high bark of laughter, underscored by Allan's deep, rich masculine chuckle.

*They're laughing!* Mara thought in wonder. *They actually like each other!*

She paused in the middle of the kitchen, holding the hand mixer, poised as lightly as a colorful silken bird caught in midflight. Her face was glowing with joy.

*This is wonderful* she thought. *This is just marvelous. Allan was right. I should have done this ages ago.*

She took a last critical look at the table in the dining room, moved one napkin a fraction of an inch to the left, touched the vase containing Allan's flowers and then went over to stand in the archway, looking into the living room. "Dinner's ready," she announced.

"Good!" Allan said, smiling at her. "I've been saving up for this all day. Mrs. Steen?" He paused by Gran's chair, offering her his arm, and ushered her into the dining room.

Mara seated them at the big old-fashioned carved wooden table and brought out the salad. As the meal progressed, Mara listened in growing amazement. She had never seen Agnes like this—so urbane, so voluble, so consciously gracious.

Agnes reminisced, narrated anecdotes and drew Allan out skillfully, asking him questions about his farm and his life, about his family and Michael. Allan was relaxed and courteous, answering her questions with quiet sincerity and listening with genuine interest to her stories about the early days in Calgary.

He looked, Mara thought, heartbreakingly handsome, sitting at the table, a strong, masculine presence in this house that had always been almost exclusively female. The breadth of his shoulders, the strength in his big hands, the deep timbre of his voice, were all so different, so satisfying, at a table that had entertained few men in the past forty years.

*It's all going so well,* she thought happily as they worked through the main course, progressing rapidly to a first-name basis, the wine and the conversation both flowing easily.

Even the gravy was perfect, for once, Mara thought, and wait till he tasted Gran's apple pie.

Allan complimented Mara solemnly on the meal, giving her a meaningful, teasing glance that made her smile, and even Agnes admitted graciously that the food was surprisingly good. She hastened to add, however, that she had taught Mara everything she knew.

After the tension of the preceding days, and the frantic work of preparing the dinner while worrying constantly about Gran's possible behavior, Mara was worn out with emotion. She ate and smiled and listened to them, loving both of them, drifting on a warm golden cloud of pleasure and relief.

Not until much later, when they were relaxing over coffee, did warning bells begin to sound in her head as a vague, formless sense of unease penetrated her happy mood.

Something wasn't quite right here. There was something about Gran....

She glanced over at Agnes, sitting primly in her place at the head of the table. Gran had dressed carefully for the occasion in her best dress of navy blue silk and her good pearls. With her silvery crown of hair and her small trim figure, she looked elegant and attractive. Her face was animated, her eyes bright, cheeks pink.

*Too* pink, Mara thought uneasily. Gran wasn't like herself. She was too—Too what?

Mara couldn't quite say what was wrong, but she felt a sudden clutch of fear, a nameless panic. She had a frantic urge to get Allan away, to separate them, to deflect Agnes from whatever she was about to do.

"Well," she said brightly, leaping to her feet, "I guess that's it. Allan, would you like to help me clear the table? Maybe we could do up the dishes while Gran has a little rest."

"Sure," Allan said cheerfully, starting to rise.

"Sit down, both of you," Agnes said. Her voice was casual and cheerful, but with a steely edge to it that couldn't be ignored. The two younger people sank back into their chairs and looked at her. She smiled, her eyes glittering in the candlelight.

"We're having a nice visit, Mara," she said. "The dishes can wait. Let's just chat for a while, shall we?"

Mara's heart began to pound, and she touched Allan's foot with her own. He responded by smiling at her and pressing his knee against hers beneath the table, unaware of her growing tension.

"So, Allan," Agnes asked casually, smiling at him over the rim of her coffee cup, "you're a widower, I understand."

"Yes," he said quietly. "I am."

"I see. How long has your wife been dead?"

"Almost two years," Allan said.

Mara poured him another cup of coffee, and he thanked her quietly without smiling this time as he stirred sugar into his cup.

"How did your wife die, Allan?" Agnes asked, her eyes bright, her face lively with interest.

"Really, Gran," Mara protested, "I don't think that Allan—"

"Be quiet, Mara!" her grandmother snapped. "How did she die, Allan?" she repeated.

Allan set his cup down and looked steadily at the older woman. "She had an accident," he said, his voice low.

"I see," Agnes said brightly, as if they were having an animated conversation about the weather. She sipped her coffee and smiled at him again. "What kind of accident, Allan?"

"Gran!" Mara said angrily. "Stop this! I won't let you—"

"What kind of accident?" Agnes interrupted

smoothly, ignoring Mara as if she weren't even in the room.

Mara knew, by now, that her worst fears were going to be realized. This was no chance conversation. Agnes already knew the answers to all of the questions she was asking, because Mara had filled her in, briefly, on Allan's history and the details of his wife's accident.

Mara looked at him anxiously. His hands, out of sight beneath the table, were clenched into fists, and his jaw muscles were knotted. Apart from this, he betrayed no outward signs of emotion.

"She fell off the porch, Agnes," he said, looking directly at the older woman.

Agnes nodded complacently. "I see. Why, Allan?"

He stared at her.

"Why did she fall? Was there something wrong with the railing? And did you know about it?"

Allan continued to stare at her in appalled silence.

Horrified, Mara sat between them, burning with shame and a slow, growing rage. She felt furious, but totally helpless, like a person caught in one of those hideous dreams where disaster is imminent but the victim is unable to make any move to save himself.

She reached over and gripped Allan's hand, glaring defiantly at her grandmother.

"Why, Allan?" Agnes repeated. "You see," she added reasonably, "as Mara's only relative, I consider it my responsibility to find out just what kind of person you are. If you're the kind of man who's that careless about your wife's safety, then that's something we should know about. Don't you agree?"

Once more she favored him with a polite, animated smile and paused to sip her coffee.

The silence in the room was so intense that Mara could hear one of the candles hissing as the wick spluttered down into a little pool of wax and then flared up again.

Finally, after what seemed like hours, though it could only have been seconds, Allan pushed his chair back and got to his feet, folding his napkin neatly and dropping it onto his plate.

Mara looked up at him in silent agony, and he touched her shoulder gently.

"If you'll excuse me," he said to her quietly, "I think I'd better be going. Thank you for the dinner, Mara."

"Allan!" Frantically she reached out to detain him and looked down the table at her grandmother. Agnes sat gracious and erect behind the low silver vase of flowers, her face serene, her eyes glowing with quiet triumph.

Mara made her decision.

"Wait, Allan," she said. "I'm going with you."

"Mara," he began to protest, his voice low and intense.

"I am," she said firmly. "I don't want to stay in this house for another minute. I want you to take me out for a drive or something, and then maybe I'll go over to Jo's place for the night. Can you just come upstairs for a minute while I change?"

Without looking back, she hurried out of the room, and Allan followed her up the stairs.

"This is the sitting room," Mara whispered breathlessly. "You can just wait here for a few minutes while I—"

"Mara, look at me." He caught her by the shoulders and tipped her chin up so that he could see her face. In the dim light of the upstairs hallway, her eyes shone with angry tears.

"Sweetheart," he murmured. "Mara, my darling…" He gathered her into his arms, brushing away the warm salty tears and kissing her face tenderly. "Don't worry about me, Mara. I'm all right. Don't do this just for my sake."

"I'm not, Allan. I'm doing it for my sake. I really couldn't stand to stay here with her after you've gone. I couldn't trust myself to talk to her."

He crushed her to him again, holding her close. Trembling in his warm embrace, she buried her face against his chest and listened to his heart beating.

"All right," he said finally, releasing her. "It's your decision, Mara. Hurry, though, before something else happens. I've got a lot of self-control, but I don't want another encounter with her if we can avoid it."

Mara vanished into her room, and emerged in a surprisingly short time, warmly dressed in jeans, boots and a pullover, carrying her jacket.

"Ready?" he asked.

She nodded.

"And you're absolutely sure about his, Mara? No second thoughts? You don't think you should stay and try to talk to her?"

Mara shook her head firmly. "Not tonight."

He followed her downstairs, taking his leather coat

from the hall closet while she paused to look into the dining room.

Agnes sat in her place at the table, exactly where they had left her. Her face was blank and expressionless, and she kept her eyes on the centerpiece of flowers, refusing to look up.

"I'm sorry, Gran," Mara said quietly. "I didn't want it to happen this way, but I honestly can't stand to stay here with you after what you just did. You've gone too far this time, Gran."

Agnes looked up then, and her eyes filled with tears. "Please, Mara," she whispered, "don't leave me alone now. You know how scared I get when I'm alone at night. Please," she said again. "I'm sorry, Mara. I really am." Her tears were flowing freely now, rolling down her withered cheeks and dropping unheeded on the tablecloth.

"Mara," Allan murmured. "Maybe we should..."

But Mara shook her head. "Tears won't work, Gran," she said coldly. "Not this time. I'll come back when I feel able to talk to you, but I don't know when that's going to be."

She took Allan's arm, her face calm and composed now that her decision was made, and walked rapidly out of the house without looking back.

# 10

Snow swirled and hissed across the road, coating the windshield heavily. Wind whipped white clouds in front of the truck, and the ditches were filled with drifts, so that it was difficult to see where the road was. Allan drove carefully, his lean brown hands gripping the steering wheel as he peered out at the narrow highway and kept his eyes fixed on the center line to give him some sense of direction.

Automatically he drove out of the city on the road that led to his farm, searching for familiar landmarks to guide him through the swirling darkness. From time to time he glanced down at Mara, sitting tense and silent beside him.

Finally he pulled over onto an approach, parked and turned to her, gathering her into his arms. She nestled against him gratefully, drawing comfort from his big, warm, male presence.

"Mara?" he whispered.

"Yes?"

"You all right, sweetheart?"

"Oh, God, Allan, she was just so awful. Worse than I'd ever dreamed she could be. I'm so sorry."

He smiled grimly. "Yeah, she sure goes for the jugular, doesn't she? Of all the topics in the world, she picked the one thing guaranteed to make me crazy.'' He was silent for a moment. ''Mara,'' he whispered finally, his lips against her hair. ''I've always felt so guilty about that railing.''

''Allan, it was an accident. You know it was. And it's part of the past. It's nothing to do with us.'' She stirred unhappily in his arms. ''I just feel so terrible that she behaved that way, and that you had to endure it, just because of me.''

''Listen, Mara,'' he said. ''My feelings weren't hurt *that* badly, you know. I decided it was time to leave because I could see that the whole situation was hopeless, and I didn't want her pushing me to the point where I might say something really damaging. Nothing that happened was your fault. The whole thing was my idea, remember? You tried to warn me, but I was arrogant enough to believe I could win her over if I just had the chance. I don't blame you for anything, darling.''

He looked down at her. Only the top of her head was visible, shining dull gold in the dim interior light of the truck.

''Are you listening, Mara?''

She looked up and nodded, her face still pale and tense with pain.

''Well, I want you to know that I don't really blame *her*, either. She's not a monster, Mara. She's just a sad, lonely old lady, terrified of losing you, trying to hang on to you any way she can. I know that her methods are pretty awful, but I can't hate her for it. God knows, if you were mine, and I was in danger of losing you, I'd fight damn hard, too, to try to hang on. She's misguided and mixed up, but when you get right down to it, she's just trying to hold on to what she loves best in the world—like we all do.''

At his words, Mara's reserve finally broke, and she sobbed against his chest. All of the tension and fear and frustration of the past months came pouring out in a flood of tears, while Allan held her, patting her back, murmuring comforting words.

Gradually the storm of tears abated, and she grew silent in his arms, trembling slightly from time to time. He searched in his pocket for a tissue and tenderly mopped her face as if she were Michael's age.

"Feeling better?" he asked her.

She nodded and gave him an embarrassed smile. "I drenched you, I'm afraid. I'm sorry, Allan. I don't usually do things like this."

"Well, it's about time," he said with satisfaction. "You needed that. You've been carrying around a lot of tension and unhappiness bottled up inside you for a long time, Mara."

"You're right, I have. And I do feel better." She turned to him and smiled, a genuine, glowing smile, looking freer and happier than he had ever seen her. "In fact, I feel wonderful."

"Good girl. You look wonderful." He kissed her warmly and then straightened on the truck seat and reached for the key in the ignition, casting her an inquiring glance. "Well, then," he asked. "What now?"

"What do you mean?"

"Which way do we go? Now that you're feeling

better, do you want to go back and talk to her, or do you still want to go to Jo's place?''

"I want to go home with you," Mara said without hesitation.

He looked at her, startled into silence.

"If that's okay with you," she added, giving him a little awkward glance.

He studied her face thoughtfully. "If we go out to the farm," he said, "we won't likely be coming back tonight. She'll be alone all night, and she's terrified of that. Are you prepared to do it, anyway?''

"Yes, I am," Mara said. "You see," she explained, frowning at the dashboard, choosing her words carefully, "I believe that people have to live with the consequences of their actions. I really do love Gran, and I'll always feel responsible for her. I can't help that, Allan.''

She turned to look up at him, her eyes wide and earnest, and he nodded in understanding.

"But," she went on, turning to stare ahead of her again, "she can't keep behaving the way she does. Nobody can be that awful and not suffer for it. Somehow she has to learn that she can't get her own way by being rude and manipulative, that she has to be nice if she wants people to be nice to her. I've been so foolish, giving in to her emotional blackmail, letting her push me around because I was afraid she'd hurt herself or get sick or something if I ever really stood up to her.''

"Mara," he warned her gently, "she still might, you know. You have to be prepared for that, dear.

She might not learn this lesson all that easily. Are
you ready to deal with anything that might happen?''

She squared her shoulders, her face cold and set.
''I have to be, Allan. Or else she'll push me around
forever. If I give in to this again, she'll just keep on
doing it. I hate the thought of her suffering and being
lonely and frightened, but, yes, I'm prepared to go
through with it.''

He considered for a moment and then looked at her
honestly. ''Okay. I'm not sure if you'll still feel that
way in the morning, but I accept your decision. I'll
take you home with me.'' He paused, and then added,
''Mick's away tonight. He's over at Jimmy's for that
birthday party. You can sleep in his bed.''

''Allan, it's such a cold, stormy night, and I feel
so…and after all this…'' She floundered, searching
for words, and then looked at him frankly. ''I don't
want to sleep alone tonight, Allan.''

He stared at her, his handsome face dimly illuminated in the glow from the dashboard. ''Mara,'' he
whispered. ''Are you sure, sweetheart? You don't
want to wait a little longer?''

''What's this reluctance?'' she asked in mock outrage. ''After all that teasing, I expected you to leap
at my offer!''

He gathered her into his arms again with a husky
laugh. ''Teasing's one thing,'' he murmured. ''Having your dreams come true is something else altogether.''

Mara smiled and kissed his neck.

He put his hand under her chin and lifted her face
up, looking down into her eyes. ''I hope you're se-

rious about this, girl. I hope you're not just planning to use me for a night's pleasure and then toss me aside. I'm not that kind of guy, you know. I'm really very respectable.''

He grinned, and his words were light and teasing, but his eyes were intent as he studied her face.

Mara smiled. ''I'm serious about this,'' she whispered. ''Really serious.''

He nodded, put the truck into gear and started off again, driving slowly through the winter storm. Mara sat close to him, lost in warmth and happiness, with her hand resting on his strong, hard-muscled thigh as the snow whipped and swirled around them.

The little farmhouse was bright and warm, a cosy island in a vast, stormy sea. They stamped the snow from their boots, built a roaring fire in the wood stove and settled gratefully in front of its glowing flame until they were warm and comfortable.

Then with a good deal of laughter and cheerful teasing, they made a bowl of popcorn and some cocoa, carrying their mugs back into the living room to settle in front of the fire again. Soon it was so warm that they took off their sweaters and Allan dimmed the lights so that the only illumination in the room was the crackling glow of the fire, visible through the glass door, casting dancing, mysterious shadows on the walls and ceiling.

He tossed some big, soft pillows onto the sheepskin rug in front of the stove, lay down and stretched out, pulling Mara gently down beside him. She sat cross-legged, leaning into the hard curve of his body, and gazed at the leaping flames while the two of them ate their popcorn and sipped the warm, sweet cocoa.

"You know, I love a fire," she said dreamily. "Almost every night, after Gran goes to bed, I build a fire and just sit there, all by myself, watching it and thinking."

"What do you think about?" he asked, caressing her idly.

"You, most of the time," she confessed. "Lately there have been nights at home when I've wanted you so much, I'd have given anything to have you there with me."

He laughed, a low, teasing sound, set their empty mugs and bowls aside and tugged gently at her long plait of hair. "You've felt that way, too have you?" he asked. "And what were you planning to do with me if I'd been there?"

She smiled at the glow of the fire. "Oh, all sorts of things. It's amazing how inventive your mind can be in front of an open fire on a winter evening. Allan," she said in sudden alarm, "what are you doing?"

"Relax. I'm just unbraiding your hair. I want to see how it looks."

She closed her eyes and felt his hands working behind her, separating the heavy strands of hair. He undid the braid, lifting and shaking her hair until it fell loose over her shoulders and covered her body in a shimmering cascade, glowing ruddy gold in the firelight.

"Mara," he muttered brokenly. "Oh, my God..." He sat up, cradling her in his arms, and buried his face in the fragrant masses of hair. Then he leaned away from her, looking into her eyes. "I love you, Mara," he said simply.

"And I love you," she whispered. "So much, Allan..."

Still looking into her eyes, he reached out and began, slowly to undo the buttons on her shirt, easing it off her shoulders. Bending forward, he brushed his lips over her throat and reached behind her to unfasten the closure of her bra.

Mara shivered as his fingertips trailed across her bare skin. Gently, gently, he took her bra off, peeling away the lacy cups to expose her firm breasts, the nipples standing erect at his touch. Quietly she looked into his eyes and kissed him, a slow, deep, yearning kiss.

It was such bliss, she thought, to be able to give herself to him freely after all the times she had resisted and turned away, even though she longed for him. But now, tonight, they were together at last, and there was nothing to come between them.

Allan leaned beside her on his elbow, glorying in the sight of her shapely, naked breasts burnished by the firelight. "So beautiful," he murmured. "So beautiful..."

He moved beside her, leaning down to kiss each breast, running his tongue lightly across the small erect nipples, and she gasped with pleasure. Then he pulled her gently down onto the pillows, and arched above her, unzipping her jeans and easing them down over her hips, tugging at her panties.

All the while he murmured to her, telling her how

lovely she was, how he adored her, how much he desired her, while his hands stroked and caressed her slowly, worshipping the lines and curves of her beautiful slender body.

Finally Mara lay naked on the soft rug, gazing up at him. Firelight flickered over her, bathing her in its radiant warmth, and the sheepskin was soft and yielding beneath her naked skin. Outside, she could hear the blizzard winds howling and sobbing around the eaves of the little farmhouse, and their small lighted area seemed like an enchanted place, a sanctuary of warmth and love and safety in the midst of the night's fury. She forgot everything, cared about nothing. She existed only for this moment, with this man whom she desired above all men. She murmured to him, soft, broken words of pleasure and endearment, lost in passion and desire, her body flaming at his sure, gentle touch and his soft loving words. She watched while he stood up to undress, and gazed at him as he towered above her in the glow of the fire.

"Allan," she murmured, "you're so beautiful, darling...such a beautiful man..."

His tall body rippled with hard, flat muscles bronzed by the firelight, and the dense curly hair on his chest and legs was tipped with gold. He looked like a sculpture, a godlike creature molded from some precious metal, rich in his strength and virility.

He was erect and rigid with desire, and Mara reached up toward him on fire with urgency, dying for him. But he refused to be hurried. He lay down beside her and drew her close, continuing to caress her and whisper to her, loving her with his hands and mouth and eyes until her body opened to him like a flower.

Then, at last, he entered her, filling her with a richness so exquisitely satisfying that she shuddered with joy. Their bodies began to move together in an ancient, eternal rhythm—a movement as old as the ages, and as new as springtime. Finally they mounted together to overwhelming heights of pleasure and, afterward, lay gasping, locked in each other's arms, kissing softly and murmuring to each other in the darkness while the shadows flickered and danced on the walls and ceiling and the winter winds howled fiercely outside the frosted windows.

Mara woke before the first light and lay in the warm bed, trying to decide what had startled her.

*It's the silence,* she realized suddenly. *That's what's different here. It's so quiet.*

She lay still, absorbing the new sensation. There were none of the city noises she had been accustomed to all her life—barking dogs and early traffic and the low, growling hum of a big city struggling to wake after a long winter night. The storm had died away while they slept, leaving the countryside muffled in snow, and utterly still. The only sound in all the world was Allan's deep, regular breathing as he lay in the bed beside her.

Mara rolled her head on the pillow and smiled tenderly at him. His profile was etched in the dim glow of the yard light outside their window, and she was surprised by the boyish, vulnerable look of his face as he slept.

Suddenly all the memories of the previous night came flooding back, and her body tingled and flamed with love. Still smiling, she gazed up at the ceiling again. Then she stretched luxuriously in the bed, touching her warm body with soft, wondering hands, remembering how beautiful he had made her feel.

"Here," he said suddenly from his pillow, "what's all this wiggling and squirming while I'm trying to sleep?"

"I'm sorry, Allan. I didn't mean to wake you."

He chuckled, a warm rich sound in the shadowy room, and drew her close to him.

"Oh, my goodness," she murmured as she felt the familiar, unmistakable, bulging firmness of him. "Not *again*. How many times is this?"

"Who's counting? Besides, it's your fault. You woke me up."

"You're going to get sick if you maintain this pace," she protested, laughing. She pulled out of his arms and sat up in bed beside him. Her hair, still unbound, fell all around her in a shining golden curtain. "You'll go into a decline and die of weakness."

"Yeah," he agreed blissfully, reaching up to stroke her breasts. "What a way to go. Lie down," he added. "I want to talk to you."

She chuckled and nestled beside him under the covers, and it was a long time before she was able to give any further thought to the peace and quiet of her surroundings.

She woke again, presently, from a soft, gentle morning sleep to find his side of the bed empty. Lights were on somewhere else in the house, a radio was playing and Allan was singing in a sweet, clear baritone that was surprisingly pleasant to listen to. Mara lay in bed feeling blissfully happy—warm and lazy and hungry.

Allan appeared in the doorway, dressed in work clothes and thick woolen socks, carrying a steaming mug of coffee. "Morning, sweetheart," he said, sitting on the bed beside her and handing her the coffee. "How do you feel?"

"I'm not sure," she said, giving him a lazy grin. "Why don't you feel me and see?"

He chuckled. "What a brazen hussy. My mother warned me about girls like you, but I could never find one."

Mara laughed and touched his cheek. "You're cold."

"I sure am. It's freezing out there. Thirty below."

"Oh, Allan," she asked, "have you been out already?"

"Certainly. I've done all my chores."

"Oh, my goodness," Mara said guiltily. "And I've just been lolling in this nice warm bed."

"Yeah. Some help you are. I invite you out here to help with the chores and you sleep all day."

She smiled, yawning and stretching. "What time is it, anyhow?"

"Nine o'clock."

"Well, that's not so bad. But I'd better get up now. I'm getting hungry."

She climbed out of bed and gathered her clothes, which she had left neatly folded on a chair the night before. Blushing at his frank, admiring appraisal of her slender naked body and shivering in the early morning chill, she hurried into the bathroom to wash and dress.

"Allan," she called.

"Yeah?" he answered in a muffled voice from somewhere at the back of the house.

"Can you braid my hair, please?"

"Love to," he said promptly, appearing in the hall-way. "Come on, sit in here by the fire."

She followed him into the living room and sat comfortably on the soft rug while he knelt behind her, brushing her hair with long, firm strokes and dividing it carefully. But the memories of the night before, the cozy warmth of the fire and the nearness of her shapely body, all kept distracting him, and it was a long time before her hair was finally braided and secured.

They breakfasted on toast and coffee, smiling across the table at each other, lost in love and tenderness.

"Are you happy, sweetheart?" he asked her.

"Oh, Allan, I can't ever remember being this happy. It just feels so...so right. You know?"

He nodded. "I know." He was quiet for a moment, and then looked at her, meeting her eyes steadily. "No regrets?"

She laughed at him with a little teasing sparkle. "Why all these question? What's this leading up to? Are you about to tell me you don't respect me now that it's morning?"

He grinned wickedly. "*Respect* you?" he said, raising one eyebrow. "Sweetheart, I'm *dazzled* by you! You have talents I never dreamed of beneath that prim schoolteacher disguise."

Mara smiled demurely and buttered another slice of toast.

He watched her, his face suddenly serious. "It's just that I worry. I know you have responsibilities, Mara, and I know you take them seriously, no matter what. And I don't want anything that happens between us to cause you any pain in the future."

She nodded in understanding and stared down into the depths of her coffee mug. Slowly her sparkle faded, and she looked sad and troubled.

"You'd better call," he suggested gently.

"Do you think I should? I wasn't going to, Allan. I was going to spend the whole day and have you take me home tonight and just walk into the house as if nothing had happened at all. That was my plan."

"I think you should call," he said. "No matter what your plan is, I know that soon you'll be getting worried. And," he added, smiling at her, "you're not going to be able to relax and enjoy your afternoon nap if you're all tense and worried."

She looked up at him, the sparkle returning to her vivid face. "Are we having a nap?"

"Certainly we are," he said with dignity. "We need a nap because we didn't get nearly enough sleep last night. And this time I don't want you wiggling around and bothering me, keeping me awake. Go and make your call."

She laughed and hugged him. "Oh, Allan, I just love you so much...."

He leaned back in his chair, watching her as she dialed the number.

Mara gripped the receiver, her heart pounding, wondering what Gran's reaction was going to be.

"Hello?" an unmistakable voice boomed in her ear.

Mara knew that voice. It belonged to Delores, Rachel's daughter-in-law, who lived two doors down from Agnes. She and her husband, Wayne, had been their neighbors as long as Mara could remember, and there was nobody else who sounded like Delores on the telephone.

"Delores?" Mara asked in bewilderment. A cold little chill touched her heart, and she shivered.

"Delores, what are you doing there?"

"Mara? Oh, thank God!" Delores said. "We've been phoning all over, but nobody knew where you—" She paused and spoke to someone in the background. "Tell them to hurry. Right in there. For God's sake, don't worry about *that*, just—"

"Delores?" Mara said frantically. "What's going on? What's happening?"

"Mara, just be calm now and listen. Wayne and I stopped in to see if Agnes wanted a ride to church because it was so cold this morning."

Delores paused again, giving muffled instructions to someone nearby. Distant thumpings could be heard over the phone, and the sound of voices. Mara waited, trembling with frustration and anxiety, and Allan came across the room to put his arms around her and pat her back reassuringly.

"Mara?" Delores's voice finally sounded again in the receiver. "Are you still there?"

"Of course I'm here, Delores. Please tell me what's happening, before I go crazy."

"I'm sorry, sweetie. There's just so much going on here, and all these people are—" Muffled voices and heavy footsteps were once more audible and then suddenly there was silence.

"At last," Delores said. "They're gone. Now listen, Mara—"

But at that moment, coming loud and clear over the phone line, Mara heard the high, keening shriek of an siren.

"That's an ambulance!" she cried. "Delores, she's hurt, isn't she? What is it? *Tell* me!"

Allan held her more closely and tried to take the receiver from her. She shook her head frantically, gripping the phone to her ear.

"We came by just before church," Delores said. "And we found her at the bottom of the basement stairs. She must have gone down to get something and fallen, and apparently she'd been lying there a long time. Maybe all night, because she was still fully dressed."

"Oh, no," Mara said softly, her face ashen.

"Well," Delores went on, "we called the ambulance and then we checked with a few of the other teachers that we could think of, but nobody knew where to find you. Not," she added hastily, "that anybody's blaming you, dear. We all know how you've looked after her all these years. It's just that none of us knew what to do, really, and it took so long for that damn ambulance to get here. They went to the wrong address, I guess. Probably Wayne's fault. He was so upset he probably gave the street instead of the avenue or something.''

"Delores, is she…is she…'' Mara choked on the words, caught in the grip of a dreadful fear.

"The paramedics said she has some bad bruises—from the fall, you know—and they think she broke her collarbone. I guess she suffered worst from the cold. They figure she was there all night, and it must have gotten really cold in your house, Mara.''

Mara nodded miserably. "The furnace is on an automatic thermostat. It turns way down overnight.'' Her voice was hushed and shaking, barely more than a whisper.

"Well, they've just taken her away. She's going to the Foothills Hospital. They said we should have you come over as soon as we could locate you in case you have to sign for treatment or anything.''

Mara nodded mechanically. "Delores, did she… did she say anything? Did she ask for me?''

"She was never really conscious, Mara. She seemed kind of…I mean, her eyes were open, part of the time, but it was like she couldn't see us, you know? The paramedics said she was in shock.''

"Oh, God. Delores, I'm out in the country. I'll be there as soon as I possibly can.''

"No rush now, dear. She's in good hands. Although I guess you should get to the hospital sometime this afternoon, if you can, just in case they…you know…''

"Yes, I will. Thanks, Delores. I'm so grateful to all of you and so sorry you had to be involved."

"What are neighbors for? Do you have someone there with you who can help you?"

"Yes," Mara said, her voice trembling on the verge of tears. "Yes, I have someone. Goodbye, Delores."

She hung the phone up slowly and turned to look at Allan, her eyes wide and tragic in her pale face. "You heard?" she asked him.

He nodded, trying to smile. "With that woman's voice I'll bet I could have heard it out in the barn."

"That's Delores. She lives two doors down from us. She's the one, remember, who's Rachel's daughter-in-law, and she and Gran have a kind of running battle all the time, but they're really good neighbors."

"Mara," he said gently, interrupting her nervous flow of words.

"Oh, Allan..." She looked up at him, her face crumpled in misery. She moved into his arms, and he held her, patting her back tenderly, gazing over the top of her head with a distant, troubled expression on his face.

"Come on," he murmured finally when he felt her tension begin to subside. "Get your things together, sweetheart. I'll take you home."

Mara sat huddled in her corner of the truck cab, wringing her gloves tensely in her hands and staring out the window at the snowy landscape. Allan cast a concerned glance at her remote profile, and then peered ahead down the road again. The snowplows had been through early in the morning, leaving huge banks of snow piled on the shoulder on both sides of the road allowance and a narrow driving lane in the center that had to be negotiated with extreme care.

"Look, Mara," he said finally, "none of this is your fault, you know. You're blaming yourself, and it's not fair. You didn't do anything wrong."

"Of course it's my fault," she said in a quiet, even tone. "I went away and left her, knowing what state she'd be in and what it would do to her. I knew, better than anybody, what effect it might have on her. It was criminal, Allan, leaving her like that."

"I'll be damned if I'll let you say that! You said yourself that she deserved to be left alone and that she should have to live with the consequences of her actions."

"But not like that! Allan, she must have lain there, in that freezing cold all night long. And all the time we were—"

"Stop right there, Mara," he warned her grimly. "I mean it. Regardless of what happened to your grandmother, don't imply that there was anything wrong with what *we* did last night. We just loved each other, and there's nothing wrong with that."

She nodded tightly, biting her lip. "I know, Allan. I'm sorry. It's just that I can't help picturing…"

"Well, don't. Quit using your imagination to torture yourself. Just deal with the reality of the situation and forget everything else."

"All right. I'll try."

"Good. Do you want to go straight to the hospital?"

She nodded, and they drove on in silence, turning finally onto the wide, cleared highway and then into busy city traffic.

"Do you want me to come in?" he asked, parking in front of the admitting doors.

Mara stared miserably out at the big hospital complex, so quiet and serene in the winter sunlight.

She shook her head. "I don't think so, Allan. It would likely just upset her. And you have to leave soon, anyway, to go pick up Michael."

"Okay. Whatever you say." He got out and came around to help her down and walked beside her to the entry.

Mara paused, gazing up at him, her eyes wide and pleading.

He looked down at her steadily. "I love you, Mara," he said. "Whatever happens, I want you to remember that."

"And I love you."

He gathered her into his arms, kissed her tenderly and then released her, turning to leave. Mara watched him stride away up the snowy walk, tall and broad-shouldered, a powerful, masculine figure in his rough work clothes.

At the truck he paused and turned. "I'll call you tonight," he said. "All right?"

"All right," she said tonelessly.

# 11

Agnes lay as small and still as a doll in the white hospital bed, her heavy-lidded eyes closed, her skin white and translucent. The bone structure in her face was very prominent, as if the skin had been stretched too tightly, and the large blue veins at her temples throbbed. An intravenous tube was dripping slowly into her arm, and pale blue oxygen tubes were inserted in her nostrils. Over one side of her forehead and cheek, a large bandage had been placed, very white against her grayish, age-spotted skin. Her arm and shoulder were also heavily bandaged and immobilized in a kind of overhead sling.

Mara stood hesitantly in the doorway, peering in at her grandmother, who had been sleeping all afternoon. She tiptoed across the room and sat in the chair, trying to be as quiet as she could, but Gran's thin, veined eyelids fluttered and opened. She gazed around blankly, taking in the bare walls, the hospital equipment, the sling on her arm and Mara sitting beside her in the chrome-and-vinyl chair.

Then her face blanched with panic, and she struggled weakly, rolling her head on the pillow and trying to pull herself into a sitting position.

"Gran!" Mara said. "Gran, don't. It's all right. I'm here. Don't move, Gran. You'll hurt yourself."

"Mara?" Agnes whispered. "Mara?"

"It's me, Gran. Just relax," Mara said, leaning over to grasp her grandmother's free hand.

Agnes looked around her again and shuddered. "I'm in the hospital," she said.

"Yes, Gran, you are."

"How did I get here? Who brought me?"

"You came in an ambulance. After last night, remember, when we left—" Mara flushed, then continued doggedly. "After we left, you must have gone down the basement for some reason, and you tripped and fell on the stairs."

Agnes stared ahead. "It was the furnace," she whispered. "It was making a funny noise and I went down to see what was the matter with it, and then I can't remember what happened. I just remember being so cold, and something hurt so bad. I think it was my shoulder."

She rolled her head on the pillow again and looked at Mara. "I'm sorry, Mara. I'm sorry for what I did and for causing you all this trouble."

"It's all right, Gran. You were just upset, that's all. Don't think about it."

"How bad am I? What did they say?"

"I only talked to the nurse. She said you're stable and that you'll be fine. Your collarbone is broken and you have a touch of pneumonia, that's all. I'm seeing the doctor later this afternoon, and I'll find out all the details then. But I think you should be out of here in a week or so."

"I'll die in here," Agnes said flatly.

"Gran, don't say that. Of course you won't. There's nothing seriously wrong with you at all."

Agnes's hand flopped and twitched spasmodically in Mara's, and her face flushed a dull, blotchy red. "I'll die in here," she repeated. "How can I go home when you're not there?"

"Gran," Mara said blankly, "what are you talking about? Why won't I be there?"

Agnes stared at Mara, her eyes widening in disbelief. "But, Mara," she whispered, "you said...you said that you weren't coming back. You said you were going away with *him* and not coming back."

Tears filled her faded eyes and began to trickle down over her temples and into her hair. Mara took a tissue from the bedside stand and dabbed at them gently.

"Gran, I didn't really mean it that way. People get upset and say things they don't mean. I'd never just walk out and leave you, like that, without making some arrangements for you. You know that, Gran. I was just so terribly angry."

Agnes squeezed her hand, rolling her head weakly on the pillow. "I'm sorry, Mara. I love you. You know that. I've never loved anyone as much as I love you. Not even Emily. But I'm just a burden to you. You'd be better off without me."

"No, I wouldn't. I love you, too, Gran."

"And you won't leave me all alone?"

"Of course not. We'll just concentrate on getting you all better, and I'll visit you every day after work, and when you're home, then we'll talk."

"I hate it here," Agnes said, glaring at the tubes and machines with a little of her old spirit.

"I know you do, Gran. But you have to stay in here for a little while."

"How long?"

"I don't know," Mara said patiently. "I have to talk to the doctor. He's on the ward just now, and he wants me to come into his office at four o'clock." She looked at her watch. "My goodness, that's just a few minutes. They'll be bringing your supper soon, Gran," she said brightly.

"Supper!" Agnes muttered bitterly. "I can imagine what *that'll* be like."

"Gran, you be nice. Everybody's trying hard to get you better, and the least you can do is cooperate."

"How did I get here?" Agnes asked suddenly.

"I told you, Gran. You came in an ambulance."

"I mean, who called the ambulance?" She looked at Mara hopefully. "Did you come home and find me?"

Mara looked at her grandmother unhappily, wondering how much to tell her. She decided, finally, that there was no point in evading the issue, because Agnes was going to find out, anyway.

"No, I didn't," she said. "Wayne and Delores stopped to give you a ride to church and found you, and they phoned a few people they thought might know where I was."

Agnes glared, speechless with indignation. "And so the whole neighborhood came over and stood around gaping at me," she said flatly.

"Gran…"

"And how *did* they find you?" Agnes asked. "Did the whole neighborhood know where *you* were, too?"

"No, they didn't. I happened to call just when all this was going on."

"I see." Agnes turned away and gazed out the window.

"Gran," Mara said, "I have to go see the doctor now, but I'll come back later."

"Tell him I want to go home," Agnes said without looking at her. "Tell him I hate it here and I want to go home."

"Yes, Gran. I'll tell him."

Mara lingered in the doorway, looking at her grandmother's sharp old profile, etched clearly against the drab hospital curtains. She waited a moment longer, but Agnes refused to look at her. Finally Mara left and started slowly down the gleaming corridor toward the doctor's office.

Dr. Holmes was youthful and boyish-looking with a round, sympathetic face behind thick-lensed glasses. On his desk was a framed photograph of a slender dark-haired woman holding a round, bald, solemn baby on her knee.

Mara smiled, thinking that if the baby were wearing horn-rimmed glasses and had a little more hair, it would look exactly like its father. With an effort she drew her attention back to what he was saying.

"It's not really serious," he said, tapping a pile of X rays with the end of a gold-plated pen, "except, of course, that her age must be considered."

"Yes, of course," Mara said.

"And she's...seventy-two, I believe you said?"

"Next birthday," Mara said. "In January."

"Hmm." He hesitated, pondering the file, and then looked directly at Mara. "You live with your grandmother, Miss Steen? May I call you Mara, by the way?"

"Of course you may. Yes, I live with her."

"Permanently?"

"Well...more or less. She raised me, you see, and then I moved away for a few years, but I had to move back after she broke her hip and needed my care."

"Yes, the hip injury is recorded in her file." He looked up thoughtfully. "I would assume that she suffers from a fairly serious degree of osteoporosis. Her bones seem to break quite easily."

Mara nodded.

"And she has no doctor of record. Is that correct?"

Mara nodded again. "She hates going to the doctor. We had a family doctor for years and years who looked after her when her hip was broken. But he died last year, and Gran refused to see another doctor. I tried to get her in for a checkup, but it was just impossible." She hesitated. "Gran can be...difficult sometimes."

"Yes, I would have guessed that." The doctor was silent, toying with his slender, expensive pen. "I spoke with her this morning after she was brought in. She was still in mild shock and had been sedated. I doubt that she remembers the conversation."

"I don't think so. She woke up just now when I was in her room and I had to explain to her where she was and how she got here."

"Yes, I see. How did she get here, Mara? What happened, exactly?"

Mara flushed and moved uneasily in her chair. She gave the doctor an unhappy, pleading look. "It's... not a very pleasant story, I'm afraid. I had a friend to dinner last night, and my grandmother was very rude to him. I was angry with her for her behavior, and when he left, I...I went with him and left her alone."

She looked up, her eyes wide with misery, and met Dr. Holmes's calm, impassive gaze.

"I know," she went on, "that it was a terribly callous and irresponsible thing to do."

"Callous? Irresponsible? To leave a healthy, fully functioning adult alone in a comfortable house that happens to be her own home? I hardly think so, Mara."

"But...she hates to be alone. She can't bear it. And I knew that."

"She's very dependent on you." It was a statement, not a question.

"Yes, she is. She was always such a strong woman, and I loved her so much. I relied on her for everything when I was growing up. But now it all seems different somehow." She looked up, trying to smile. "What you'd call 'role reversal,' I guess."

He smiled back. "So where does that leave you?"

"Pardon?"

"I mean, how much freedom do you have, Mara? To live your own life as an adult?"

"Very little, really. You see, Gran's my own responsibility. There's no way to avoid that."

"And you have no relatives who can help share the burden?"

"None at all. I was illegitimate and my mother was an only child and died when I was born. And my grandfather had died years before. There's always been just the two of us."

Dr. Holmes nodded thoughtfully, took the cap off his pen and began drawing aimless little circles on his desk blotter. "And she can't live alone?"

"No. She's terrified to be alone. I think it's gotten really bad since she broke her hip. Now she's obsessed with the idea that she might be hurt, all alone, and nobody would find her, so she'd just lie there and die."

Mara was silent a moment. "It just occurred to me," she said miserably, "that what's happened now is going to confirm her worst fears. It's actually happened again. Now she'll be more paranoid than ever."

"That's certainly likely. I'm not aware of your economic situation. Is there any possibility of some sort of paid companion?"

"She'd never even consider it. She hates strangers in the house. She's always so rude and abrasive when she meets new people, and she just won't give them any kind of a chance to get to know her. She's so stubborn."

"So I assume that she wouldn't adapt well to some sort of housing complex for independent seniors? Some place where she could have her own suite or room but live in a community atmosphere?"

Mara shook her head. "She's always said that

she'd rather kill herself. She wants to stay in her own house." She looked over at the doctor with sudden curiosity. "Why are you asking me all these questions, Dr. Holmes? Does this have anything to do with her present condition?"

The young doctor gave her a frank, boyish smile. "Not really. More with yours, I guess. You look as if you're under a considerable strain, Mara. The sole care of an elderly, dependent woman can be very taxing. I'm just exploring ways that the burden on you might be eased."

"Dr. Holmes, you don't know how many nights I've lain awake, going over and over these possibilities by the hour. There's just nothing that I can see as a solution."

"Except living with her and continuing to care for her yourself."

"Yes. That's all I can see."

"Hmm." Dr. Holmes pushed his heavy glasses back up on the bridge of his nose and consulted the file briefly. "All right," he said. "We'll be keeping that collarbone supported for a few days and giving her treatment for the pneumonia. It's really quite a mild case, and she has an excellent constitution." He gave Mara a keen glance, and she nodded slowly. "She could easily live another twenty years or so in quite good health, you know," he said gently.

Mara nodded again and looked down wordlessly at her hands, clenched tightly in her lap.

"Well," Mara said finally, getting to her feet, "I guess I'd better get back to her room. She's going to need help eating her supper, and I doubt that the nurses have time for that kind of individual care."

"Mara…"

"Yes?" She paused in the doorway.

"Mara, at the very outside, I can keep her in here for about ten days. Not much of a respite for you, but I'm afraid it's the best I can do."

Mara looked at him in surprise, and he met her eyes directly, his round, ingenuous face open and earnest.

"Just be sure," he said with a sudden smile, "that you and that friend of yours take full advantage of these ten days I'm giving you."

Mara flushed a delicate pink. "Thank you, Dr. Holmes," she murmured. "I'm sure we will."

All at once she smiled at him, a warm, grateful smile that brightened the room long after she was gone, and left him gazing fondly at the picture on his desk of the pretty young woman with the fat, solemn baby.

"So," Allan said, reaching down idly to caress Mara's cheek with his lean brown hand. "It's going to be Thursday, is it?"

"Thursday or Saturday," Mara said. "It depends on the outcome of the tests they're doing tomorrow. Dr. Holmes said that if he wasn't satisfied with the test results, he might keep her till Saturday and run another check on her."

"Wouldn't that be great? Then Mick could go back to Jimmy's for the weekend and we could have next Friday night, too."

"I know," Mara said, smiling at him. "Do you think I haven't already figured that out?"

He grinned. "I'll bet you have. When will you know?"

"Not till Thursday. Dr. Holmes said he'd call me at school in the morning if he's planning to release her on Thursday."

"Maybe," Allan suggested hopefully, "you could talk them into leaving the phone off the hook."

Mara laughed and shifted her weight to lean back against his legs, reaching up to grasp his hand and kiss the strong, callused palm.

They were in the living room of his little house in their favorite place near the wood stove. Allan sat in a leather armchair with a sheet of newspaper over his knees, whittling one of the tiny puppies he was making for Michael's birthday. Mara was curled up on the rug at his feet, sewing a patch on his jacket sleeve with neat, careful stitches.

"She's been in there over a week," Allan complained, "and all we've gotten out of it is one night."

"Two nights," Mara corrected him. "Unless, of course, you've changed your mind and decided I shouldn't stay tonight."

He laughed softly and reached down to tug at her long braid. "Are you kidding? Wait'll you hear the plans I've got for you tonight."

Mara smiled to herself and kept her head bent over her sewing.

"It's just that we should have had a lot more time together," he said. "Just one weekend, out of all those days, and now she's coming home and everything's going to be the same as it was before.''

''Allan, I just don't like the idea of staying here while Michael's at home. I couldn't be comfortable with it. I wish I had my sewing machine here,'' she added. ''This would be so much easier on a machine.''

He looked idly down at the work in her hands. ''How could you sew that sleeve on a machine? Wouldn't it just get all stitched together?''

''My machine has a free arm. It slips over like this—'' she demonstrated, sliding the sleeve over an imaginary sewing machine arm ''—and then you can just stitch the surface that's on top.''

''I'll be damned,'' he said, picturing that. ''What a neat idea. Do you sew a lot?''

She nodded, frowning in concentration as she threaded her needle. ''I make almost all my own clothes. I love sewing. Do you think they mind?'' she added.

''Does who mind what?'' he asked, baffled, as he often was by the quick, darting flights of her agile mind.

''Jimmy's parents. Do they mind having Michael there all weekend?''

''They love it. They've always wanted him to come over, but he used to be so shy that I could never talk him into going. He's come a long way since school started.''

Mara smiled up at him. ''I know,'' she said softly. ''It makes me so happy, Allan.''

He smiled back, looking down fondly at her gentle face. "So," he asked, "what happens now?"

"When?"

"When she comes home. Do I get to see you any more, or are we back to total secrecy?"

"I don't know," Mara said, looking troubled. "I've tried to talk to her about it, quite a few times, but she just refuses to discuss it. She just absolutely ignores anything I say about you."

"Well, she can't ignore me forever, sweetheart. I'm not giving up and I'm not going away. She's just going to have to accept that."

Mara was silent, pushing the needle through the heavy fabric with sharp, jabbing movements.

"I want you, Mara," he went on. "All the time. You know that."

"Allan…"

"I know. You always say we can't talk about it, because we don't know about the future. But when *can* we talk about it, Mara? I want you here. I want you to live with me and let me look after you. I want to have you in my bed every night, not just when you can sneak away. When can we talk about *that*, Mara?"

She trembled at the passionate conviction in his voice. "Allan, I know. I understand how frustrating this is for you. But there are a lot of things that—"

"How about a little trailer?" he asked suddenly. "I know the house is too small, and I can't afford a major renovation right now. But what if I moved a little trailer out here for her to live in, hooked it up to my well and septic system…?"

Mara shook her head wearily. "You're just like Dr. Holmes. Always coming up with these great ideas, except that none of them will work. Not for Gran. They might work for other people, but she's so…" Mara paused, searching for words. "Allan, she'd *hate* living out here. She doesn't like the country and she wouldn't have cable TV or her friends down at the corner store and," Mara added bitterly, "Gran's not the type to suffer in silence. If she's miserable, she wants everybody around her to know all about it."

"Yeah. I know." He stared at the fire in moody silence for a moment, then levered his long body out of the chair and wandered restlessly across the room to look out the window.

The wind moaned and shrieked around the sturdy little frame house, whipping dense clouds of snow that piled in drifts along the fence lines and against the buildings. The sky was dark, although it was early in the afternoon, and icy gusts of snow hissed against the windowpane, driven by the howling prairie blizzard.

Mara got up and went to stand beside him, leaning quietly against him in the circle of his strong arm. He rested his chin on top of her head, and they looked together at the storm that raged beyond the window.

Mara shivered, thinking that the storm was like some dreadful, primeval creature, stalking them, probing all the cracks and openings of their little shelter to find an entry. Pulling her into his arms, Allan kissed her eyelids and the tip of her nose and gave her a long, lingering kiss on the lips that left her, as always, weak and shaky with longing. Then he set her gently aside, went to the closet and took out his heavy coat and fleece-lined boots.

Mara leaned back against the window ledge and stared at him, aghast. "Allan! You're not going *out* in that storm?"

"I have to, sweetheart. The cows will all be drifting in from the west field and packing along the fence line. I have to open the gate so they can get into the corral and find some shelter."

"But…but you might get lost out there. You can hardly see your hand in front of your face, Allan."

He smiled. "I've lived on this farm for a year or two, darling. I think I know my way around even in a storm. I'll be back right away."

The door whipped and jerked in his hand like a living thing, and it took all his strength to slam it shut. Mara stood shivering, her arms wrapped around herself, although it was warm in the little house. She peered out through the frosted pane of the living room window, long after his big body was swallowed up in the swirling whiteness.

She wandered back to pick up her mending and finished patching Allan's jacket sleeve. Neatly she put away the sewing basket and supplies and then gathered the jacket into her arms, hugging it and burying her face for a long time in the heavy fabric.

Then she went out into the kitchen to make herself a cup of coffee and stood at the counter, sipping it slowly, looking out the window at the storm that roared all around the house. She felt a deep, hopeless sadness and a sudden terrible loneliness. She peered desperately into the blank, swirling whiteness, longing for Allan to come back.

Allan plodded into the billowing snowstorm, keeping the wind at his back, placing one foot carefully in front of the other. He found it a weird sensation, moving through that world of whiteness. It was white overhead, beneath his feet, all around him. After a while he even lost track of where the ground was and wasn't sure where to place his feet. He was becoming disoriented, beginning to lose his balance, when he stumbled into something waist-high, firm but yielding, and recognized it as a cow's flank.

He pushed and kicked his way through the mass of cattle packed against the fence, taking some comfort in their dense warmth. When he reached the fence, he climbed over it and felt along the inside until he found the gate. He slid the latch open and strained and pushed the gate against the heavy drifted snow, wide enough for the cows to move haltingly inside, following one another blindly, nose to tail.

*I'd better check and make sure the chop house door is closed tight,* he thought. *Otherwise, sure as hell, as soon as the storm dies down, they'll all crowd in there and eat grain until they bloat....*

He continued down the fence line to the chop house and fumbled along the side to the door, which was securely latched. Weary of the constant buffeting of the wind, and the brutal cold, he opened the door and let himself inside for a rest. He switched on the light, upended a five-gallon pail and sat on it, looking about him. The small building was unheated, but the absence of wind and snow made it seem almost cozy.

He could smell the rich, musky scent of burlap and chopped grain and hear mice scurrying around, doing whatever mice did to survive in the bitter cold. Last summer's cobwebs hung from the icy rafters like dirty, tattered lace. Allan wondered briefly what spiders did in the winter, and then abandoned the thought.

He hunched over on the pail, holding his frozen hands between his knees to warm them, and gave himself up to the bitter frustration that gnawed at him. Allan was a powerful, capable man, accustomed to planning a course of action and seeing it through. He was single-minded and goal-oriented, and his goal just now was extremely simple.

He wanted Mara.

He pictured her in his mind, concentrating with loving detail on her sweet freckled nose, her wide gray eyes, the shy, teasing way she had of looking up at him.

Smiling in the dim half-light, he warmed himself with more intimate memories. He had, he now knew, been correct in his first instincts about her. She was quiet and reserved in public, but in bed she was an absolute delight. Playful, loving, impulsive, inventive—she was everything a man could ever fantasize. Just thinking about it caused the familiar stirring in his groin and made him shift awkwardly on his improvised chair, uncomfortable with longing.

But it was more than just sex. Far more.

This woman, he knew, wasn't just a partner for

lovemaking. She was made to be a man's partner in everything—in business, in travel, in work and play. She was lover, mistress, companion, friend—everything he had ever wanted, more than he had dreamed of finding.

But he couldn't have her.

Grimly he pictured the relentless old lady who stood between them, keeping him from the woman he wanted and needed. He recalled Agnes's spare, erect figure, her dignity, her forced gaiety and mechanical politeness. And then, frowning again with bitter anger, he remembered her final rudeness, her terrible insinuations.

*How did she die, Allan?*

Allan clenched his big fist and pounded it on his knee with helpless misery. For a long time he had suffered deep, painful guilt over his wife's death, believing that with more care, he could have protected her and kept her safe. And just as he was beginning to learn to deal with her death better, to accept it as a sad and terrible accident, but not his fault, the old woman's words had brought back all the grim, bitter memories.

Mara had helped him. Her generous love and acceptance had restored his faith in himself and in life and convinced him that happiness was possible, after all. If he had any residual guilt regarding his late wife, it was only because he knew that he hadn't loved her enough, that his love for her had been nothing like the overpowering, passionate adoration that he now felt for Mara.

But that wasn't his fault, either. A man couldn't

make himself love someone. It just happened or it didn't. And for Allan there was nobody in the world but Mara.

Having found her at last, it drove him wild with frustration to know he couldn't have her. He was beaten, thwarted, defeated by a tiny little gray-haired woman just half his size. How could a man fight an enemy like that?

And the most infuriating thing, he realized, was that the very qualities in Mara that made him love her were the qualities that made their situation impossible. Her loyalty, her loving faithfulness and dedication to duty, her sense of responsibility—all those things were going to hold her tied to the old lady forever.

*God,* he thought wearily. *I can't stand it any longer.*

Shaking himself in helpless frustration, he got to his feet and gave the pail an angry kick, sending it clattering against the wall. He opened the door and latched it carefully behind him, hunching his shoulders and grimacing as he plunged back into the storm.

He felt his way along the fence to the open gate and then hesitated. The blizzard, by now, was howling with such force that he quite literally couldn't see his hand in front of his face. He knew that if he continued along the fence to his right, he would arrive at the Quonset, and then at the workshop, where there was a kerosene heater that he could light to warm the building and protect him from the cold. The house, on the other hand, sat alone on the prairie, somewhere off to the east, lost in the billowing gusts of snow, with only its own little picket fence around it to serve as a rough guide.

Allan pondered. If he went on up to the workshop, he knew he'd be safe in there, but who knew when the wind would ever die down enough for him to get back to the house. Maybe not till morning, and Mara was all alone in there. If he took too long getting back, she might get worried and decide to come out looking for him. And she didn't know her way around the farm. She could wander out onto the prairie and never find her way back.

Just the thought of it was enough to suck the breath from his body and make his knees go weak with terror. He touched the corral fence once more, as if for a final benediction and launched out into the shrieking wind.

Mara paced restlessly through the little house, peering out the frosted windowpanes, trying to find a place where she could get a glimpse of the world outside. But there was nothing anywhere but furious, whirling snow.

*He's been gone so long,* she thought. *Surely it shouldn't take this long to open a gate.*

She shivered, feeling as if she would never be warm again, and huddled in her sweater, gazing out the living room window with a brooding expression.

*Maybe I should go out and look for him. Maybe he's fallen or hurt himself somehow, and he'll just freeze to death out there.*

Galvanized by sudden terror, she ran to the door and began to tug on her boots and parka. Then she paused, realizing that there was no sense to what she was doing.

If he was lost out there, Mara could never find him. And if he couldn't find his way back, how could she?

With the sudden deep, painful illumination that accompanies times of crisis, Mara realized how much she loved this man. Her feeling for him was something that came from the very core of her—a deep, wrenching, aching need that nobody else could ever satisfy.

Moving slowly, her face drained of color, tense with fear, she went through the house, switching on all the lights in every room.

*Please, Allan,* she prayed silently. *Please see the lights and find your way back. Please, darling, please come back.*

Taking those first steps into the icy, swirling world of whiteness was the same sensation as plunging off a high diving board. He had the feeling that he was abandoning his body to the laws of physics and the forces of nature—whatever happened next was beyond his control.

It was a feeling Allan hated.

He struggled on into the blinding snow. Ice caked on his eyebrows and eyelashes, and the scarf that covered his mouth froze and cracked with every breath. When he lowered it, the wind caught his breath and flung it back over his shoulder, leaving him feeling hollow and limp. The cold was brutal. He could feel his whole body turning to ice.

*It's too long,* he realized in sudden horror. *I've been*

*walking too long. Somehow I must have missed the house, gone past it already. But what direction is it? Jeez, I'm out on the open prairie and I don't even know what direction I'm going. Mara...Mara, darling...*

By this time he was convinced that she would be out in the blizzard somewhere, looking for him. She was always so impetuous.

But she'd never find him. She'd wander around until it was too late. And there was nothing Allan could do to help her.

"Mara!" he shouted aloud. "Mara! Where are you?"

But the wind caught his voice and threw it away as if he had never spoken.

Doggedly he plodded on, trying to keep himself moving in a straight line by placing the heel of one boot squarely against the toe of the other with each step. But the snow was drifted to his waist in places, and he stumbled and floundered.

He had a sudden impression of bulk nearby, off to his right, like a huge ship passing a small one in heavy fog. Something glimmered faintly through the blowing snow. He struggled toward it, blinking and squinting into the wind. More lights gleamed, and tears filled his stinging eyes as he realized that she had been wise enough to pull back the curtains and switch on every light in the house to guide him back home through the storm.

He found the door, wrenched it open and stumbled into her arms.

\* \* \*

Mara murmured aloud in relief and joy as she tugged off his parka, knelt to unlace his boots, threw aside the ice-encrusted scarf, chafed his hands between her own.

"Come on, come inside by the stove. Allan, you might not have found your way back. You could have died out there! Oh, Allan…"

Tears ran down her cheeks. He held her, his hands stiff and clumsy with cold, and tried to draw warmth from her body.

"Come on, Allan, you're almost frozen. You have to get warm." She dragged him down the hallway to the bedroom. His legs were as heavy and unyielding as fence posts, and his feet tingled with the prickling agony of slowly returning circulation.

Awkward with haste, Mara peeled off his clothes and pushed him into bed. Then she undressed with quick, jerky movements, tossing her clothes onto the floor with his in a disorderly heap. She climbed into bed on top of him, trying to warm all of him with her slender naked body. She rubbed against him, ran her bare feet up and down his legs and held his cheeks between her palms, kissing him and holding her face against his.

Allan hugged her tightly, closing his eyes in bliss as heat began to flood his icy body. With the warmth came a surge of strength and power and a fresh wave of the stormy frustration that had been tormenting him for weeks. It gathered, intensified and focused. He rolled her over silently and made love to her with a violent urgency that brought them both to a wrenching, shuddering climax. Afterward, still silent, he cradled her in his arms.

"Mara," he whispered, "I never knew till I was out there just now how much I love you. I'd die without you, darling."

"I know," she said quietly. "I know, Allan. When I thought I'd lose you, I felt the same way. I could never love anyone the way I love you."

She reached out to switch off the lamp and lay in the circle of his big, hard-muscled arms. She looked with love and sorrow at his handsome, clean-cut profile, dimly illuminated in the eerie half-light created by the storm, and leaned over to kiss him gently.

He stirred, gathering her closer. She rested her face against his broad chest and drew the covers up around his shoulders.

The wind howled and moaned, rocking the little house like a ship on a storm-tossed sea. The noise softened, dimmed, grew lulling and soothing until Mara's thoughts were rambling and vacant. Then she nestled in the delicious warmth of Allan's strong arms and finally drifted off to sleep.

# 12

"And then," Michael said, "Miss Steen said that Jason was being bad, and she—"

"Don't hold your fork that way, Mick," Allan interrupted, looking across the supper table at his small son. "Remember the way I showed you?"

Michael nodded and frowned with concentration, trying to remember how to hold his fork.

"What was Jason doing that was bad?" Allan asked.

"He was burping. Real loud."

"On purpose?"

"Yeah," Michael said. "He can do it real good. Like this," he added, giving a creditable imitation of Jason's accomplishment.

"All right, all right," Allan said hastily. "So what did Miss Steen do to him?"

"She made him sit in the corner behind the screen, and she said he couldn't come out until we finished finger painting."

Michael herded all his peas into a little pile and covered them quickly with a lettuce leaf, glancing up cautiously to see if his father had detected this criminal activity.

But Allan was gazing at the darkened window with

a fond, wistful expression on his face. "She made him sit in the corner, did she?" he asked finally, turning to smile at his son. "And what did Jason think about that?"

"He was real mad. But then Miss Steen had to go down to the office to answer the phone, and Jason came out from behind the screen when he wasn't supposed to, and Marcy…"

"She had to go to the office?" Allan interrupted again. "For a phone call?"

"Yeah. And when she came back, Marcy tattled and said that Jason…"

Allan sat silently, barely listening as Michael chattered on.

The doctor said he'd call her at work if he was going to release her grandmother today. Damn!

Not until now did he actually realize how desperately he had been hoping for one more night with her, how much he had been looking forward to tomorrow.…

"Mick, how did Miss Steen look after she came back from the office?"

Michael pondered. "She looked kind of sad. And when Marcy told her about Jason, she just said, 'That's all right.'"

*Poor Mara,* Allan thought. *I'm sitting and feeling sorry for myself, but she's the one who has to deal with it.*

"Why, Dad?" Michael asked, looking up at his father's tense, preoccupied face. "Is something wrong?"

"No, Mick, nothing's wrong," Allan said automatically. "Eat your vegetables," he added, "*including* the peas you hid under that lettuce leaf."

Michael sighed and returned to his meal.

Allan cleaned the kitchen, did the dishes and tucked Michael into bed, singing him a song and reading from his favorite tattered storybook. Finally he went back into the silent kitchen and dialed Mara's number.

She answered the phone on the third ring, a little breathlessly. "Hello?" she said.

"Hi, sweetheart. How's my girl?"

"Allan. I wasn't expecting to hear from you tonight." He heard the cautious, reserved note in her voice and contrasted it with the free and joyous spontaneity of their phone conversation the night before.

*Oh, Mara,* he thought, his heart aching for her. *This is going to be so hard for you, and there's no way for me to make it any easier.*

"Is she home?" he asked.

"Yes. We just finished eating, and I'm getting her settled in the living room. How are you?"

"Fine. I sold ten steers today at the auction yard. Got a real good price. How'd you like a trip to Hawaii during the Christmas holidays?"

"You're joking."

"Well...maybe a little. But I'd love to see you in a grass skirt. How is she, Mara?"

"Oh, fine. A little weak, you know, and awfully glad to be home."

"Have you talked to her yet?"

"About what?"

"About anything. About me. Come on, Mara, you promised."

"I know, Allan, but I don't want to upset her when she's just gotten home, and I—"

"Sweetheart, I'm not asking you to give her an ultimatum or have any big scene. I'm just asking you to let her know that I'm going to be part of your life, and it would be so much more pleasant if she'll just accept that. We agreed that was the best approach for now, didn't we?"

"Yes, we did, Allan. You're right. I'll talk to her."

"Tonight?"

"Yes. Tonight."

"Good. And get ready for that trip. Buy a bikini."

"Allan…"

"Good night, darling. I love you."

"Me, too. Good night, Allan."

He heard the click as she hung the phone up and stood quietly for a moment with the receiver in his hand, staring at the opposite wall, his finely molded features drawn and tense with concern.

"Who was that?" Agnes asked from her nest of pillows.

"It was…" Mara hesitated, battling her reluctance, and then looked directly at her grandmother. "It was Allan."

"Oh," Agnes said flatly. Her face set into familiar, rigid lines. "What did *he* want?"

"Just to know if you were home and how you're feeling."

"I'll bet," Agnes said bitterly. "I can just imagine how concerned *he* is with my welfare."

"Gran," Mara pleaded, "he's really nice. He's the nicest man I've ever met, and I really care for him. He matters a lot to me, Gran. I wish you could just—"

"I want to go to bed," Agnes said petulantly. "I'm worn right out. Help me up, would you?"

"Gran, can't we talk about this? Please?"

"I'm tired and I want to go to bed, and the last thing I want to talk about is that...that..." Agnes's voice faltered as she searched for a sufficiently vile epithet to describe Allan Williamson.

"Gran, he's such a good man. If you'd just—"

"I've had enough of this. I'm going to my room, whether you'll help me or not." Agnes heaved against the sofa and gave a sharp yelp of pain as she jarred her injured shoulder.

Mara uttered a little cry of alarm and rushed to help her grandmother to her feet, steadying Agnes and supporting her as she walked haltingly through the house to her room.

"My own bed is going to feel so good," Agnes said with satisfaction. "Mara, could you just turn on the electric blanket for me, please? I get so dizzy if I try to bend over."

"Of course, Gran." Mara moved softly about the room, helping Agnes to get undressed and ready for bed. They were gentle and polite with each other, and Agnes clung to Mara for a moment after she was finally settled in bed, whispering her gratitude and her joy at being home.

"I know, Gran. I know. Sleep now."

*Well,* Mara thought, *we're not going to be doing any more talking about Allan tonight.*

With the strange combination of love and frustration that she so often felt when she was with Agnes, she took a last look at the old lady's face against the pillows, sighed and turned out the light.

Mara stared down at the fat little shepherd who was planted stubbornly in front of her, staff in hand, robe askew, looking up at her with relentless determination.

"Your mother said *what,* Jason?"

"She said I was supposed to be one of the Wise Men. She doesn't want me to be a shepherd."

"But…" Mara still stared at him, completely baffled, trying to absorb this new development. Aware of the disruption in their pageant rehearsal, a number of the other children, all dressed in various costumes, crowded around to watch.

"A Wise Man," Jason repeated firmly.

"But," Mara repeated, completely at a loss, "but why should it matter to your mother whether you're a shepherd or a Wise Man?"

"My mother says it's better to be one of the Wise Men. She says shepherds wear ugly costumes, and if I'm a Wise Man, I can wear her velvet dressing gown and her gold belt, and my Grandma Rossiter is coming to watch me, and she'll be taking pictures of me, so my mother wants me to be one of the Wise Men."

A light slowly dawned. Mara remembered Jason's

mother, a large glossy, aggressive woman, not accustomed to having her wishes ignored.

"I see," she began, her voice quiet. "And which of the Wise Men does your mother think you should be, Jason?"

"The one who carries the gold box," Jason replied promptly.

The children whispered and murmured, and Mara looked quickly over at Jamie, the quiet little boy who was Michael's friend. Since Michael's transformation, Jamie was now the shyest, most withdrawn child in the room, and Mara had deliberately given him a coveted role in the pageant. Jamie, to the envy of the others, was the Wise Man who carried the box of gold. The box was actually just an old toffee tin of bright stamped metal, but it fascinated the children, and they all considered Jamie incredibly lucky to be the one carrying it. And Jamie himself, as he led the slow procession toward the manger, wearing his tinfoil crown and carrying his treasure box, seemed to radiate a new pride and confidence.

But now, as he heard plump, confident Jason calmly announcing his intention of taking away both the role and the gold box, Jamie's face crumpled in sorrow. A tear coursed slowly down his cheek, and he wiped it on the sleeve of his father's shabby black brocade robe, which trailed on the floor behind him.

"Jason," Mara said, "we already have someone for that part. Jamie's the one who carries the gold box."

"I know," Jason said, unimpressed. "But his robe is ugly, see? And mine will be really nice. My mother says she'll hem it and everything, so I'll look like a real Wise Man. Jamie can be a shepherd.''

Evidently considering his cause already lost, Jamie was now sobbing openly, though quietly. With great care, he placed the gold box on the piano bench and began, sadly, to remove his oversize robe.

"Wait, Jamie," Mara said. She turned back to Jason, who returned her gaze implacably and fired his final shot.

"My mother said that if I don't get to carry the box, she's going to come down and see you."

"She said that, did she?" Mara kept her face expressionless. "Well, Jason, I think that's a really good idea. You tell your mother to come down and see me, all right? Jamie, put your costume back on."

"But I want to carry the box *today*!" Jason wailed. "My mother said I can! She said you have to let me carry the box!"

"Jason," Mara began, "you just can't—"

Jeff and Lisa, busy up in the wings transforming seven small children into candy canes, looked at each other in alarm. Jeff leaped off the stage and approached the small tableau with a lithe, rapid step, smoothly interrupting Mara in midsentence.

"Now," he said calmly, "what's all this? What's going on here?"

Children clustered around, jostling one another, shouting all the details to him.

"Jason gets to carry the box!"

"His mom said!"

"Jamie hasta be a shepherd and he's crying."

Mara stood looking on, wondering how Jeff

planned to deal with this. The young man shot her a cheerful grin over the children's heads and knelt in front of Jason. "What are you now, Jason?" he asked.

"I'm just a dumb ol' shepherd."

"And what does your mother want you to be?"

"She wants me to carry the box."

Jeff nodded thoughtfully. "I see. Well, we'll have to change you two around, then, I guess, but it doesn't really seem fair to me."

Jason glowed with triumph and moved toward the gold box on the piano bench.

"I mean," Jeff added casually, "it doesn't seem fair to me that Jamie should get to be a shepherd when Miss Steen picked you first."

Jason paused, and looked up at him suspiciously. "Why? What's so great about being a shepherd?"

Jeff stared at the fat little boy, his boyish, handsome face a mask of comical disbelief. "What's so great about being a *shepherd*? Don't you *know*? Haven't you heard the Christmas story?"

"Yeah," Jason said with some belligerence. "Sure I have."

"Well, you must have forgotten, then. The shepherds were really special." Still kneeling in front of the small boy, Jeff lowered his voice to a whisper. "The shepherds got to see the *angels*, Jason. They were the luckiest ones of all."

Jason hesitated, clutching his staff. "Didn't the Wise Men see the angels?"

Jeff shook his head emphatically. "Never. All they saw was the star." He lowered his voice even more.

"The shepherds even heard the angels *talking*. And they were outside sitting around their *campfire*, and they saw the bright lights from heaven and everything."

"Yeah? They had a *campfire*?" He was listening, wide-eyed and openmouthed, mesmerized by Jeff's hypnotic dark eyes and his low, persuasive voice. With sudden decision he turned back to the group of children. "You can keep your dumb ol' box," he said loftily to Jamie. "*I* get to be a *shepherd*."

Jeff approached Mara, who'd watched his performance with deep interest. Lisa stood nearby, holding an armful of pine boughs.

"See how it's done, my girl?" he said to Mara. "No fighting. Just a little finesse, that's all it takes."

Mara smiled ruefully. "I know. You're right, Jeff. But I still would have liked to have a little chat with his mother."

"I don't see why. She sounds to me like a woman to avoid at all costs. Coming up to finish the candy canes, Lisa?" he added, taking the pine boughs from her and smiling down at her.

"In a minute," Lisa said, turning away from him without returning his smile. "I'd like to ask Miss Steen something."

"Okay," he said, obviously deflated by her reaction. He strode away and vaulted lightly onto the stage while the two women stood watching him.

"Lisa," Mara said gently, "it wouldn't hurt you to…to be a little nice to him. Just sometimes. He's trying so hard."

"He just wants to be a big brother," Lisa said bitterly. "I don't want a big brother."

"How can you be so sure of what he wants?"

"Miss Steen, you know who he is. He could date anybody in this city. He knows all those girls...the ones who drive their own sports cars and go to Hawaii during Christmas break to get a tan. Do you really think he's actually interested in a girl who's going to be a single mother? A girl who's going to earn her living waiting on tables?"

"How will you ever now if you won't give him a chance?"

Lisa looked at Mara, her face imploring. "This is hard enough. All of it," she whispered. "I don't need *that* kind of pain, besides everything else."

Mara studied the girl's face, amazed, as she always was, by Lisa's beauty. Now in her fourth month of pregnancy, Lisa seemed to glow with an inner light that made her hair and face and eyes shine and gave her pearly complexion a pure, translucent radiance. To the observant eye, her figure was beginning to round slightly, but was easily disguised by the sloppy, baggy clothes that all the high school girls wore. Her face, Mara had noticed, was frequently strained and tense, but she remained as pleasant, soft-spoken and helpful as she had always been.

"You said just now that you wanted to talk with me about something. What was it, Lisa?"

"I was just wondering... I mean, I was going to ask you..." She paused, flushing painfully.

"What is it, Lisa?" Mara repeated. "What did you want?"

"Well—" the girl took a deep breath "—I'm almost four months along now and I'm starting to show a little. I'm going to have to tell my father soon. And you said, a long time ago…you said that when I—" She broke off and gave Mara a pleading glance.

Mara's heart sank.

"It's all right," Lisa said hastily, catching Mara's expression. "You don't have to. Honest, Miss Steen. I can do it. I'll tell him myself. That's okay."

"Of course I'll come with you, Lisa," Mara said, ashamed of her own cowardice. "I did promise you and I meant it. It'll help a lot for you to have another adult, especially a woman, there with you when you tell him. You just say when you want to do it."

"Really, Miss Steen?" Lisa's face brightened with gratitude. "That'd just be so—" Her voice broke.

"Of course," Mara said, patting the girl's shoulder. "When, Lisa?"

"I don't know. As soon as we can, I guess. I want to do it now while I'm still feeling brave. How about tonight? After school? I can come down and help you with the afternoon kids after my math class, and then we could—"

"And then I'll give you a ride home and we'll tell him." Mara paused. "It's Friday, Lisa. Will he be at home?"

Lisa nodded. "He hurt his back last week. He's been home from work all week."

"Lisa!" Jeff shouted from somewhere behind the curtains. "I'm drowning in candy canes up here! How do you attach the holly at the bottom?"

Lisa smiled, looking relieved and almost happy. "I'm coming, Jeff," she called.

Mara watched her climb the stairs and disappear behind the curtains. She frowned anxiously, thinking of the afternoon ahead with deep reluctance.

The two of them sat in the front seat of Mara's little car, looking out at the modest bungalow where Lisa lived with her father.

"He's a mechanic," Lisa explained. "He's worked for over thirty years at Simpson's Garage downtown, and he's going to retire in just a few more years."

Mara stared at the blank, unrevealing facade of the house.

"What's he like, Lisa?"

The girl frowned, pondering the question, and Mara felt a twinge of sympathy and recognition.

*I always feel like that,* she thought, *when anybody asks me what Gran is like.* It was so hard to describe Gran without making her sound awful, and yet she wasn't awful, really. Lots of times she was even lovable. She was just...Gran.

"Well," Lisa said slowly, "I guess you could call him...hard. Stern, maybe, is a better word. And uncompromising. Not loving at all, but not cruel, either. He never backs down on an issue, and I can't coax and tease and get him to give in, like other girls can with their fathers."

"You don't have him wrapped around your little finger, you mean?"

Lisa smiled grimly. "I sure don't. When he says something, he means it. Period. End of argument. But he's fair and he always warns you of the consequences in advance. He's not mean or anything. Just firm.''

"Well," Mara said with relief, "that doesn't sound too bad. Let's go talk to him."

"Okay." Lisa clenched her hands tightly into fists and then relaxed them, flexing her fingers and turning to give Mara a tight, nervous little smile. "Well, here we go," she said. She was pale and trembling but resolute.

"Here we go," Mara agreed, getting out of the car and walking beside Lisa up to the front door.

Lisa let herself in with a key and entered a small living room decorated in a sparse, conventional manner with department store furniture. A man sat in one corner in a shabby recliner chair, watching television. At their approach he looked up, startled, and then watched in silence as Lisa crossed the room and turned off the television.

"Dad," she said, "this is Miss Steen, one of my teachers at school."

"Hello, Mr. Stanley," Mara said, smiling at him.

He smiled back courteously and extended his hand. "Pleased to meet you, Miss Steen. I'd get up, but I'm afraid it still involves quite a bit of pain. Have a seat."

"Don't worry about getting up," Mara said warmly, shaking his outstretched hand and sitting down on the sofa near his chair. It was easy, she thought, to see where Lisa got her pure, classical beauty. Malcolm Stanley must have been incredibly handsome at one time, a blond god of a man with fine, regular features and a nobly shaped head and brow. He was graying, now, and his face was set in grim, humorless lines, but when he smiled there was still a lingering trace of the old, heart-stopping good looks he must have had when young.

"Do teachers frequently make house calls, Miss Steen?" he asked Mara, "or is this a rare honor?"

"This is a rare honor," Mara assured him solemnly.

Lisa fussed over her father, putting an extra pillow behind his back, bringing his pipe, offering to make a pot of tea. Finally he waved her away impatiently and turned to look at Mara again.

"A rare honor, is it? And to what, exactly, do I owe this rare honor, Miss Steen?"

Mara met his glance and felt a sudden overwhelming sympathy for Lisa. He did, indeed, look like a stern, uncompromising man—a man who didn't allow weakness in himself or others and who wouldn't easily tolerate failure or wrongdoing.

"I think, Mr. Stanley," Mara said quietly, "that Lisa has something to tell you."

He swung his cold blue gaze to his daughter, who sat nervously on the edge of her chair.

"Does she now? And what could she have to tell me that's serious enough to require the use of reinforcements?" He cocked a sardonic eyebrow. "Eh, Lisa?"

Lisa was silent, trembling in her chair, her face pale with fear and unhappiness.

Malcolm Stanley looked back at Mara, his eyes glinting with grim humor. "Well, Miss Steen? Is someone going to explain this mystery, or am I supposed to play guessing games?''

Mara looked up at him and drew a deep breath. ''Mr. Stanley,'' she said, ''Lisa is pregnant. That's what she wants to tell you.''

A shadow passed over his handsome, lined face. The jaw muscles tensed and knotted and the blue eyes hardened. Apart from this, he displayed no outward signs of emotion. ''I don't believe you,'' he said flatly.

''Well, it's true. Lisa is four months pregnant, and I've come with her, as a friend and a teacher, to tell you this so that we can all discuss the situation and make some plans for her future.''

Malcolm seemed not to have heard Mara's words. He looked at Lisa, who sat miserably in her chair. ''Lisa?'' he asked sharply. ''Is this true?''

Lisa nodded.

''Speak up, girl!''

She looked up, her blue eyes filling with tears. ''Yes, Dad,'' she whispered. ''It's true.''

He stared straight ahead, ignoring both women, gazing unseeingly at the opposite wall. ''Who's the father?'' he asked finally.

''That doesn't matter,'' Lisa said in a low, barely audible voice. ''It's a boy I don't even see anymore and don't want to have anything more to do with.''

He didn't answer and continued to stare off into space with a brooding expression.

''Mr. Stanley…''

At Mara's tentative words he whipped around and confronted her, his face dark with rage. ''Discuss the future, did I hear you say, Miss Steen? Make some plans?"

Mara nodded unhappily.

"And what future does she have now? Eh, Miss Steen? Her future was bright enough before, wasn't it? Top of her class, city prize for languages, all kinds of college scholarships just waiting for her...but what future does she have now? Answer me that, Miss Steen."

"There's no reason she can't—"

Ignoring Mara, he turned to his daughter again. "Four months, Lisa? Is that what you said?"

Lisa nodded, swallowed hard and then murmured, "Yes, Dad. Four months. I'm due in May."

"You're due in May." His voice was flat and heavy with sarcasm. "Due in May," he repeated.

He was silent for a moment, thinking, and then he addressed himself to Lisa once more. "I know you, girl. I know how stubborn and strong-willed you are. If you've had four months to think about this, you've come to some conclusions. I want to know what they are."

Lisa looked up at him, her lovely face pale and agonized. "Dad, please..."

"Tell me, Lisa," he said with implacable calm. "Just tell me what your plans are, please."

Lisa was silent, twisting her hands together between her knees.

Her father watched her coldly. "Both you and your spokesperson here appear to have lost the power of intelligent speech," he observed. "Let me help you.

There are, after all, a limited number of options. Do you plan to have an abortion?"

Lisa shook her head, and her shining golden hair flew and settled softly around her shoulders.

"I see. You must intend, then, to give the child up for adoption?"

"No," she said.

"Good God," he breathed. "You're planning to *keep* it. You stupid girl. You're going to ruin your entire life over a moment's foolishness with a boy who means nothing to you."

"Dad, please listen to…"

"There's nothing to listen to. Why should I listen to you? I would request, please, that you listen to *me*, Lisa. Listen very carefully, because I won't repeat myself. Look at me, please."

Lisa looked up and met his steely glare with a brave, unflinching gaze.

"Lisa, you know that I always mean what I say?"

She nodded, still looking at him steadily.

"And you're aware that what I say now is and will remain my final word on the subject?"

"Yes. I am."

"Good. Then listen carefully. I will support you in the decision to have an abortion and the topic will never be mentioned between us again. If you choose to have the child and give it up for adoption, you may live here while you do so and carry on with your educational plans afterward with my help and support."

He paused, his face cold and austere, while the other two watched him in silence. "If," he continued, "you decide to have the child and keep it, then you will leave my house. I will disown you and disclaim you. I will have no wish ever to see you or the child, and no financial obligation to either of you. The choice is yours."

When he finished speaking, the three of them sat for several endless moments in a silence so profound that the ticking of the clock on the mantel was clearly audible, almost unbearably loud.

Finally Lisa got to her feet and moved quietly toward the door.

"Lisa," Mara whispered. "Where are you going?"

Lisa looked back over her shoulder, her face calm and composed. "To pack my things," she said.

"Wait a moment, Lisa," Malcolm Stanley said. He turned to Mara. "When does this semester end, Miss Steen?"

"The first week in January. Then there's exams and then the semester break."

"I see. Thank you." He turned back to Lisa. "You may live here until the end of this semester when your exams have been written. By the semester break, unless you've changed your decision, I will expect you to leave the house. In the meantime, I will ask you not to speak to me at all—about anything. I prefer to forget the fact that I have produced a daughter like you."

"Mr. Stanley," Mara began indignantly, "that's just so—"

"Don't, Miss Steen," Lisa interrupted. "Thank you for trying, but there's no point. He means what he says. And the choice is mine, after all."

''But,'' Mara began helplessly, ''it's all so…'' She paused and gazed earnestly at the grim, older man. ''Look at her,'' Mara pleaded. ''She's just eighteen years old, and she'll have herself *and* a baby to look after, and no way to support herself. How can you possibly…?''

''You heard her, Miss Steen. The choice is hers. We all have to live with our choices, don't we? And Lisa is no exception. She, too, will live with her choice.''

His voice was calm and unemotional. Looking at his hard, implacable face, Mara felt sad and chilled, and understood at last what Lisa had tried to tell her. There was no softness here, no possibility of changing or relenting. If Lisa wanted to keep her baby, then she would be on her own by mid-January, and that, quite simply was the way it would be.

Mara gathered her handbag and gloves and got slowly to her feet, giving a curt nod to Malcolm Stanley and walking with Lisa to the door.

''Thanks so much, Miss Steen,'' Lisa murmured in the front hall. ''It really helped a lot having you here.''

''I didn't do anything, Lisa. Not a thing.''

''Nobody can *do* anything. But you gave me the courage to tell him, and now that it's over with I feel so much better.''

She did, in fact, look much more relaxed. The strained, tense look was gone from her eyes, and her young face was smooth and calm again.

Mara hesitated. ''Lisa…how are you ever going to manage?''

"I'll be fine." Lisa smiled reassuringly. "You'll see. Something will work out. I'll get a job somewhere and I'll be fine."

*I doubt it,* Mara thought. *I really doubt it.*

But she refrained from voicing her fears. Instead, she paused in the doorway, looking at the slender girl and thinking about a more immediate concern. "Will you be all right here after I leave? I mean, will he be angry or anything?"

Lisa shook her head, setting her soft curtain of hair swinging again. "Oh, no. He means what he says. He'll never mention it again. In fact, he won't talk to me at all. He'll just ignore me completely and expect me to be gone by semester break. And if I'm not, he'll just quietly pack up all my things and lock me out of the house."

"Oh, Lisa—" Aching with sympathy, Mara hugged the blond girl and patted her smooth, pale cheek and then started down the snowy walk toward her car.

"Miss Steen?" Lisa called from the doorway.

Mara turned.

"Thanks again," Lisa said. "I'll see you tomorrow night at the pageant."

"Really? Are you coming tomorrow night, Lisa?"

"Of course," Lisa said. She smiled suddenly and, for the first time in months, Mara saw the old impish sparkle on the girl's face. "There's just no way Jeff could manage the candy canes without me."

Mara smiled back as the door closed, then started toward her car again. Her smile faded and her face was full of sorrow as she put the little car into gear and drove slowly away.

# 13

Mara darted about behind the closed curtains on the big stage, looking lovely in heels, a clinging, high-necked red wool dress with a wide gold belt, and a sprig of holly in her honey-colored hair. She felt the same combination of emotions that she always experienced on Christmas pageant nights—a mixture of tension, excitement, nervousness, relief and sheer childlike enchantment.

Children milled about in the wings, arguing in loud stage whispers, scuffling, pushing and demanding attention and help from Jeff, Lisa, Mara and the three harried mothers who had volunteered to assist with costume changes. Mara paused once to peep out through the curtains at the huge auditorium, which was rapidly filling with people.

Agnes was there in the front row, regal and stately in black velvet and pearls, still wearing her shoulder sling. Unseen behind the curtain, Mara smiled down at her fondly. Agnes had never missed a single Christmas pageant since Mara had started teaching. She considered them wonderful entertainment and applauded extravagantly for every act.

Still peering cautiously out into the room, Mara saw Allan enter and make his way to a seat near the center of the room. Her heart turned over, and she glowed warmly with love as she always did whenever she saw him. He was so handsome in his dress slacks and leather jacket—tall, erect and sun-browned, and other women's eyes followed him as he moved quietly through the room. Mara watched him, too, warmed by private, intimate memories of those arms, those lips, that big-hard-muscled body. There was, she thought, something deliciously exciting about observing him like this when he had no idea that she was watching him.

"Mara!" Jeff called. "Do you have a list of the candy canes? We're missing one!"

Mara hurried over, program in hand, to count candy canes. Jeff and Lisa were working efficiently as a team, dressing the group of children in their complicated striped outfits and giving last-minute instructions. Lisa, for once, had shed her blue jeans in honor of the occasion and wore a calf-length white skirt and a white-and-silver top. With a spray of white poinsettias pinned in her golden hair, she looked like a snow princess.

Jeff, Mara could see, was watching the graceful girl with quiet intensity. He could hardly keep his eyes off her. He, of course, wore his customary jeans and sweatshirt. Mara often wondered if he owned any other clothes. But someone, possibly Lisa, had pinned a cluster of holly leaves and berries at the neck of his sweatshirt, so that he, too, looked cheery and festive.

"All right," he said briskly. "Reindeer are ready, snowflakes are ready...right, Lisa?"

"Right," she said.

"This girl," Jeff told Mara solemnly, "is marvelous. I mean it. A veritable model of efficiency and diplomacy. With a little training from the right person, she could run her own corporation."

"Sure, Jeff," Lisa said bitterly, turning on her heel and walking quickly away.

Jeff watched her and then turned to Mara, his face sober for once. "No matter what I say, it's the wrong thing," he said. "Where's my other candy cane, Mara?"

Mara consulted her list. "I don't know, Jeff," she said finally. "I'll just have to check and see."

A frantic search and some hurried telephone calls revealed that a candy cane had succumbed, that very day, to chicken pox. Jeff and Lisa immediately went into a huddle, choreographing the necessary changes to the candy cane routine, while Mara rushed away to oversee the installation of the reindeer antlers.

The kindergarten Christmas pageant was complicated every year by the fact that the two groups of children, Mara's morning and afternoon classes, never practiced together. Each class did its own rehearsals and memorized its own routines, and even Mara, who organized the program, wasn't sure how it was all going to work out until the evening of the actual performance.

*Fortunately,* she thought, fitting cumbersome antlers onto small, wiggling heads, *we have the world's most indulgent audience.*

"Mara!" Jeff whispered from the other side of the stage. "Come on! It's almost starting time!"

"Oh, my goodness," she breathed, looking at her watch in dismay. "Nathaniel! Where are you?"

"Here I am." A small fair-haired boy materialized at her knee, nattily turned out in a miniature gray suit, highly polished shoes and a plaid bow tie.

Mara smiled down at him. "Nathaniel, you look so handsome. Are you sure you know your verse?"

He nodded solemnly.

"Good boy. You wait here now till I come back and tell you. All set?"

He nodded again.

Mara walked out to center stage, took a deep breath and motioned to Jeff, who pulled the curtains open.

She smiled at the enthusiastic burst of applause and stood looking out into the packed hall, waiting for the noise to subside. Her eyes sought out Allan, who gazed up at her admiringly, grinned and gave her a private thumbs up sign.

Bolstered by his presence, and the look of loving pride on his face, Mara delivered a small speech of welcome to the audience and then introduced Nathaniel, who was to recite the opening verse.

She exited amid fresh applause, and Nathaniel marched to center stage as stiff as a robot. He searched the crowd until he located his own parents and then stood staring at them in wide-eyed panic, like a rabbit caught in the glare of oncoming headlights.

"Welcome, welcome, one and all," Mara prompted softly from the wings.

He swung his head toward her. "I have to go to the bathroom!" he whispered loudly.

"Right after you say your verse," Mara murmured. "Welcome, welcome..."

"I have to go now!" he implored, even more loudly, standing rooted to the floor at center stage.

Mara went swiftly to the piano, sat and began to play "Jingle Bells," motioning to the audience to join in. Lisa, meanwhile, came out quickly and removed Nathaniel, to the accompaniment of more applause and a wave of suppressed laughter.

When the little boy reappeared, looking much relieved, he said his verse perfectly, setting the tone for the rest of the evening. Everyone performed on cue, kept time to the music and remembered their parts. Only one set of antlers fell off, and the absent candy cane was hardly missed.

When the program ended, amid thunderous applause, Mara went down to the doorway, flushed with triumph and limp with relief, to greet the departing parents.

Allan paused on his way out, holding Michael's hand, and gave her a brief hug.

"Well done, sweetheart," he whispered. "And you look just lovely."

Mara smiled gratefully and nestled close to him for a moment. "Thank you. I'm so glad it's over."

"Do you want to come out with us for ice cream?" Allan asked. "Just to celebrate a little?"

Mara smiled wistfully. "I'd love to, but I have Gran with me."

"She can come, too!" Michael said.

Mara sensed a sudden movement at her side and saw Agnes standing nearby, gazing coldly at Allan.

"Hello, Mrs. Steen," he said courteously. "How are you feeling?"

"Better, thank you," Agnes replied in a flat, level tone.

"That's good. Mara?" Allan gave her a significant, questioning glance.

Mara was painfully aware of Agnes, stiff and disapproving beside her, and of Allan, waiting expectantly. She hesitated.

"Hey, Mara," Jeff said urgently, materializing at her elbow, "how about if we all go out somewhere for something to eat? Hi, everybody," he added, smiling at the other two adults, and then turned to Mara again. "See," he explained in a low voice, "Lisa's never going to go out with me alone, but I thought maybe if everybody was going…"

"But…" Mara began helplessly, looking at her grandmother's stiff, expressionless face, and Michael, bouncing with excitement beside Allan. "I know," Mara said finally. "Let's all go to our place. All right, Gran? Won't that be fun? Allan, you and Michael can just follow us over. Jeff, you know where we live?"

"Sure," he said. "Lisa and I will tidy up and be right over." He paused. "Thanks, Mara," he whispered.

Mara, Allan and Agnes sat stiffly around the living room, holding coffee mugs in their hands. The only person present who felt no tension at all was Michael. He lay on the floor with a glass of orange juice, gazing blissfully up at the shining Christmas tree in the corner.

"That's so pretty," he breathed. "Isn't it, Dad?"

"Yes, son," Allan said. "It's a beautiful tree." He smiled politely at Agnes, who ignored him and addressed herself to Michael.

"When I was your age," she said, "we used to go out into the forest with my father to cut down our own tree and bring it home on a sleigh pulled by two horses."

"Really?" Michael asked, wide-eyed with wonder. "Did you get to ride on the sleigh, too?"

Agnes nodded. "After a while. When we got tired of walking."

Michael smiled at her. "We never even had a tree last year," he said. "But we are this year. Dad bought it already, and it's a great big tree, and Miss Steen is coming out tomorrow to help decorate it. Aren't you?" he asked, turning to Mara.

"Mick…" Allan began warningly.

Agnes turned to glare at Mara. "It's the first *I've* heard about it," she said. "I thought you were going with me to take Rachel her Christmas gifts tomorrow. Or is that too hard to fit into your schedule?"

"Gran—"

Then, to Mara's intense relief, the doorbell rang, and she ran to admit Jeff and Lisa, both cheerful and rosy-faced with cold.

Mara led them into the living room. "Gran," she began, "Allan, this is Jeff and Lisa."

Allan smiled a greeting, but Agnes said nothing.

Mara looked at her grandmother. She was sitting in her chair, stiff and silent, staring at Lisa with a strange expression of startled, fixed intensity.

"Gran?" Mara said. "Is something the matter?"

"Pardon?" Agnes shook herself a little, looked vaguely at Mara and then seemed to pull herself together. "No," she said finally. "No, it's all right. Lisa just...reminded me of someone, that's all."

She nodded to the two young people, trying to smile, but her face was still pale and intent, and Mara looked at her occasionally with concern.

Allan got up quietly, went into the kitchen and refilled the coffeepot. Then he brought mugs to Jeff and Lisa and handed around the plate of cookies. Mara looked up at him, smiling her thanks, and he paused to touch her cheek gently. Agnes saw the little loving gesture, and her face darkened.

Fortunately, Mara thought, no party could be a complete disaster when Jeff was present. Jeff was able to clown his way through anything, even an occasion as awkward as this one. He launched cheerfully into his repertoire of impersonations, doing outrageous takeoffs of political figures, movie stars and various school dignitaries. In a very short time he had Michael rolling on the floor in fits of giggles, Allan laughing heartily and the three women, even Agnes, smiling and chuckling.

Mara was intensely grateful to him and even sorry when Michael grew sleepy and Allan announced that it was time for them to be going. Jeff and Lisa left at the same time, and Mara stood on the step, waving to all of them, hugging herself against the cold. Then she came back inside and began quietly to tidy away the dishes.

Agnes helped her, still silent and unusually thoughtful.

"Gran," Mara said finally, "what is it? Something's bothering you, isn't it?"

Agnes turned to her, a wondering expression in her eyes. "I can't believe you've never noticed it," she said.

"Noticed what, Gran?"

Agnes went to the piano and brought back the silver-framed picture of Emily, Mara's young mother. "Look," she said softly. "Just look, Mara."

Mara studied the picture and her eyes widened. "Oh, my goodness," she said. "I see what you mean. There *is* a remarkable resemblance, isn't there?"

"She's just the image of Emily," Agnes breathed. "Just like having her right here in the room."

Mara was still pondering. "What an amazing coincidence," she said, almost to herself. She looked up at her grandmother. "Gran," she said softly, "Lisa's pregnant."

Agnes stared at her, speechless.

Sitting in the big armchair by their glowing Christmas tree, Mara repeated what she knew of Lisa's situation and of the reaction of her father to her pregnancy while Agnes listened with concentrated attention.

"And this boy," she asked, "this Jeff...it's his baby?"

"No, Gran, it's not. She has no relationship any longer with the baby's father."

Agnes looked at her blankly. "Then what's this

boy doing with her? Doesn't he know she's pregnant?''

"Yes, he knows. He just…cares about her, that's all.''

"He won't for long," Agnes said bitterly. "Wait till she starts showing and she's an embarrassment to him. Then see how fast he runs in the other direction.''

"He might not," Mara said staunchly, although she knew that Gran's words echoed her own secret fear. "Not all men are shallow and rotten, Gran.''

"Most of them are," Agnes said flatly. "Especially *his* kind.''

"What do you mean, his kind?''

"Mara, you know who he is. You know who his parents are. Everybody in the city knows them. People like that don't allow their sons to get involved in socially embarrassing situations. Just wait and see," Agnes said coldly. "That poor girl is in for more heartache if she gets involved with a boy like him.''

"Well," Mara said, "she seems to share your opinion, so I don't think there's much danger of it. Come on, Gran," she added, suddenly overcome with weariness, "let's finish up and go to bed, shall we? I'm just worn out.''

"Yes," Agnes said with cold sarcasm. "And you've got a big day planned for tomorrow, don't you? But no time for poor Rachel, that's for sure.''

Too tired to start an argument, Mara ignored this, stacked the dishes in the sink and climbed the stairs to her room.

* * *

"Aren't these little ceramic angels just beautiful?" Mara breathed, enchanted. "And every one has a different little musical instrument." She held a tiny angel up against the fragrant pine boughs, awed by its delicate perfection.

Allan came over to stand beside her, lithe and easy in jeans, moccasins and a denim shirt. He looked at the dainty little ornament in her hand with a fond, faraway smile.

"You know, I can still remember these from way back when I was Mick's age," he said. "They were my mother's, and I always thought they were just magic. I could stand and look at them for hours. The little trumpet really works," he added. "My mother used to let me take it off and blow into it sometimes if I was really careful."

Mara raised herself on tiptoe and kissed his cheek. "I'll bet you were just the sweetest little boy," she said. "I wish I could have known you then."

"No way," he said, grinning. "If there's a girl like you around, I'd rather be a *big* boy. Big boys have a lot more fun."

"Allan!" she protested, tossing a significant glance in Michael's direction. But Michael was absorbed in unpacking ornaments, lifting the fragile glass balls from their cardboard compartments with great care and lining them up on the couch for Mara to hang on the upper branches.

The little boy squatted on the rug and looked up at the tall bushy tree with the angel on the topmost branch glowing softly in a cloud of pale gauze. "This is so pretty," he said blissfully. "This is just the best tree in the whole world."

Allan smiled and turned aside from his scrutiny of a faulty string of lights to ruffle the little boy's hair.

"Dad, will we leave the lights on for Santa?"

"Well, sure," Allan said. "How else can Santa see to leave the presents and fill your stocking?"

"Santa's magic," Michael said placidly. "He can see in the dark or anywhere. But I want him to see how pretty the lights are."

"I always left the lights on for Santa," Mara said, climbing on a stepladder to reach the upper branches with a rope of tinsel. "And then, after he came, he turned them out so I couldn't peek if I got up in the night."

"Did you ever get up in the night?" Michael asked with deep interest.

"I tried not to. But sometimes I just couldn't stand waiting, and I'd get out of bed and tiptoe downstairs to look at the tree, but it would be all dark and quiet down there, and then I'd know that Santa had already come."

"What did you do then?"

"Then I went back upstairs and fell asleep, so I could get up early in the morning and open my presents." She smiled, remembering, and then returned to her task. "Hand me that pink one, could you please, Allan?"

"I wish you could be here on Christmas morning when I open my presents," Michael said. "It would be so much fun if you could come."

"I know, dear, but I can't."

"Why not?"

"Because," Mara said gently, "if I came here, then my grandmother would be all alone."

"But if you don't come," Michael argued, "then Dad and me will be all alone."

"But you'll have each other," Mara pointed out. "Gran wouldn't have anybody at all if I weren't there."

Michael pondered this and then brightened. "Why can't she come, too? Then we could all be together?"

Mara and Allan exchanged a glance.

"I don't think so, dear," Mara said. "She likes to be at home for Christmas. Older people are like that. They don't like to leave their own houses very often."

"But you'll come out right after Christmas to see all my toys?"

"Just as soon as I can," Mara promised.

"Okay. Look at this little snowman. He has a tiny little hat and everything."

"Oh, Michael," Mara said in delight. "Isn't he darling! Hang him down there, all right? These higher branches are just about full, aren't they?"

"Yeah," Allan said, laughing up at her as she stood on the ladder. "They sure are."

"You be quiet," Mara said cheerfully. "I like a tree to look well decorated. None of these sparse, tasteful Christmas trees for me."

He chuckled and held up his arms to lift her down, holding her tenderly and kissing her face and throat while Michael looked on, beaming.

"Michael," Mara said, "do you think you can finish hanging all these ornaments on the lower branches, now?''

"Sure. They're easy to reach. See?''

"Good boy. Your dad and I have to go out and finish up some chores, but we'll be back soon.''

"Mara,'' Allan protested, "I already…''

She turned and shot him a meaningful glance, and he grinned slowly.

"Right,'' he said. "We have a few things to tend to, Mick, so you just keep working on the tree, okay?''

"Okay, Dad,'' Michael said absently, already absorbed in his task.

Mara and Allan bundled up in warm clothes and waded hand in hand across the snowy yard to the barn. The day was cold, but clear and sunny, and the cattle stood quietly in the corrals with steam rising from their shaggy bodies.

"He seems so small to leave all alone in the house,'' Mara said. "I always worry about it.''

"I know what you mean,'' Allan said. "But he's been used to it for a long time, and he's really good. He knows not to touch the stove or anything, and he knows where to find me if he needs me, so I don't worry all that much anymore.''

He pulled the barn door open and followed Mara inside, letting the door swing shut behind them. Mara stood blinking in the dim, dusty interior and sniffed the pleasant scent of hay, cattle and leather.

Allan turned to her, his dimple sparkling, his blue eyes dancing wickedly beneath the peak of his cap.

"Okay," he said. "You've got me out here. Now what are you planning to do with me?"

"Oh, Allan," she said, "I just couldn't stand it another minute.... Allan, darling," she murmured, moving into his arms and beginning to kiss his neck and face.

He held her, responding to her surging passion, whispering and stroking her face, moving his big body against hers, kissing her and thrusting his tongue into her mouth.

Her breath came in short little gasps, and she shivered against him. "I dream about this all the time," she whispered. "All the time when I'm away from you and I'm tired of working or Gran's being awful, I just think of being close to you like this...."

"Me, too," he murmured. "All the time. You know," he added softly, "I think we have far too many clothes on. Let's shed a few layers, shall we?"

She nodded eagerly and then paused in dismay, finally becoming aware of their surroundings again.

"But, Allan, it's *cold* out here."

He chuckled softly against her neck. "Wait'll you see my new invention," he whispered.

She pulled back in his arms and looked up at him, puzzled.

Still smiling, he led her toward one of the box stalls, opened it with a flourish and motioned her inside.

"It's an incubator," he explained. "If I have any more calves come along out of season, like that one we pulled last month, and it's freezing cold outside, then I can put them in here and keep them warm until they're stronger.''

Mara peered inside. He had built a low roof over the box stall, creating an enclosed space about eight feet square and five feet high. A big infrared light bulb was suspended from the ceiling of his improvised "incubator," and when he switched it on, the bulb bathed the little box with a warm, rosy glow.

Mara looked up into his laughing eyes and smiled. "That's what I love about you," she said. "You're a man who's always prepared for any emergency."

"And this," he said solemnly, "is a real emergency. At least for *me*."

Mara laughed and spread their heavy parkas on the straw, then crawled into the little lighted space. Allan followed her and closed the door behind him, and they lay gazing at each other in the soft pink glow of the lamp.

Slowly, lovingly, he undressed her, taking his time, as he always did, exposing her body as if it were a precious gift to be unwrapped for his pleasure. Finally she lay naked in their soft nest of hay and jackets, and he lay beside her, looking down at her, running his big hard hands down over her stomach and thighs while her skin burned at his touch. He buried his face against her breast, and she smiled down at him, stroking his thick sandy hair, loving the feel of it against her skin.

Unable to control his rising passion, he tossed his own clothes aside, stripping rapidly down to his shorts, and she looked with pleasure at his hard, powerful, masculine body, tinted ruddy bronze by the light of the overhead lamp. He was so large that he seemed to fill their whole tiny room with maleness and virility, and Mara reached toward him longingly, running her hands lightly over his thick, muscular thighs and his hard flat belly, caressing the bulge in his shorts.

"Oh, Mara," he gasped, "sweetheart, you know I love it when you touch me like that."

Slowly, lovingly, he unbound her hair and pulled it loose around her, then bent toward her again, stroking and sucking her small, firm breasts until the nipples stood taut and erect, kissing her mouth, running sure, gentle hands over her body.

She arched to his touch, moaning with pleasure, lost in the richness of sensation. The little space that enclosed them was filled with the scents and sounds and warmth of their love, and there was no world anywhere, except this tiny realm of pounding rhythm and tingling pleasure and deep, singing, breathless joy.

"Allan," she whispered. "Darling…darling…"

He held her, still breathing hard, his face buried in her soft masses of hair, murmuring broken, incoherent words of endearment.

For a long time they lay in the warm pink glow of the lamp, their naked bodies entwined, kissing and stroking each other softly in the peaceful, gentle aftermath of passion. Finally Allan pulled away and leaned on one elbow, looking down at her. He brushed her hair away from her face and cupped her cheek tenderly in his hand, smiling into her eyes.

"Merry Christmas, darling," he whispered.

She smiled back sleepily. "Merry Christmas. I think that was the nicest present I've ever had."

He grinned and reached for his shirt. "You're sure easy to please. If that's the kind of present you like, there's thousands more where that one came from."

"Thousands, Allan?"

"Damn right. Here, let me braid your hair again. You're so beautiful, Mara."

"You're not so bad yourself," she said. "Of course," she added thoughtfully, "It could just be that red lamp. It's a very flattering light."

He chuckled and tugged gently at the heavy strands of hair.

They opened the door of the box stall, and the chill in the barn came flooding into their cozy space, causing them to dress rapidly. Allan crawled out of the little cave first and reached in to help Mara clamber to her feet.

She emerged and looked around, blinking. "Why do I feel so guilty?" she asked. "Like I've been doing something really naughty?"

"Haven't you?"

"Nothing we haven't done before. But today I feel so…so deliciously wicked."

He grinned. "Yeah. I know what you mean. I think it's because it's a hiding place, sort of, you know? And it makes you feel like a kid in a secret place, doing something you know you shouldn't be doing."

They smiled at each other. Without speaking they moved into each other's arms for a long, slow, tender kiss and then separated reluctantly.

"We'd better get back to the house," Mara said

finally, "before Michael gets worried and comes looking for us."

"You're right. We'd better." He started toward the door and then looked back at her. "Damn! I almost forgot. There *is* one chore we have to do. For real, I mean. I'd been planning to bring you out here later to help me."

"What's that?"

"I forgot to gather the eggs this morning."

"Okay," she said. "When it comes to chores, I'm learning that there are worse things than gathering eggs."

"Like what?"

She considered. "Well…for instance, I *hate* filling feed pails."

"Yeah," he said, surprising her. "So do I. But there's no feed pails today. Just a few eggs to gather."

She followed him out into the frosty afternoon, so rich and contented and filled with his love that the whole day seemed touched with gold. The sky arched overhead, an incredible, endless, azure sea, and the sun shone warm and still on the drifted fields of snow, tinted with delicate blue shadows in the prairie hollows.

They entered the chicken house, musty and warm and dancing with dust motes in the sunlight that streamed through the dirty windowpanes. Most of the hens were huddled together on the slanting rows of roosts, while an intrepid few still squatted in the high bank of rough wooden boxes, filled with straw, that served as nests.

Allan handed Mara the pail, knowing that she liked taking the warm brown eggs from the nests and depositing them carefully in the bucket.

"Look," she said cheerfully. "There's lots today, Allan. They must be gearing up for Christmas."

He chuckled. "More likely," he said, "they're just trying to avoid becoming Christmas dinner."

She moved along the bank of nests, laughing and talking, and then stopped abruptly.

"Oh, great," she said grimly. "The world's meanest chicken, on duty as usual."

Mara looked down at the big red hen, whose hard yellow eyes stared back at her with unwinking malevolence.

"Come on," Allan scoffed. "She's just a pussycat."

"Easy for you to say," Mara replied bitterly. "She doesn't try to take *your* arm off at the wrist every time you go near her."

The hen ruffled her feathers defiantly and made a low, dangerous chirruping sound.

"Mara," Allan said firmly, "any woman who can handle Jason can certainly handle that chicken."

Mara grinned. "You're absolutely right."

She held her breath and reached out suddenly to thrust her hand under the big bird. The hen clucked once, heaved herself to one side and then settled back placidly, ruffling her feathers comfortably and staring off into space.

Mara looked up at Allan in considerable satisfaction. "Piece of cake," she said smugly.

"Of course. I've been telling you for a month that all it takes is some assertiveness."

Mara felt around beneath the big hen. "And there's one…two…three… Allan!''

"What?" he asked, alarmed by her tone.

She looked up at him, wide-eyed. "Allan, there's a square egg under here! She laid a square egg!"

"No kidding?" He arched a sardonic eyebrow, and the dimple popped into his cheek. "No wonder she's bad-tempered if she's going around laying square eggs. That'd be enough to make anybody cranky, wouldn't it?"

"Allan," she insisted earnestly, "I'm not joking. There's really a—" She withdrew her hand gently and stared down at it, speechless with amazement. Resting on her palm was a tiny square box, still warm from the hen's body, wrapped in gold foil.

"Well, I'll be damned," Allan said, looking down at it with deep interest. "Look at that. She *did* lay a square egg."

"Allan…?" Mara looked up at him, here eyes wide, her heart pounding. "Allan?" she whispered.

"If that poor old girl went to all that painful effort," he said casually, "the least you can do is to open it and see what's inside, don't you think?"

With trembling fingers, Mara removed the gold foil to reveal a square brown velvet box. Breathlessly she snapped the lid open and then gasped. A huge diamond solitaire sparkled against the rich velvet, catching a beam of sunshine from the window and blazing with a fiery glow in the dim, musty building.

"Oh!" Mara breathed, moving the box around and

watching as the colors flamed in the big stone. "Oh, it's beautiful...it's just so beautiful...."

He reached over, lifted the ring carefully from its velvet nest and slipped it onto her left hand, looking into her eyes. "I love you, Mara. And I want to marry you."

"Allan..."

"Don't," he said, leaning down to kiss her, closing her lips with his own. "Don't say it, sweetheart. Not today. Please don't say anything. Just wear the ring and tell me you love me."

"I do love you. I love you so much." She crept into his arms and buried her face against his chest, her heart bursting with love, her eyes blurred with happy tears. He held her tenderly, stroking her hair in the winter sunlight.

# 14

"Here she comes!" Jo shouted in mock alarm as Mara entered the teachers' lounge and took her lunch bag from her cubicle. "Quick, everyone, sunglasses on or your eyes will be permanently damaged by the glare."

"Come on, Jo," Mara protested cheerfully. "It's not *that* big."

"It's pretty big," Jo said. Then she added darkly, "It's a hell of a lot bigger than mine."

"People are so competitive," Mara said, settling into a chair near Jo's worktable. "Don't you know that it's not the size of the ring, it's the thought that counts?"

"Yeah," Jo said, grinning. "And I think he likes you."

Mara smiled back. "I think he does," she said softly, her cheeks pink.

"Besides the rock," Jo asked, frowning down at the worktable, "how was your Christmas?"

"Oh, nice. Really quiet. Just Gran and I, you know." She looked at the worktable, strewn with a huge mass of tiny, intricate plastic pieces.

"What's this one? It's new, isn't it?"

Jo nodded absently, poring over a lengthy instruction booklet. "A Christmas gift from my sons. It's a 1400 cc Harley Davidson motorcycle, and I have to build the whole thing from scratch. Motor and everything," she added, happily.

"My goodness," Mara said, gazing at the bewildering array of odd-shaped little parts. "How do you even know where to start?"

"I don't. But I'm working on it." Jo leaned back in her chair, her booted feet up on the window ledge, and looked at Mara over the top of her reading glasses.

"So," she asked, "how's Granny adjusting to this latest development?"

"The ring, you mean?"

"Yeah. The ring."

"We haven't talked about it."

Jo swung her feet off the window ledge, and the front legs of her chair landed with a thump on the floor. She stared at Mara. "You *haven't talked* about it?"

Mara shook her head.

"And you've been wearing the damn thing for... how long? Three weeks? Surely she's noticed it. I mean, in a good light, it's clearly visible at two hundred yards."

"I know. Of course she's noticed it. She just... won't talk about it. I keep trying to bring it up and get her to react so we can start talking and make some plans, but she just won't."

"Hmm."

Mara looked miserably at her friend. "I don't know

what to do, Jo. She scares me. She's being so... gentle, you know?''

"Well, that's not so bad, is it? Maybe she's just adjusting to reality. Give her a little time and she'll come around. I always said she would.''

"Maybe,'' Mara said, unconvinced.

"Where the hell is this little piston? Can you see anything that looks like this?''

Mara leaned forward to study the tiny diagram. "Everything looks like that,'' she said.

Jo chuckled. "Some help you are. Eat your lunch, you love-struck child.''

After lunch Mara returned to her classroom to find Jeff and Lisa sitting on the floor at the back of the empty room, chatting companionably and cutting up bits of brightly colored felt.

"Lisa,'' Mara said in surprise. "What are you doing here in the middle of the day? Don't you have exams?''

Lisa looked up at her and smiled. "I wrote my last one this morning, so I thought I might as well stick around and help you this afternoon. Jeff says you're making hand puppets, and it sounds like fun. Besides,'' she added gloomily, "it's not much fun at home these days.''

Mara nodded in sympathy and turned to Jeff. "Did you find enough mittens?''

"Yeah. There were twenty-six odd ones in the lost and found, and they let me have all of them.'' He pulled a woolen mitten over his hand, attached a wide felt mouth and two large goggling eyes and turned it around so that it was staring solemnly at Lisa.

She chuckled. "Wait, it needs eyebrows. I'll cut some. Where did we put the black felt?"

Jeff handed her a square of felt, and Lisa cut two large, bushy eyebrows and attached them over the puppet's eyes. "See?" she said. "Now he looks just like Mr. Parker, the French teacher."

Both young people collapsed in laughter, and Mara turned away to hide her smile. The resemblance was, in fact, remarkable.

"How much does Rod pay for his place, Jeff?" Lisa asked casually, reaching for a square of white felt and beginning to cut careful small circles for puppet eyes.

"Rod?"

"You know, the one you told me about in your English class who's got no money and is going to school on scholarships?"

"Oh, him. One-ninety. Why?"

"Well, it's semester break next week, and that's it for me." She looked up at Mara. "He really means it, Miss Steen."

"Lisa, I think you might as well start calling me Mara. This is hardly a student-teacher relationship any more."

Lisa smiled shyly. "I guess not. But it'll feel funny calling you by your first name."

"Not for long. You'll get used to it."

Jeff was looking in bewilderment from one woman to the other. "I got lost about four sentences back," he complained. "Who means what?"

"Lisa's father," Mara explained gently. "He won't let her live at home anymore."

Jeff stared at them. "Why? Because of the baby?"

Lisa nodded. "I do have a choice. Abortion or adoption. Then I could stay at home. But not if I want to keep my baby."

"You're kidding," he said incredulously. "You mean, you have to leave *now*?"

Lisa nodded. "Next week. By semester break, he said."

Jeff's face grew pale, his nostrils pinched and white with anger. "And what about your last semester?"

"I guess I won't be able to graduate. If I'm living on my own, I'll have to get a job to support myself, and the baby's due in May, so—"

"I can't believe it!" He looked at Mara. "Can't anyone talk some sense to this man?"

Mara shook her head. "You haven't met him, Jeff. He's a hard man."

"Miss Steen...Mara," Lisa corrected herself, blushing, "you get the semester break, too, don't you?"

Mara nodded. "A whole week of holidays. Today's the last day of classes."

"I was wondering," Lisa said shyly, "if you could...sort of help me look for a place. I don't really know how to go about it, or how to negotiate a lease or any of the things I should know."

Jeff was cutting out bits of felt with quick, furious snips of the scissors. Finally he set the work aside and looked up, his face dark with anger.

"I can't *stand* this," he said. "Any of it. It's just so bloody stupid and cruel." He turned to Lisa. "How are you going to support yourself? Will he help?"

"Not a penny. I've made my choice, he says."

"How about Kevin's parents?"

Lisa flushed scarlet and shook her head violently. "I wouldn't ask. Never. I don't want them—or him—to have anything to do with my baby. Ever!"

"Okay. So what do you plan to do?"

"I don't know. I'll find something. I'm fairly capable, and my marks are really good. I'll get a job. And after the baby comes—"

"Lisa," he said in despair, "you don't know what you're talking about! You're just a baby yourself!"

"No, I'm not," she protested. "I'm over eighteen. Lots of girls are supporting themselves by that time. And if I can get a job, even at minimum wage, and a place like Rod's..."

"I'd die," Jeff said grimly, "before I'd see you living in a place like Rod's."

"Why? What's wrong with it?"

"Oh, nothing," he said bitterly. "Just that it's freezing cold in winter and full of bugs in summer, and he shares a bathroom with the two prostitutes who live in the other basement suites."

"We'll find you a place, Lisa," Mara said, disturbed by the terrified look on the girl's delicate face. "I'm busy earlier in the week, but toward the weekend we'll go apartment-hunting. Will that be soon enough?"

Lisa nodded gratefully, and the two young people went back to cutting out puppet parts.

Mara could tell that Jeff was controlling himself with a visible effort. Nevertheless, by the time the first kindergarten children arrived, he had begun clowning with his goggle-eyed puppet again, making it talk and nip at the children until they screamed with laughter.

Allan sat in a corner booth, watching with pleasure as Mara hung her jacket by the entry door and then came hurrying toward him among the crowded tables. She looked beautiful in tailored gray flannel slacks and a soft gray sweater the same color as her eyes, with a delicate spray of silvery flowers knitted into a front panel. Her face was pink with cold, and her eyes shone as she smiled at him across the busy restaurant.

"Hi, dear," she said breathlessly. "Am I really late? There was a long lineup just to get into the parking lot."

"No problem. You look so good, you're worth the wait. And we've got lots of time. I'm supposed to pick the boys up at the skating rink in about an hour."

"Oh, good. I was afraid I'd ruined our lunch."

"Is that the sweater Agnes knitted you for Christmas?"

Mara nodded. "Isn't it lovely? I can't believe how much work it must have been for her, especially after she broke her collarbone and had to work with that sling on. But I just love it."

"It's beautiful," Allan said sincerely. "And," he added, grinning, "what's inside isn't so bad, either."

"How would *you* know?" Mara said with dignity, picking up a menu. "How hungry are you, by the way?"

"Starving. I want the steak sandwich, but I wish they had french fries with it."

Mara frowned, considering. "How about if you get

the steak sandwich, and I'll get fish and chips, and then I'll trade the chips for your baked potato?''

"Great. Who gets the dessert?''

"What is it?'' Mara asked.

"Tapioca pudding.''

Mara made a face. "You can have it,'' she said. "I hate those little gluey fish-eyes.''

He chuckled, and Mara smiled back at him, waiting while the waitress filled their coffee cups and took their order.

"Allan,'' she said finally, "I did it.''

"Did what?''

"I told her. Last night.''

He set his cup down and stared at her with a great joy dawning in his eyes. "Really, sweetheart? What did you say? Tell me the exact words.''

"I told her that we were going to get married in June right at the end of the school term, and that I'd be moving out to the farm then, and she had to give some thought to what plans she wanted to make for the future.''

He toasted her silently with his coffee cup, beaming his approval. "And how did she react?''

"I don't know,'' Mara said, her sparkle fading a little. "Not in way I would have expected. She said that was fine with her, that she would make her own arrangements and that I wasn't to worry about her.''

Allan looked at her, puzzled by her response. "But, Mara, that's great! Why do you seem so down about it?''

"I don't know, Allan.'' She hesitated, looking at him with troubled eyes. "She was just so...different somehow. No tears, no scenes—nothing. She even wished me happiness and *kissed* me. It was spooky, Allan. Really spooky.''

The waitress brought their salads, and Allan smiled politely at her, waiting until she left again to turn to Mara.

''I think she's just kept you scared all these years, and you've been worrying about nothing. Call her bluff, and she reacts perfectly normally.''

''That's what Jo says,'' Mara told him doubtfully. ''I wish I could believe it.''

''Believe it, sweetheart. We're getting married! I'd like to stand up and tell everybody in the restaurant.''

Mara chuckled. ''Don't you dare.''

''So, what are you doing this afternoon?'' he asked as they finished their salads and the entré arrived.

''Well,'' she said, giving him a teasing smile, ''since I'm going to be a bride, I thought I'd better start doing a little shopping. I need a hope chest.''

''What are you buying?''

''Oh, lots of things. I'd like to start looking at china patterns and pick up some linens and towels—things like that.''

He smiled at her tenderly. ''Isn't it wonderful? Life with you is going to be so…Mara, I'm the luckiest man in the world.''

''Well,'' she said cheerfully, ''I think I'm not doing all that badly, either, you know.''

They finished their meal, chatting and laughing, and Allan signalled for the bill.

''By the way,'' he murmured to Mara, ''while

you're doing all this shopping, don't forget the really important stuff.''

''What stuff?'' she asked, puzzled.

''Oh, you know. Sexy nighties, sheer negligees, little bikini panties...''

''*All* essential to marital success,'' Mara said with a smile.

''Certainly,'' he agreed placidly, guiding her across the restaurant and helping her into her jacket.

''Goodbye, darling,'' he murmured, lingering beside his truck. ''I'll call you tomorrow night.''

''All right, Allan. Hurry now or you're going to be late.''

''Black lace,'' he called, pausing by his open door. ''I really love black lace.''

''Go!'' she said, laughing at him.

Still smiling, she watched him drive away.

Then her smile faded. Motivated by a sudden impulse, she went back into the restaurant lobby, fumbled in her pocket for a quarter and dialed her home number.

Come on, Gran, she thought impatiently, listening to the monotonous ringing. Answer the phone. I know you're home. You said you'd be cleaning cupboards all afternoon....

There was no answer. Her face shadowed with sudden concern, and she retrieved her quarter, dialing once more with exaggerated care.

Still no answer.

Her face drained of color. In the grip of a sudden, cold terror she turned and ran across the snowy street to the parking lot.

* * *

The house was clean and silent. If Agnes had made a start on the cupboards, there was no sign of it. The kitchen was orderly and empty, bathed peacefully in afternoon sunlight.

"Gran?" Mara called. Her voice echoed in the quiet house. "Gran, where are you?"

Mara's feeling of dread intensified. She shivered, though the house was warm, and forced herself to walk down the hallway to Gran's bedroom. But every step was an effort. Her feet were leaden with reluctance, and her whole body felt cold and stiff.

She knew what she was going to see even before she opened the door.

Agnes lay in her bed, wearing her best nightgown, her eyes closed, her old face serene and peaceful against the pillows. On the bedside table was a glass half-full of water and one of the little plastic containers in which Agnes got the pills that her doctor had prescribed, long ago, for nights when she had trouble sleeping.

The container was empty.

Mara stood for what seemed like ages, gazing down at the small, fine-boned face against the soft embroidered pillows. She heard someone crying softly and realized that it was herself. Finally, sobbing openly, she turned aside, stumbled into the kitchen and reached blindly for the telephone.

The hours that followed were a confused blur of faces and voices, of uniforms and screeching sirens and helpful hands, of demands and questions and information. Mara was helpless in the midst of it, allowing herself, as if in a dream, to be questioned and passed from hand to hand, given coffee and food and sedatives, placed in someone's car and taken to the hospital.

During all that nightmare time, all that she was clearly conscious of was a terrible, overwhelming need for Allan. She yearned, more than anything, to feel his strong arms around her, hear his comforting voice, curl up against him and cry until she fell asleep.

But she was unable to talk about him, and none of the neighbors knew his name, so nobody could call him.

At last all the noise was over and all the people were gone and all the movement ceased and everywhere, there was nothing but silence. Mara shook herself, sat up and took stock of her surroundings. She was in a hospital room, she realized, but she wasn't in a bed. She was sitting in a chair. Someone else was in the bed. She sat erect, blinking in the dim, shaded light and peered, bewildered, at the high chrome-sided hospital cot.

The person who lay there was so tiny that the mound under the covers was hardly perceptible, just a small, slight length. The head was crowned with silver curls, and the profile was sharp and delicate....

It was, Mara realized in confusion, her grandmother lying in the hospital bed.

But how...why...?

Gradually her head cleared and certain facts registered in her mind. Agnes was in bed. Tubes and cords were attached to her body and her breathing was being monitored.

She was breathing. She wasn't dead.

Mara felt a flood of joy and thankfulness, and a relief so intense that it left her feeling limp and breathless. She sagged in the chair, too weak to cry, gazing at the small, still shape in the high bed.

A bright light switched on overhead, dazzling her. She blinked and looked toward the door. Dr. Holmes stood there, neat and crisp in a shirt and tie under his starched white lab coat. He smiled at her gently.

"Hi, Mara. Feeling better?"

"I…I guess so. I feel a little dizzy."

"It'll pass. We gave you some light sedation, but it's wearing off quickly."

"And Gran?"

"She's going to be fine."

"Oh," Mara breathed. "Oh, thank God. I was so afraid…"

He nodded briskly. "I'm just finishing my rounds. Rest here for fifteen minutes or so, and then come down to my office, all right? I'd like a word with you before you leave."

"All right. Thank you, Dr. Holmes. Please leave the light on."

After he left, Mara sat for a few moments longer in the soft chair, trying to orient herself and collect her thoughts. But when she recalled the events of the afternoon, she felt a stirring of horrible, remembered panic and a rising nausea.

*Dear God, it was awful*, she thought. *It was so awful. Allan, I want you. Where are you, darling? Allan.…*

And then she remembered that Gran had done this

dreadful thing because of Allan. This was Gran's final word, her absolute response to Allan and to the loving, happy future that he promised for Mara.

At last Gran had made her statement.

Mara got to her feet, moving slowly, like an old, old woman. She halted across the room and stood by the bed, leaning on the chrome side rails, gazing intently down at her grandmother.

Agnes looked serene and peaceful, her old face smooth and delicate against the crisp hospital linen. The blue veins at her temples throbbed slowly, and her skin looked translucent, incredibly fragile.

Mara stood for a long time, looking down at the small, fine-boned face that was so much like her own. Finally, she reached out a gentle hand and touched the soft cheek, brushing it lightly with the backs of her fingers. Slowly she caressed the snowy curls and patted the thin shoulder that jutted beneath the hospital sheet.

"All right, Gran," she whispered at last. "All right. You win."

Then she turned and walked slowly out of the room.

Dr. Holmes was in his place behind his desk, toying, as usual, with the slim gold pen. He looked up when Mara entered, and motioned her to a seat.

They looked at each other in silence for a moment, and then he pushed his chair back and placed the pen on his desk. "Well," he said, "she made a genuine attempt. It was no bluff."

Mara nodded. "I'm sure it wasn't." She smiled a

wretched little half smile. "Gran's a very thorough person. She doesn't do things halfway."

"That's certainly true in this case. She took enough pills to put away three or four people."

"But she's still alive."

"Yes, she is. Just through sheer luck. She must have assumed that you'd be away a lot longer than you were. As it was, the medication had barely begun to take effect when you called the ambulance, and we got her stomach pumped out before any real harm was done."

Mara nodded again, trying not to cry. "It was so lucky. Just on impulse I tried to reach her by phone, and when there was no answer, I left for home right away. I must have called just a few minutes after she..." Her voice trailed off.

"But," he said, "we do have to consider the fact that people who try once usually try again. And the second time, if they're serious about it, they usually succeed."

"That's all right." Mara said. "She won't be trying again."

Something in her voice caused him to glance up at her sharply. "You're sure about that?"

"I'm sure," Mara said quietly.

He picked up his pen, twirling it slowly between his fingers and eyeing Mara in thoughtful silence. "I believe," he said casually, "that you're wearing a ring I haven't seen before."

"Yes," she said, meeting his gaze steadily. "But I won't be wearing it any longer."

"Mara..." he said, and all at once, his professional

manner dissolved and he was just a troubled young man, confronted by a miserable, insoluble problem. "Mara, don't do that. Please don't do that."

"What would you do in my place, Dr. Holmes?" Mara asked. "Tell me what you'd do."

He sat in silence, staring at the pen in his hand, unable to answer.

Finally Mara got to her feet, murmured her thanks and turned to go.

"Mara, she's really in no danger and all her vital signs are stable. I can keep her in here for a day or two, but no longer."

"That's all right. It doesn't matter. I just need—" Mara paused and took a deep breath. "I just need one day. Tomorrow I have to go and...see someone."

She sobbed suddenly and rushed from the room.

The young doctor half rose from his chair and then sank back, staring helplessly at the door. He looked at the picture on his desk of the sweet-faced young woman with the plump, solemn baby and then gazed once more at the empty doorway.

"Damn," he muttered aloud. "Damn!"

His desk was piled with work, but for a long time he sat without moving, staring off into space, twirling the gold pen between his fingers.

Mara drove slowly into the setting sun, her heart aching with sorrow and loss. The prairie on this winter afternoon was almost unbearably beautiful. The bitter cold had ended as suddenly as it had begun, and a balmy wind blew over the mountains, filling the wide blue sky with feathery pastel clouds and forming sparkling crystals of rainbow brightness where it danced on the endless surface of powdery snow.

She turned at the red granaries and started down the lane. High overhead an owl wheeled and circled against the setting sun, riding the warm air currents. The big bird was graceful and solitary, intent on some mysterious prey. Suddenly it folded its wings and dropped like a stone, rising almost at once with a small furry animal clutched in its hooked talons.

Mara shivered and pulled into the farmyard, driving over to park in front of the house. She trudged up the steps, knocked once and stepped inside, taking off her snow boots and walking through the house to the kitchen. Allan and Michael were both there, and their faces reflected identical expressions of startled delight at her unexpected appearance. Michael, however, was the first to recover.

"Miss Steen, look what Auntie Diane sent me for Christmas! It was late, in the mail, and it just came today!"

Mara knelt on the kitchen floor beside him, where he was playing with a complex array of colorful, oddly shaped building blocks.

"What is it?" she asked, bewildered.

"It's a whole space station! See, these little guys are the arts…asters…what is it, Dad?"

"Astronauts," Allan said.

"Right," Michael said. "Asternots. And this is their little house, where they live up in space, and the cupboards where they keep their food—and everything."

"My goodness," Mara said. "What a complicated thing, Michael."

"And here's where they get the gas for their space-ship. See the little hose? And here's—"

"Mara," Allan said, "is anything the matter?"

She looked up at him, her face pale and tense. He had covered the wooden surface of the kitchen table with newspaper, and the paper was littered with bits and pieces of a pump engine, which he had disman-tled and was repairing. His lean brown hands were stained with grease, and there was, Mara noticed, with a sudden, aching flood of love and tenderness, also a smear of grease across the bridge of his nose.

She got slowly to her feet, took a tissue from her jacket pocket and leaned against him, tenderly wiping the black stain from his face.

"Sweetheart?" he asked again.

She shook her head, not trusting her voice, and poured herself a cup of coffee from the pot on the stove.

Allan watched her in growing alarm. Finally he pushed himself away from the table and got to his feet, looking down at Michael. "Mick?" he said.

"Yeah, Dad?" Michael asked absently, placing a small yellow astronaut tenderly in a plastic bunk bed.

"Mick, don't touch any of this stuff on the table, okay? Mara and I are going outside for a little while, down to the barn. We'll be back soon."

"Okay, Dad. Look, his helmet even comes off."

"I should hope so," Allan said, trying to smile, though his face was tight with worry. "Who'd want to sleep with that big helmet on?"

Silently he took his jacket from a hook by the door, led Mara through the house to put her boots on and walked beside her through the gathering twilight to the barn. The air was balmy and caressing, and the sunset sky swirled around them in a vivid sea of rose and lilac and turquoise. They walked hand in hand without speaking.

Allan latched the door behind them, and Mara sat on a small pile of hay bales near one of the mangers. He sat beside her, putting an arm around her and drawing her close to him.

"Okay," he said finally. "Shoot."

"It's Gran," she said.

She looked up at him, needing to see his face, but he stared straight ahead, and all she could see was his handsome, clean-cut profile, finely etched against the dim, cobwebbed interior of the barn.

His arm tightened around her. "What about her?" he asked.

"Well," Mara began, struggling to keep her voice steady, "I've told you how strange she's been acting ever since I came home wearing the ring. She just pretended it didn't exist, sort of, and I was getting really scared by her attitude. She wasn't like herself at all. She was so gentle and thoughtful and just…different, you know?"

He nodded, still holding her close against his big body.

"And then I told her about our wedding date, and she was so…I told you all that yesterday…. And after we left the restaurant, I was just leaving to go shopping and I thought I'd give her a call to see how she was, and there was…there was no answer, so I went right home—'' Her voice broke, and he held her close, waiting silently.

"Oh, Allan, it was so awful. She'd taken a whole bottle of pills, and she was almost—I called the ambulance and they pumped her stomach out, and she's going to be all right, I guess. She's a lot better today. But, Allan, it was just so terrible.''

She turned to him, burying her face against his chest. He held her, stroking her hair gently and gazing into the distance above her head with a grim, brooding expression.

"Did she really mean it?'' he asked suddenly. "Or was it just a bluff?''

"She really meant it. The doctor said that she took enough pills to kill several people. And she had no idea I'd be back so soon. I'd told her not to expect me until late in the afternoon.''

"I see.''

"Allan…'' Mara leaned back in his arms and looked up at him, her eyes wide and pleading.

He returned her gaze, his face quiet and drawn with pain. "Say it, Mara,'' he said gently. "You might as well say what you've come to tell me.''

She closed her eyes and took a deep breath. "I've come to tell you that I can't marry you, Allan. I can't stand any more of this, and there's no other choice that's possible to make. I'm so sorry, Allan.''

Her voice broke, and she began to cry. He sat silently beside her, holding her tenderly and murmuring to her until she managed to compose herself. Then, for a long time, they sat side by side silently, lost in unhappiness.

Finally he spoke in a soft, remote voice. "That's the way you want it, then, Mara?"

"No!" she burst out. "I love you and I want to live with you and sleep with you every night and have your babies and be your wife. It's *not* the way I want it! But I've thought and thought about it, over and over, ever since Gran did what she did, and I know that this is the way it has to be. There's nothing else for me to do, Allan."

"Sure there is. There's always a choice, Mara. You do have another option, you know."

"Oh, I know that," she said bitterly. "We could ignore this and go ahead with our plans. And then she'd do it again. Even Dr. Holmes says she would. And he says that people who try a second time usually succeed." She turned to him, her eyes blazing with passionate despair. "Tell me honestly, Allan. Tell me what kind of chance we'd have for happiness together with something like that hanging over us. You've felt guilty for years over a loose railing. How guilty do you think I'd be knowing that she was dead and it was my decision that killed her?"

"All right," he said tonelessly. "I've known for a long time that we were in war, that old lady and I. And she's won the war. I'll give up. She can have you, but only because I'm the one who loves you the most."

Mara looked up at him miserably.

Allan turned to her, his eyes dark with pain. "I'll give up, Mara, but only for your sake. Your grandmother can win, because I love you far more than she does. I could keep fighting, but I'd rather give you up, if I have to, than see you torn to pieces like this."

Tears rolled silently down her cheeks and dripped unheeded onto the front of her jacket. He reached out and wiped them away gently with his hand. "I'll always love you," he told her simply. "All my life, till I die, I'm going to love you, Mara."

"Oh, Allan…" Slowly she took the ring from her finger and handed it to him.

He turned away with an abrupt, angry gesture. "For mercy's sake, Mara, have some pity! Don't try to give it back to me! What do I want it for? Just to remind me for the rest of my life that I can't have the only woman in the world that I want? Keep the ring, Mara."

She nodded and slipped the diamond into the pocket of her jacket. Then she got to her feet slowly and turned to look at him.

"Goodbye, Allan."

He looked up at her directly, his face tight and cold, and the anguish in his eyes was almost more than she could bear.

"If this is goodbye, Mara, then it has to really be goodbye. No more visits or phone calls or anything. It would kill me, do you understand? I love you far too much to be able to endure any kind of casual, friendly relationship. I don't want to see you again."

"I know," she whispered. "I couldn't bear it, either. Just hearing your voice would be enough to—" She stopped abruptly, bit her lip and walked toward the door. She unlatched it and paused. ''What will you tell Michael?'' she asked without looking around.

''I'll think of something. Go now, Mara, please.''

She nodded, swallowing hard, and stepped out into the calm prairie evening, walking across the silent farmyard to her car.

During the time that they had been inside the barn, deep twilight had flooded in and covered the land. Early stars winked overhead in the vast, dark blue bowl of the sky, and each prairie hollow was a deep, silent pool of mystery.

Mara drove toward the city, numb with pain, too weary to think. Tears blurred in her eyes, turning the city lights on the horizon into sparkling pinwheels and soft whirls of color. Finally she pulled over to the shoulder, rested her forehead on the steering wheel and sobbed briefly. Then, resolutely, she wiped her eyes, squared her shoulders, slipped the little car into gear and drove on again.

*That's it,* she told herself. For the past few months it seemed she'd cried a lot. But no more. She'd never cry again. She was dead inside now and dead people don't cry.

Silent and composed, with a bitter anguish far too deep for tears, she entered the city traffic and drove toward her lonely home.

# 15

Mara awoke in beaming winter sunlight that fell across her bed like a golden coverlet. She stretched sleepily, feeling a childlike pleasure in the warmth and brightness of the morning. Then, as she came fully awake, the old aching misery flooded her and throbbed painfully in her mind. She rolled over in bed, moaning quietly, and pulled the covers up around her head to block it all out—the sunlight, the memories, the day ahead of her.

Little more than a week had passed since her last few moments with Allan, but it seemed like a lifetime. She longed for him all the time, with a steady, relentless hunger that never diminished and never left her mind. Through all her waking hours, she longed for the sound of his voice, the touch of his hands, even just a glimpse of his face. Scattered errant memories tormented her at odd moments. She would see, suddenly, the clean plane of his cheek, the line of his long back, the way his hair parted and fell across his forehead, and the pain would crush her like a physical blow.

She thought about him constantly, wondered how he was, yearned to hear from him that he was all right. From the bottom of her heart, she hoped that he wasn't suffering as terribly as she was, because, she thought, it had all been her fault.

*I should never have allowed it to happen. I knew I wasn't free to love anybody. I knew Gran was never going to let me go. Yet I let him fall in love with me just because I was selfish and lonely. But, oh, God, I wanted him so much. And I still do. I still do.*

A dozen times she picked up the telephone, searching for some excuse to call him, just so she could hear his voice. But then she would remember his final words to her and slowly replace the receiver, her face pale with misery and loneliness.

Mechanically she went about the business of living. She brought Agnes home from the hospital, cleaned the house, prepared meals and cared for the old lady with competent, brisk attention. Agnes was pathetically grateful for all that Mara did and tried hard not to be a bother. She curbed her tongue, followed Dr. Holmes's orders with no argument at all and did everything that Mara asked of her without comment or complaint.

Her suicide attempt was never mentioned between them. By tacit agreement they avoided speaking of it and pretended that their lives had never been disrupted by such terrible trauma. Nor did they mention the ring that had disappeared from Mara's hand.

Mara was certain that Agnes had noticed the absence of the ring, but nothing at all was said. Agnes crept quietly about the house, small and childlike, unusually quiet and thoughtful. Obediently she took her medicine, ate her meals and went for slow, careful walks in the mild winter air. She and Mara were cautious and considerate with each other, talking quietly about unimportant things.

If Agnes was aware of her granddaughter's unhappy, faraway expression from time to time or the moments when Mara excused herself and rushed upstairs to her room before a fit of black misery could overtake her, the old lady said nothing.

Neighbors dropped in to visit, chatted briefly in a tense, embarrassed kind of way and left as soon as they could decently escape. Mara spent the semester break catching up on her schoolwork and planning for the next term. For once she hated the holiday and longed for it to end so that she could get back to work and have something to occupy her mind.

Now, as she lay in her bed, she cast her mind cautiously back over the past dreadful week and ahead to her plans for the day.

Just one day at a time, she had decided. If she could just live one day, then she could live another, and sometime, after she'd lived enough days, then maybe it wouldn't hurt so terribly.

*Allan, I love you, my darling. I hope you're well. I wish I could just hear your voice, just once, and know that you're all right. I love you, dearest. I love you....*

She struggled to banish the thoughts of him from her mind and forced herself to face the day. It was Saturday, almost the end of the semester break. Today she had promised Lisa that they would go together to look for an apartment.

Well, Mara thought, that was something, at least. She had a plan. It would fill in the whole day, and then there was just tomorrow, and then she could go back to work.

Moving slowly and listlessly, she heaved herself out of bed, dressed in jeans and a heavy, fleece-lined red sweatshirt, brushed and braided her hair and trudged down the stairs to have breakfast with her grandmother.

Lisa stood in the center of the shabby, dingy room, looking around. Jeff, who had insisted on being included in the apartment-hunting expedition, leaned in the doorway, scowling furiously.

"This isn't so bad," Lisa said bravely. "It's not as bad as the others. If I just scrubbed it out and got a rug or something to cover that big crack in the floor...."

"Lisa," Jeff said, "it's horrible. It's awful. You can't even think of living in a place like this."

"I can't think of living anywhere else," Lisa said calmly. "We've been to every place on the list. This is the last one. And even this is more than I planned to spend."

Mara looked around at the tiny apartment, feeling desolate. The single room that made up living room, bedroom and kitchen was covered in stained, peeling wallpaper and carpeted with a filthy scrap of fabric of indeterminate color. In the kitchen end several of the cupboards had doors that hung crookedly or were missing altogether, and the crack that Lisa had mentioned ran diagonally across the floor, three inches wide and packed with dirt. The taps in the stained sink dripped constantly with a sad, monotonous rhythm.

A rusty rod in a doorless opening formed the closet, and the bathroom, Mara noticed with a shudder, was foul-smelling and crusted with ancient grime.

"I could scrub it all clean and buy an old couch to sleep on," Lisa said earnestly, "and have a crib here beside me for the baby."

"Lisa," Jeff said, "this is four floors up, and there's certainly no air conditioning in this building. It'll be stifling hot in the summer. Too hot for a baby."

"There's a park just a few blocks away. I could carry the baby to the park in the evening when it's really hot and stay there till it cools off."

"Oh, Lisa…" Mara began.

"Come on," Jeff said suddenly. "I can't stand this. Let's get out of here."

They clattered down the shabby, grimy stairs and went back out onto the street, breathing the fresh air gratefully. At Mara's car they paused and looked at one another. Lisa's face was wet with tears.

"Oh, Mara," she whispered, "what am I going to do? What *can* I do? It's just so awful—" She broke off, her hand to her mouth, her shoulders shaking.

Mara hugged her and pushed her gently into the car. "Don't worry, Lisa," she said. "We'll think of something. Don't worry, dear. Let's go to my place and have a cup of coffee."

Lisa gave her a small, tearful smile. "That'd be nice." She looked bleakly out through the window.

"After the afternoon we've spent," she added, "it'll be nice just to go somewhere clean."

Mara nodded grimly. "Those places were pretty terrible, weren't they?"

"Yes. Terrible."

Jeff sat silently in the back seat, staring gloomily out at the front of the dingy apartment building.

They drove in silence through the city streets, all thinking their own thoughts as the blocks of houses slipped by.

"Gran," Mara said, "this is Lisa Stanley, and this is Jeff McLaren. You met them after the pageant, remember?"

Lisa smiled shyly and murmured something in greeting.

Agnes looked at the fair, slim girl with a tender, wistful expression. "Hello, Lisa," she said. "I hear you've been out apartment hunting."

Lisa nodded and gave her coat to Jeff to hang in the closet.

"Well? Any luck?" Agnes asked, leading them into the sunny kitchen and sitting with the two young people at the polished oak table, while Mara busied herself preparing a pot of coffee.

"No," Lisa said in a low voice. "Not really."

Jeff sat quietly for once, still wrapped in his brooding silence, while Lisa and Agnes chatted together casually and Mara bustled around the kitchen, setting out cups, cream and sugar and a plate of homemade oatmeal cookies. As she worked, she listened to them, amazed by the gentle, compassionate tenderness that

Agnes, usually so cold and reserved with strangers, showed toward this young girl.

With genuine interest, Agnes questioned Lisa about her life, her plans, her relationship with her father and her decision to keep her baby. She inquired about Lisa's health and the progress of her pregnancy, and Lisa responded freely, grateful for this motherly concern after all her months of loneliness and worry.

Finally the warmth and comfort of the clean, shining kitchen and the kindness that surrounded her was too much for Lisa. Her careful reserve broke, and she began to cry, resting her face on her folded arms.

Mara came across the room to slip her arm around the girl's quivering shoulders. "It was the apartments we looked at," she explained in a low voice to her grandmother. "They were pretty depressing, Gran."

"They're all so awful, Mrs. Steen!" Lisa wailed, raising her tear-stained face and looking at Agnes. "Anything I can afford is just so terrible! I wouldn't mind for my own sake, but to think of taking a little baby into one of those places...."

Agnes reached across the table and patted the girl's hand gently. "Don't cry, Lisa," she said. The older woman was silent for a moment, her delicate face concentrated in thought. Then she turned to Mara. "Why can't she live with us for a while, Mara? We've got all kinds of room. She could have the suite in the basement. It's furnished and everything, Mara, and nobody's used it for years. And we could look after her, so she could finish school, too."

Lisa shook her head violently, setting her blond ponytail swinging. "No, no, I couldn't...."

Jeff looked up at the older woman, his dark face lighting with joy. "Mrs. Steen," he said fervently, "that's just wonderful of you!"

Mara was staring at her grandmother, thunderstruck.

"Gran!" she said. "Gran, you've always said you couldn't stand to have anyone else in the house. *Always!* I would have offered long ago if I'd ever thought there was the slightest chance you'd agree."

"I always told you," Agnes said calmly, "that I didn't want a *stranger* in the house. But this is just a sweet girl with a baby. Do you know who you remind me of so much?" Agnes asked Lisa shyly. "You look so much like my daughter Emily. I'll have to show you her picture. You're just the image of Emily."

Lisa smiled gently at the older woman and touched her trembling hand. Agnes smiled wistfully, moving the salt shaker around on the polished surface of the table. "It would be so nice to have a little baby in the house again," she said. "You were such a sweet baby, Mara."

Jeff sat looking on, thoughtfully sipping his coffee. "If Lisa were to live here," he said finally, "then you wouldn't be alone, Mrs. Steen. Mara would be free to live wherever she wanted."

Mara and Agnes both stared at him, wide-eyed.

Mara was the first to recover. "It wouldn't work, Jeff," she said slowly. "It would be too much responsibility to put on Lisa if she's also going to be finishing school, and she'll have the baby to deal with...and there's too much for her to look after in this big house. She couldn't do it all alone."

"She could," he said quietly, "if I was living here, too."

"Now wait just a minute, young man," Agnes began with a touch of her old spirit. "I never said that *you*—"

"Mrs. Steen," Jeff interrupted her, "please, just hear me out. You said there's a self-contained suite in the basement of this house. I could live down there, and Lisa could have Mara's room. She'd help with the housekeeping to earn her board, and I'll do all the heavy work around the house and yard." He grinned with something approaching his old cheerful nonchalance. "I'm really quite a handy kind of guy, you know."

Agnes looked at him steadily. "I know where you come from," she said. "I know what kind of home you grew up in. Why would you want to move into my basement?"

"Because," he said with quiet sincerity, "I care about Lisa. I want to be close to her and look after her. And I'd like Mara to be free to live with the man she loves."

Agnes ignored this, still studying his face. "Lisa's pregnant," she said. "She's going to have a baby. Are you still going to care about her when she's not slim and pretty any more, when she's nine months pregnant, and later when she's tired out because the baby's been crying all night and she hasn't had any sleep?"

"Yes," he said. "I am."

Mara was stunned by the tone of quiet conviction in his voice. She looked more closely at him and realized that the struggles and agonies of reaching this decision had turned Jeff from a boy into a man. He was no longer a laughing, teasing adolescent, but a mature man whose face had been sculpted into hard firmness by his own private hours spent wrestling with pain.

Maybe, she thought wonderingly, maybe it could work.

Jeff, however, was still considering practicalities. "I want Lisa to graduate and go on to university after the baby's born," he said in this new, crisp voice that was so unlike the old, teasing Jeff. "So she won't be able to contribute financially to the upkeep of the household. I'll have to do all that. I can quit school, get a day job and take night classes to get my degree."

"Oh, Jeff," Lisa said. She looked over at him, her face shining with a sort of wondering tenderness. "I can't have you giving everything up for me."

"He wouldn't have to," Mara said slowly, "if there was somebody else in the house to share expenses, too."

Agnes looked at her a little bitterly. "Go on, Mara," she said. "I don't seem to have any say in any of this. Who else do you plan to move into my house?"

"Rachel," Mara said.

Agnes stared at her, startled into silence.

"Rachel could use the den on this floor, so she wouldn't have to climb the stairs," Mara went on earnestly, "and she'd be company for you all the time, and with her pension and the amount of rent she has to pay at the nursing home, plus your pension, there'd be enough that neither Jeff nor Lisa would have to have full-time jobs. They'd contribute by looking after both of you and taking care of the house."

The others were silent, listening to her and watching her animated face.

"Don't you see?" Mara went on. "This is the way the world should be. Everybody should be doing this. There's millions of old people forced to leave their homes because they're no longer able to look after the physical necessities of running a household. And there's millions of young people—students, and single mothers, forced to live in terrible poverty just to keep a roof over their heads and food on the table. Why don't they all get together and cooperate and help one another?"

Agnes looked around at the three young people. "I'm not...not a very nice person sometimes," she said, her voice low and unsteady. "You all know what I did, and you know how difficult I've made life for Mara. I've thought so much about things, ever since I..." She looked pleadingly at Mara, who nodded gently.

"We know. Go on, Gran."

"I just know that it was wrong to hurt her when I love her so much, but I've always been so...so afraid of being alone."

"You won't be alone, Mrs. Steen," Lisa said. "You'll have a whole houseful of people to look after you."

"And Rachel, Gran," Mara said. "Think how

much fun you'd have, with Rachel living right here in the house. You've always gotten along with her so well.''

Gran's mouth twitched in a semblance of a smile. ''As long as she doesn't cheat at solitaire,'' she said. ''It drives me crazy when Rachel does that.''

''She'll be closely supervised,'' Jeff promised solemnly.

Agnes grinned in spite of herself and then looked over at Mara with a sad, wistful expression. ''So you'll be free to go, Mara,'' she said. ''Will I ever see you again?''

''Oh, Gran, of course you will. The farm's just a few miles out of town, and I'll be coming in to work every day, anyway. I'll be over here all the time. Especially,'' she added with a smile, ''when you people have a *baby* here.''

''If you have any enterprise at all.'' Jeff observed, ''you should have a baby of your own before too long. You won't need to borrow *our* baby.''

Mara smiled at him, her eyes shining. Then she turned to Agnes.

''Gran,'' she said quietly, ''it's all up to you. None of this will happen if you don't want it to. It's your house, and you have the final word. What do you think?''

Agnes returned her gaze steadily. ''Are you telling me, Mara, that if I say 'no' to all of this, if I say I want you to stay here and for life to go on as it always has, then you'll stay?''

''Yes, Gran, I will. I promised you that I'd stay, and if you ask me to, I'll honor my promise.''

Agnes sat silently, thinking, while the others waited.

Finally she spoke, looking firmly around the table. "It wouldn't always be wonderful, you know," she said. "As I said, I'm not always a very nice person. We'd have fights and disagreements and get on each other's nerves and even hate each other sometimes."

"Just like in any family," Jeff pointed out.

"But," Agnes continued, "Rachel is my best friend, and you—" she turned to Lisa, smiling "—are just so much like my Emily that it's almost a miracle. Isn't she, Mara?"

Mara smiled. "In looks, maybe, Gran. But I tend to suspect that Lisa has a lot stronger personality than my mother had."

Agnes nodded thoughtfully and turned to Jeff. "And *you*," she went on crisply, fixing him with a stern eye, "seem to be all right, provided you behave yourself."

"I'll stay in the basement all the time," he promised her solemnly, his eyes dancing with mischief, "and just come up every now and then to beat you at Scrabble." He grinned. "I see that you have a well-worn Scrabble board over there and I have to warn you that I'm a world-class player. You don't stand a chance."

Agnes snorted at this impudence, trying not to smile, and turned back to Mara.

"All right," she announced. "I'll try it. Just till the baby's born, mind you, and then we'll see."

"Oh, Gran!" Mara got up and ran around the table to hug her grandmother.

"Leave me alone!" Agnes protested, pushing her away. "I just said we'd see, that's all!"

Mara kissed her again, and Agnes smiled at her granddaughter and patted her cheek with rare gentleness. Mara turned away, her eyes misty, and went into the living room, motioning Jeff to follow her.

"Jeff," she whispered, "how can I ever thank you? This is just so marvelous, so absolutely—"

"Quit babbling," he said cheerfully, "and go pack your suitcase."

"Suitcase?" she asked blankly.

"Mara, most of Lisa's stuff is in your car. I know she doesn't want to go back home tonight. And, knowing what your grandmother's like, I think it might be wise to strike while the iron's hot. I'll run back to the apartment and grab a few things, and Lisa and I will stay here right away, tonight, just so she can see that it's going to work. We don't want to give her a chance to start brooding about things and change her mind."

"Do you really think that's a good idea?" Mara asked dubiously. "Right away, tonight?"

"Sure." He leaned toward her confidentially with all of the old sparkle back in his handsome face. "I'll even let her win the first Scrabble game," he whispered. "Just as the supreme sacrifice."

Mara laughed, feeling, all at once, happy and optimistic and as light as air.

"Of course," he added with mock concern, "we *do* have the problem of where you're going to sleep tonight, once we throw you out of here. Do you know anybody who likes you enough to give you a bed for the night?''

"Oh, Jeff..." She looked up at him, her eyes wide and imploring. "Jeff," she whispered, "I haven't even seen him since we said goodbye. What if he doesn't want me?''

"Then he's crazy," Jeff said comfortably. "Go on, Mara. Go to the farm. We'll all be fine here.''

"But what if—''

"Go!''

Silently she nodded and hurried upstairs to pack her suitcase.

As if in a dream, Mara drove westward through the darkness of the winter night. The moon had risen and stood overhead so high and full that it looked like a bright coin tossed into the sky, bathing the sleeping, snow-covered prairie with a soft, silvery radiance. The evening was mild and sweet, one of those deceitfully springlike nights that occasionally visit the prairie, even in January.

Each snowy hilltop shone platinum in the moonlight, and the frosted sagebrush trimmed the flat landscape like a delicate stitchery of lace. Mara drove steadily into the darkened countryside, her headlights picking out a long golden pathway in front of her, while the mysterious, dusky land rolled off into the blackness on both sides of the road. The big diamond on her finger caught and reflected the moonlight in bright, fiery sparks—the only flash of color in all that silvered landscape.

She looked straight ahead through the windshield,

gripping the wheel tightly. After all the turbulent emotions of the past months, she felt almost detached and strangely peaceful. She made no plans, formulated no thoughts. She just drove quietly through the winter night toward his farm.

When she pulled into the farmyard and parked by the house, she saw with a little jolt of surprise that Allan was sitting out on the front step in his fleece-lined denim jacket. Taking advantage of the unseasonal mildness of the evening, he had come out to the veranda to sit in the pool of light cast by the overhead lamp and whittle on the last of Michael's family of puppies.

He threw his head up as he heard the sound of an engine approaching and stared out into the darkness. But, with the bright light shining overhead, he was unable to see Mara's car. Knowing that he couldn't see her, either, Mara stood for a moment by the gate, her heart pounding wildly, and drank in the sight of him—his big, muscular body and finely sculpted face and strong brown hands.

"Who's there?" he called.

She tried to answer, but she was unable to speak.

"I said, who's there?" he called, more sharply and started to rise.

"It's...it's me," Mara said, walking up the pathway and into the pool of light.

He looked at her, his eyes piercing, his face suddenly pale. Slowly he sank back onto the step.

"Hi," Mara said, standing hesitantly in front of him.

"Hi," he said curtly. He looked down and began

to whittle again at the the block of wood, his big hands trembling slightly.

"May I sit down?"

"Sure." He moved over a little to make room for her, and Mara sat beside him, not touching him. Allan said nothing, carving silently on the body of the tiny wooden dog.

"How have you been?" Mara asked.

"Fine. You?"

"Fine," she said, her voice shaking a little. "Just fine."

"That's good."

"Allan…" She paused, took a deep breath and began again. "Allan, I have to tell you something. A lot of things, actually. First of all, I—" She clenched her hands nervously in her lap, wondering where to begin.

Beside her Allan made a quick, startled movement and reached over to grasp her hand, holding it so the diamond sparkled in the light.

At his touch Mara's heart melted and her whole body grew weak. She forgot everything she had planned to tell him. All she wanted was to creep into his arms, nestle as close to him as she could and never, ever move away from him again.

"What's this?" he asked, staring down at the ring.

"It's my engagement ring," Mara whispered.

"Yeah?" he asked, dropping her hand and feigning disinterest. "Are you engaged?"

"I hope so."

"Who's the lucky guy?"

"Just the most wonderful man in the whole world. The man I love more than anything."

Carefully he set the knife and carving block on the step beside him and turned to look directly at her. "Maybe," he said slowly, "you'd better say what you came to tell me."

In a low voice she sat beside him, still not touching him, and told him everything that had happened— Lisa's apartment hunting and Gran's amazing suggestion to have the girl live with them and then Jeff's inspiration and her own idea about Rachel and Gran's tentative agreement to try the new arrangement.

"So," Mara concluded, "they wanted to get me out of the house tonight to give it a try, and I have no place to stay, so I just thought you might not mind if I…" Her voice trailed off.

She sat beside him, not looking at him, rigid with fear.

*He's so quiet. Why doesn't he say something? Why won't he touch me? Oh, God…he doesn't want me. I've ruined it by hurting him so badly. It's gone….*

A sob caught in her throat, and she choked it back, turning to look up at him. He was staring straight ahead, his fine profile set and still, his tanned cheeks wet with tears, gleaming silver in the moonlight.

"Allan," she whispered in wonder. "Allan, darling, you're crying."

"Yeah, I guess I am." He brushed at his face and turned to her with a rueful smile. "Isn't it awful what love does to a man? I've got no control at all. Weak as a kitten."

"Oh, Allan…"

Then she was in his arms, with his mouth kissing her passionately and his body crushed against hers as if he could never hold her close enough. Blissfully she gave herself up to the embrace that she'd hungered for, that she'd thought she would never feel again. Over and over she murmured his name, caressing his hair and cheeks and lips, pouring out all of her love and longing.

"Listen," he whispered suddenly in her ear.

They were both silent, locked together, their faces touching. Far off in the distance, on some lonely prairie hilltop, a coyote howled plaintively, singing his melancholy lament into the vast moonlit stillness.

"Poor old boy," Allan murmured against her cheek. "He thinks it's mating time."

As they listened, another coyote answered, not quite so distant, and the two of them set up a sweet, mysterious chorus that carried clearly on the soft winter air.

"She's answering!" Mara whispered. "Listen. She's calling back to him."

Allan's arms tightened around her. "I'll be damned," he murmured. "Maybe it *is* mating time. What do you think, sweetheart?"

"It might be," she agreed solemnly, smiling to herself against his chest. "It *feels* like spring tonight, doesn't it?"

"I think," he whispered huskily, "that we'd better go inside and check this out."

She laughed, and he lifted her, carrying her easily in his arms, and took her inside the small farmhouse.

Long after the lights in the little house dimmed and

flickered into darkness and the whole wide landscape was still and empty, the pair of coyotes called to each other, their wintry song of love echoing sweetly across the silvered prairie in the magic moonlit night.

From the bestselling author of
*THE BABY FARM*

MIRA®

# KAREN HARPER

# DOWN TO THE BONE

Deep in the heart of a small Amish community lies a secret someone thought was buried forever. But one woman may have just unknowingly uncovered it....

As Rachel Mast begins to dig up the past for answers, someone is equally determined to keep it buried. Someone who won't stop at murder to keep the truth hidden....

"A compelling story...intricate and fascinating details of Amish life."
—Tami Hoag on Karen Harper's *DARK ROAD HOME*

*On sale mid-July 2000 wherever paperbacks are sold!*

New York Times **bestselling author**

# JAYNE ANN KRENTZ

## BETWEEN THE LINES

Amber Langley married for all the right reasons. There was no passion to break her heart, no love to risk losing—just a sensible agreement with her boss, prominent businessman Cormick Grayson. But Amber's plan was not working out quite as neatly as she had intended. Because the heat in Gray's eyes made her suspect that there was more to this relationship than a polite living arrangement. Can Amber risk falling in love with her own husband?

"If there's one thing you can depend on, it's the humor, passion and excitement of a Jayne Ann Krentz novel."
—*Romantic Times Magazine*

*Available the first week of July 2000 wherever paperbacks are sold!*

MJAK595

**The house on Sunset was a house of secrets...**

# SHADOWS AT SUNSET

The house on Sunset Boulevard has witnessed everything from an infamous murder-suicide to a drug-fueled commune to the anguish of its present owner, Jilly Meyer, who is trying to save the house and what's left of her wounded family.

Coltrane is a liar, a con man and a threat to everything Jilly holds dear. Jilly has to stop Coltrane from destroying everything she cares about—including her heart. But to do that, Jilly has to discover what Coltrane is *really* up to.

# ANNE STUART

"Anne Stuart delivers exciting stuff for those of us who like our romantic suspense dark and dangerous."
—Jayne Ann Krentz

*On sale September 2000 wherever paperbacks are sold!*

# MARGOT DALTON

| | | | |
|---|---|---|---|
| 66522 | FOURTH HORSEMAN | ___ $5.99 U.S. | ___ $6.99 CAN. |
| 66441 | THIRD CHOICE | ___ $5.99 U.S. | ___ $6.99 CAN. |
| 66421 | SECOND THOUGHTS | ___ $5.99 U.S. | ___ $6.99 CAN. |
| 66265 | FIRST IMPRESSION | ___ $5.99 U.S. | ___ $6.99 CAN. |
| 66047 | TANGLED LIVES | ___ $5.50 U.S. | ___ $5.99 CAN. |

*(limited quantities available)*

TOTAL AMOUNT                                                    $_____
POSTAGE & HANDLING                                        $_____
($1.00 for one book; 50¢ for each additional)
APPLICABLE TAXES*                                           $_____
<u>TOTAL PAYABLE</u>                                               $_____
(check or money order—please do not send cash)

---

To order, complete this form and send it, along with a check
or money order for the total above, payable to MIRA Books®,
to: **In the U.S.:** 3010 Walden Avenue, P.O. Box 9077, Buffalo,
NY 14269-9077; **In Canada:** P.O. Box 636, Fort Erie, Ontario,
L2A 5X3.

Name:_____
Address:_____ City:_____
State/Prov.:_____ Zip/Postal Code:_____
Account Number (if applicable):_____
075 CSAS

   *New York residents remit applicable sales taxes.
    Canadian residents remit applicable GST and provincial taxes.

MIRA